Praise for the Woodfalls Girls novels

Misunderstandings

"A beautifully woven story of a love that can withstand anything."
—Molly McAdams, *New York Times* bestselling author

"Funny, real, moving, and passionate, *Misunderstandings* is a MUST-READ for New Adult contemporary romance fans."
—*New York Times* bestselling author Samantha Young

"Sweet and sexy! Great characters and an intriguing romance . . . So good!" —*New York Times* bestselling author Cora Carmack

No Attachments

"Allow me to summarize *No Attachments*: Great story. Amazing characters. Awesome read." —*Book Freak Book Reviews*

"Readers will spend the first half of this story on the edge of their seats and the last half hugging a box of tissues."
—Priscilla Glenn, bestselling author of
Back to You and *Emancipating Andie*

"Sweet, beautiful, funny, and heartbreaking all rolled into one amazing story." —Tara Sivec, *USA Today* bestselling author

continued . . .

Misunderstandings

A Woodfalls Girls Novel

TIFFANY KING

BERKLEY BOOKS, NEW YORK

THE BERKLEY PUBLISHING GROUP
Published by the Penguin Group
Penguin Group (USA) LLC
375 Hudson Street, New York, New York 10014, USA

USA • Canada • UK • Ireland • Australia • New Zealand • India • South Africa • China

penguin.com

A Penguin Random House Company

This book is an original publication of The Berkley Publishing Group.

Library of Congress Cataloging-in-Publication Data

King, Tiffany.
Misunderstandings / Tiffany King.
pages cm.—(A Woodfalls Girls novel)
ISBN 978-0-425-27479-8 (pbk.)
1. Homecoming—Fiction.   2. Electric power failures—Fiction.   3. Elevators—Fiction.
4. Relationships—Fiction.   5. Miscommunication—Fiction.   I. Title.
PS3611.I5863M57   2014
813'.6—dc23
2013049250

FIRST EDITION: May 2014

PUBLISHING HISTORY
Berkley trade paperback edition / May 2014

PRINTED IN THE UNITED STATES OF AMERICA

10 9 8 7 6 5 4 3 2 1

Cover art by Lóránd Gelner / Getty Images
Cover design by Lesley Worrell
Interior text design by Tiffany Estreicher

ACKNOWLEDGMENTS

Being a writer is a solitary job, but creating a book is a group venture. As writers, many people play a part in helping the words we see in our heads make it into the hands of the readers. I will be forever grateful to everyone who makes this possible.

To my husband: for being my first reader, editor, and critic. Thank you for always believing in every story I write. I know I'm not the easiest person to work with, but I appreciate that you never give up on me. None of this would be possible without you.

To my Ash: You make me feel special every time you read one of my books. I started this journey because of you, and I could not imagine ever doing it without you.

To my Ryan: You are my creative inspiration.

ACKNOWLEDGMENTS

To Hollie Westring: for always making time for me and my stories. I am so thankful for the forces that brought us together.

To Kevan Lyon: for helping me reach a dream I never thought was possible. I am incredibly fortunate to have you in my corner.

To Kate Seaver: for believing in me. You will never know the impact your words had on me. You make me strive to be a better writer.

To Tara Sivec: for being my sanity. You are my sounding board. You make me laugh when I need it most, and you are the voice of reason when I begin to doubt myself. Thank you for always being my friend.

To my amazing Wolfpack: for inspiring me each and every day. Your kindness and support are what make this the best job in the world.

To all my readers: Thank you for giving me an opportunity to do what I love the most. Without you, my stories would cease to exist. Your support allows me to carry on.

Finally, to the three amazing people who completely changed my life, Carol Kunz, Adam Kunz, and Jennifer Armentrout. Your helping hand when I least expected it took my breath away. I will never be able to thank you enough for standing by me.

1.

The rain was coming down in steady sheets as I stepped from the yellow taxi that had deposited me in front of Columbia Center in Seattle. "Keep the change," I said to the driver as I reached back inside the taxi to pay my fare. I stood momentarily with the rain pelting my face, tilting my head back to see the top of the tallest building in the state of Washington—all seventy-six floors of it. I knew that fact because I looked it up on the Internet. I needed to get an idea of what I would be dealing with. Not that my friend Rob, who I was here to see, worked on the top floor, but it was close. His office was on the fifty-second floor, which meant a long torturous elevator ride. Something I wasn't looking forward to at all. Back home in Woodfalls, Maine, the tallest building was the three-story Wells Fargo bank they had built across from Smith's General Store a few years back. I was attending college at the University of Washington at the time, but back in Woodfalls it was big news. My mom, the town's resident busybody, made sure I received daily updates about the construction. Now, as I stood here, the building in front of me made our little bank back home look like a dollhouse.

The rain was beginning to find its way down the generic yellow raincoat I had purchased from the Seattle airport just that morning. The pilot had gleefully informed us before landing that Seattle was having its rainiest September in years. The irony that the rainiest state in the country was having its rainiest year in history was not lost on me. Why wouldn't it be cold, rainy, and miserable? It matched the way I felt about this place. Of course, that wasn't always the case. When I first arrived in Seattle three years ago, I was a greenhorn from my podunk hometown. That was why I had chosen UW. It was as far away from Woodfalls as I could possibly get without applying to the University of Hawaii. Three years ago, I had decided that nine months of rainy weather was a fair trade-off to finally be surrounded by civilization. That and it was hundreds of miles away from my often annoying but well-intentioned mother. The endless array of restaurants, museums, and stores and the music scene had tantalized me, making me vividly realize just how lacking and uncultured Woodfalls was. Everything about Seattle intrigued me, making me never want to leave, but Puget

Sound was by far my favorite thing about being there. On the weekends I would haul my laptop and textbooks down to one of the cafés on the waterfront. I would spend hours drinking coffee and working on schoolwork. That is, when people-watching didn't distract me. That trait is something I had obviously inherited from my mom. Still, everything had been going along just the way I had imagined it would. It was liberating to be out from under my mom's thumb and the prying eyes of everyone back home. Here I could be my own person, with my own life. Then everything went to hell. I met Justin Avery—the whirlwind hurricane who left my head spinning and my stomach dropping to my knees like I was on a roller coaster.

My thoughts were broken when a wave of water splashed up from the road, soaking my pants from the knees down. "Terrific," I grumbled, looking down at the ruined pair of strappy sandals I had just bought. This was what I got for abandoning my typical attire of jeans and Converse shoes.

Stepping away from the offending curb before another rogue wave of nasty puddle water could finish the job, I focused on making it into the building without busting my ass, or, worse yet, breaking my neck. The fake leather that had seemed so smooth and comfortable when I bought the sandals was now doing a great impersonation of a roller skate. My toes were also threatening mutiny from the cold, only adding insult to injury. This was the gajillionth reason why I had vowed never to return to Seattle. The city and I had bad blood between us.

The only reason I was standing here now was for Melissa and Rob, my two best friends from college who had demanded that I be here for their engagement party. I'd tried every feasible excuse I could come up with—"I'm sick," "I'm out of the country," "I can't get off work." No excuse seemed to stand up to Melissa's bullshit meter.

"You're one of our best friends. You have to be here," Melissa insisted.

"No. I hate you. I'm not your friend. I never was your friend," I said.

"I wish you could see the world's smallest violin I'm playing for you right now. Come on. Pull on your big-girl panties and stop hiding."

An uncomfortable silence interrupted the conversation before Melissa finally spoke up again. "I'm sorry, Brittni. I'm a bitch for even saying that. I just mean you can't let what happened dictate your life forever," Melissa had reasoned. "Besides, you're my maid of honor. I need you. Just think of this trip as a test, like dipping your toes in water. Chances are you'll hardly see him, and if you do, it's not like you guys even have to talk."

"Maybe," I said. "I'll talk to you later."

"You mean you'll see me lat—" Her words were cut off as I ended the call.

"Maybe" was the best answer I could give at the moment. The only hope I had left was my boss.

"It's a good time to go since I'll need you more next month," Ms. Miller, my principal at Woodfalls Elementary, had stated. "Mary Smith has her wrist surgery scheduled for October and won't be able to return to work until February. I swear, I've never seen someone so damn gleeful over a surgery. I'm sure it has something to do with that god-awful book-reader thingy she got for Christmas. She's always crowing about some new author she's discovered," Ms. Miller added, looking perplexed. "Me, I need an actual book in my hand, not some electronic doodad that will most likely come alive and kill me in my sleep."

"I'm thinking now might be a good time to lay off the science fiction flicks," I had countered dryly as I tried to squish the unease that had settled in the pit of my stomach. That was that. Ms. Miller was the only obstacle left. It seemed fate wanted me in Seattle.

Now, two weeks later, here I was with my shoes squishing across the tile floor of Columbia Center. It was glaringly obvious that nothing good could come from me returning to Seattle. I skirted around a security guard and headed for the women's bathroom so I could survey the damage.

"Holy shit," I muttered when I took in my appearance in the long expanse of mirrors that lined the wall. I looked like a drowned rat. My long hair, which I had painstakingly straightened earlier, had been replaced with my typical corkscrew curls that were the bane of my existence. "Damn," I sighed as I pulled my compact from my purse so I could repair my makeup-streaked face. This was just another sign I shouldn't be here. If my friend Rob hadn't been expecting me for lunch, I would have chalked it up as a lost cause and headed back to my hotel. At the moment, I'd gladly trade my soaked clothing and frozen toes for solitude in my hotel room.

"Get a grip, wimp-ass," I chastised myself out loud, ignoring a startled look from a form-fitting suit-clad woman before she hustled out of the bathroom. "Yeah, keep moving. Nothing to see here but the freako talking to herself in the bathroom," I said, grabbing a handful of paper towels to mop up my feet and legs. Tressa, my best friend back in Woodfalls, would have a field day if she saw what a mess I was, and Ashton, my other friend, would laugh and make a joke about it. I was supposed to be the one who never got frazzled and always held it together. Tressa was the more dramatic one of our trio. She made snap decisions often, never giving any thought to the consequences. Growing up, I was often left holding the short end of the stick in most of her escapades, but I didn't care. I envied her fearless attitude. I could have used an ounce of her fearlessness at the moment. I was the cautious one. The overanalyzing, skeptical, glass-is-half-empty kind of girl. Only once had I thrown caution to the wind, and it had bitten me in the ass. That one mistake was never far from my mind. How could it be? I left town and ran back home because of it. Being back at the scene of my troubles didn't help the situation. I needed to get my act together. Two years was a long time ago. I needed to buck up or whatever shit they say to get someone to stop freaking out.

I pulled my brush from my bag and ran it through my damp blond locks, cringing as it tugged through the tangled curls that had taken over my head. After a futile moment of trying to make my hair look more dignified and less like a refuge for wayward birds, I gave up and threw it in a clip, which at least made it so that I no longer looked like the bride of Frankenstein from those cheesy black-and-white movies. I added a layer of my favorite lipstick and finally felt halfway normal.

"You got this," I said, pivoting around and striding out of the bathroom. I ignored the eruption of laughter from the two giggling girls who were entering as I was leaving. Obviously I would be their comedic relief for the day.

I straightened up, finding the backbone that had liquefied and all but disappeared the moment the plane's wheels had touched down on the wet tarmac that morning. "Screw him. He doesn't own the city. I have every right to be here," I told myself as I headed for the long bank of elevators to the right of the bathrooms. A small crowd of people hurried onto one of the elevators as the doors slid open. I declined to join the overflowing box, waiting instead for the next elevator, which would be less crowded. Being closed in with a group of strangers wouldn't cut it for me. I couldn't stand being in confined spaces anyway, but elevators and I had a hate/hate kind of relationship. I hated them, and if the seventh-grade hand-crushing incident was any indication, they hated me too.

"No problem. The doors will open and you will step inside. Nice and easy," I whispered to myself. I knew it would require all my will and strength to remain sane on the elevator as it carried me up fifty-two floors to Rob's office. As is always the case with my luck, he couldn't have been on the first five or so floors, making the stairs a viable option. N-o-o-o-o-o, it had to be practically up in the clouds.

The ding signifying the arrival of the next car prompted me out of my inner whine-fest. I took a deep breath as if I were about to jump into water before cautiously stepping aboard the elevator. I exhaled a sigh of relief as the doors slowly closed and

I found myself alone for the impending ride up. This was a good thing in case my hyperventilating, I-wish-I-sucked-my-thumb-or-at-least-had-a-stiff-drink elevator behavior decided to surface.

My relief was short-lived when a hand reached between the closing doors, causing them to reopen.

"You know, sticking your hand in like that can result in serious injury." Personal experience had me pointing that out before the words locked in my throat.

All the air escaped from my lungs and I wheezed out a startled swear word as the elevator doors slid closed, trapping me inside with him. I would have gladly shared the ride with a couple of brain-starved zombies instead of him.

Our eyes locked as all the animosity and hatred from two years ago radiated off him in waves.

"Justin," I squeaked out in a voice that was totally not my own.

"Selfish bitch," he greeted me with venom dripping from each word as he punched the button for the fifty-second floor with the side of his fist.

I cringed as the elevator walls began to close in on me. I knew he hated me. He had all but shouted it in my face the very last time we'd been in the same vicinity. His eyes and words had cut me like razor blades. Every syllable had traveled across the quad until all the students who had been lounging around had turned to stare at us with morbid fascination.

Justin was the love of my life.

2.

October 2010

I met Justin on a drizzly October day during my sophomore year at UW. I disliked him on sight. He was covered in equal amounts of tattoos and girls who giggled at every word that dripped from his lush lips. Everything about him screamed *bad boy*, from his ripped jeans and pierced eyebrow to his painted-on white T-shirt. This, combined with his smoking a cigarette, pretty much sealed the deal for me. I'd lost my grandma to lung cancer a year ago. Ironically, she'd never smoked a day in her life, but my grandpa had smoked like a chimney before he passed away when I was five. Turns out all that crap they say about secondhand smoke isn't some mystical fairy tale. That shit really does kill.

I ignored Justin and his admirers as I ordered a strawberry Danish and a coffee before setting myself up at a table under a large umbrella. I had a paper due the next day in my Teaching in Diverse Populations class. Usually, I preferred the café here to the library because it was closer to the dorms. Besides, my dorm room that morning had proved to be more of a distraction than an actual study haven. My roommate, Melissa, was a total sweetheart, but her constant interruptions made getting anything written nearly impossible. She was buzzing about some big Halloween party at Alpha Delta Phi the following week and freaking out about what kind of costume she should wear as she frantically searched the Web for something original that would catch the eye of some guy. I told her to go as a Victoria's Secret angel and she'd be all set. "You know, sexy panties and bra—add in a pair of wings and you'll have all the attention you want."

"I don't want to attract that kind of attention," she wailed, glaring at me.

"Hey, you said you wanted to snag a hunk. Your words, not mine," I pointed out dryly as I closed my MacBook. I lifted my backpack from the floor and stowed away my laptop and books.

"What about this one?" she asked, whipping her computer around to reveal a person covered in purple balloons.

"You want to go as an atom?" I asked, slinging my backpack over my shoulder.

"They're grapes, not an atom, smart-ass."

"So wear the bra and panties underneath and then you can pop the balloons at an opportune time."

"Shut it," she snorted, throwing a pillow at me. "Wait, where are you going?" she asked as I headed for the door.

"Look, I love you despite the fact that you're a total spaz, but seriously, you make studying damn near impossible," I answered, throwing her a kiss.

"Do you want me to order you purple balloons?" I heard her call through the door as I headed down the hall.

I shook my head. She was a mess, but surprisingly, we'd really hit it off after a few initial speed bumps last year. Melissa's vibrant and enthusiastic personality reminded me of my friend Tressa. Every emotion she was feeling was always on display for the world to see, like she was throwing up the Bat-Signal or something. Everything was a big deal whether it was good or bad. I was the polar opposite, not wanting the whole world to know every little detail about me. On our first night as roommates, I'd watched her with morbid fascination as she had buzzed around our room chattering nonstop about the great year we were going to have, and how we would be the best of friends. After hours of endless chatter, she had finally fallen asleep in the middle of regaling me with stories of all the parties and hot guys we would be exposed to now that we were in college. While she snored loudly in the bed next to mine, I vowed that first thing in the morning, I would do everything in my power to switch roommates, but by the time the next morning had dawned bright and early, she didn't seem nearly as bad. Of course, that was probably because she woke me with a steaming cup of coffee from the small kiosk near our dorm. Anyone who recognized the importance of a morning hit of caffeine couldn't be all that bad. I won't lie, though; during the next few weeks I did question the sanity of that decision. Now, a year later, I was glad I didn't follow through with my initial plan. Sure, there were still times she wore on me, but she was pretty terrific all the other times. Even if she did act like a hyped-up Red Bull junkie most of the time.

Leaving Melissa to her costume dilemma wasn't that much of a hardship. Despite the dreary day, I enjoyed sitting by myself at one of the cafés just off campus. I was supposed to be doing my schoolwork, but people-watching kept distracting me while I sipped my coffee and nibbled on a sinfully good Danish that practically melted in my mouth.

I was halfway through my second cup of coffee and finally working on my paper when the annoying squeals from a nearby table broke my concentration.

"What about this one?" a girl asked in one of those fake baby-talk kinds of voices that got on my nerves. I could practically hear her eyelashes batting.

"Well, sweetheart, I designed that one when I was seventeen. The other half is here," a masculine voice drawled behind me.

"Oh my God. On your thigh? I want to see," another voice squealed so loud that I'm sure dogs halfway across the state were sent into a barking frenzy.

"I'm not that easy, babe," the same masculine voice chuckled as he answered. "What are you willing to trade?"

"Oh brother," I said, louder than I intended. The sudden silence behind me clued me in that my comment had been heard. Now was one of those times I wished my best friend Tressa were here. She hated when girls made an ass of themselves by fawning over some guy. Better her making the loud-mouth comment than me.

"You mean, like, I'll show you mine, if you show me yours?" the same piercing voice asked after a few awkward moments had passed.

I waited to hear what his response would be, completely annoyed with myself for paying attention to their conversation. I fought the urge to turn and look at Mr. Sure of Himself to see what had the two girls so entranced.

"You have no interest in seeing my art?" he asked into my ear, making me jump.

I silently berated myself for jumping. "Excuse me?" I asked, taking in his rugged appearance. He had nice eyes, I'd give him that, but the typical bad-boy getup made any interest I might have had go down several notches. It seemed like he was trying too hard to portray his image. Even the drenched white T-shirt that showed his six-pack abs and a well-defined chest covered in tattoos was a complete turnoff. I wondered what he would have done had it not been raining. Suddenly, I found myself laughing at a mental picture of him using a garden hose to soak himself down.

"What's so funny?" he asked, seeing that I was trying not to laugh. Without waiting for my answer, he pulled out an empty chair. The heavy metal squawked loudly across the concrete as he scooted himself toward the table.

"Why don't you sit down," I said sarcastically. "And get rid of the cigarette," I added, not caring that I didn't even know him.

His lips quirked at my testy tone before looking down at the cigarette. I expected him to scoff at my demand or even ignore it, but he surprised me by using the sole of his shoe to put it out. He earned a few more brownie points by placing the butt in his pocket versus throwing it on the ground.

"Won't your 'girlfriends' wither away into a pile of simpering drama now that you've left them?" I asked, casting a look over my shoulder, where the two blond bombshells were staring daggers into my back.

"Nah, they're cool," he said, flashing them a smile, which must have been laced with some kind of potion considering the way they both smiled back at him with such adoration. I was disgusted. He was nothing but a flirt who treated women with little respect.

"I think I'm going to hurl," I commented, making him turn his attention back to me.

He laughed. "You're hard-core. So, I'm getting the sense you don't like me. Is it because I interrupted your studying, or have we maybe hooked up before? Because I definitely think I would have remembered that."

"Please, I shudder at the thought. Does that crap actually work?" I sniped. The fact that he was callous enough to find nothing wrong with flirting with me while he was on some weird ménage-a-trois date was irritating as hell.

My comment only spurred more laughter from him. "I think you just broke my heart," he said, clutching his chest.

"I'm sure your Playboy bunnies will be more than willing to repair it."

"How about you make it up to me by going out with me?"

This time it was my turn to laugh. "Um, no thank you."

"Why not?" he asked with genuine curiosity.

"Because I don't like you," I answered, stating the obvious.

"How do you know? You don't even know me."

"Maybe not directly, but I know your type."

"My type?" he asked, ignoring the calls he was getting from the girls at the other table.

"Okay, let's forget for a moment how you're over here flirting with me while your fan club over there is cooling their heels waiting for you. I'm a little puzzled what they see in you, but the fact that they're dumb enough to actually share you makes me believe you must be an out-of-work musician or something like that. Guitar player, right?"

He threw his head back, laughing loudly at my analysis. "Wrong on both. I couldn't play an instrument to save my life. Not to mention, I'm pretty much tone-deaf. As for your first assumption, neither of them is my girlfriend. I met them at a party last night and agreed to meet up for coffee today. But enough about them. I'm curious to know why you came up with these assumptions?" he asked, sitting back in his chair and folding his arms across his chest while he casually crossed his ankles.

"Hmm, could it be the Barbie twins you're stringing along? You may not think you're dating them, but they sure think something is going on," I said, deliberately cutting my eyes in their direction. "Or, it could be all the ink. Is it a fetish, or are you just blatantly seeking attention? Your whole persona screams *misunderstood tortured soul.* I'm guessing your parents ignored you and this is a vain attempt to get their attention," I added with complete disinterest. A hint of what almost looked like disappointment flashed in his eyes but was gone in a second, convincing me I was imagining things.

"Are you one of those fortune-tellers?" he drawled. "Hey, what number am I thinking of? Kidding. What about you? Gotta be a psych major, right?" he asked, raising his pierced eyebrow, which I failed miserably at ignoring.

"Education," I answered, holding up my Teaching in Diverse Populations book.

"And you moonlight as some kind of psychoanalyzer? Watching and judging everyone?" he asked.

I bristled at his description. I wasn't some busybody who clucked her tongue judgmentally anytime someone did something I disagreed with. That was my mom's thing. Not mine. Okay, so I liked to watch people, but that was different. It's not like I ever said anything negative, at least out loud. God, was he right? Did occasionally thinking snarky thoughts while nosing into people's business make me no different than my mom? It had to be different. Besides, who didn't do that? Was there a sane person who could actually walk through

Walmart without judging someone? I pondered these questions as Mr. Wet T-Shirt continued to eye me.

"I'm just observant," I finally answered lamely. "So, if you're not some misunderstood musician, what are you?"

"Like, what species? Well, when I was younger I pretty much assumed I was a monkey, but as I got a little older I was convinced either my parents were from another planet or I was. Recently, it's come to my attention that I might also be part ass," he answered cheekily.

"Funny," I answered, sitting back in my chair.

"I'll have to tell you what I am the next time I see you," he answered, standing up as his blond companions called his name again in unison. "By the way, I'm Justin," he said, holding out his hand.

I held out my own hand, reluctantly. "It's been interesting."

"What, you're not even going to give me your name?"

"It's not like we'll be seeing each other again," I answered, knowing I sounded like a total bitch. I didn't see any point in encouraging something that was never going to happen.

"You never know. Maybe next time."

"That all depends on how many girls are in your entourage. If there *is* a next time, which I highly doubt," I pointed out, tugging at my hand, which was still clasped in his.

"Well, until then," he said, giving my hand one last squeeze before releasing it. He strolled away from the table, not bothering to look back.

I could hear Barbie One and Two pouting about his absence

as they headed in the opposite direction from where I was sitting. I didn't turn around, even though for some insane reason I wanted to. I knew I'd never see him again, and most likely he'd forget about me before he even got to the next block. I might have come off as a total hag, but it was smart not to give in to the charms of some playboy. No matter how handsome he was. Yep, I'd definitely dodged a bullet.

3.

Present Day
11:18 AM

The air whistled from my lungs rapidly as I struggled to come to terms with seeing Justin. I knew I would be running into him eventually, but I was still unprepared for this sudden appearance. Yeah, we shared the same best friends. I just thought I would have more time to prepare myself. If Satan himself had popped up and said, "Welcome to hell," I don't think I would have been more shocked. It was bad enough I was riding in a steel death trap held up by tiny cables that supposedly could handle a certain weight, but I felt like a mouse dropped into a box with a snake. There was no escape from the one person I could honestly say hated me. I focused on keeping my breathing slow and steady to try to ease the sudden feeling that I would pass out.

I could feel Justin's stare burning a hole in me as I worked to keep my eyes averted from his. I concentrated instead on finding the button for Rob's floor, but they all seemed to blur together in a haze. Then I realized Justin had already pushed the button for the fifty-second floor. Of course he was going to see Rob. Why else would he be in this elevator at the same time as me? That asshole Rob. This was a setup. I was going to kill him. He knew how Justin felt about me, about our history. Did Rob think we would all show up to his office and make up and then head to lunch like nothing had ever happened? Justin had made his feelings quite clear two years ago. Even the passing of time and having lunch together wasn't going to erase the past hurt or the words we had shared.

"What the fuck are you doing here?" he bit out as I clutched the rail inside the elevator.

Bristling at his tone, I lashed out even though I knew I shouldn't rise to the bait. "Why, do you own this building now? Did you suddenly become a self-made millionaire while I've been gone? Perhaps you finally grew some balls concerning your art," I sniped out pointedly, looking at the newest tattoo on his neck. I knew it was a low blow, but I couldn't have stopped the words if I tried.

"Huh, look who's talking, sweetheart," he drawled condescendingly.

I fought the urge to punch him and wipe the sarcastic look off his face. The injustice of the whole situation was total bullshit. He'd refused to ever own up to his part and instead let it tear us apart. I know what I did was awful, but he had set the wheels in motion. Not that I even needed to justify my actions. My decisions were mine to live with, but that didn't mean the burden was mine to carry alone.

"It's nice to see you're still an asshole," I said, watching the numbers above the door light up with each floor we passed. Only twenty floors left and I could get back on an elevator going down. I'd take a cab to Melissa's and let her know what I thought of her fiancé's interference.

"And I'm not surprised you're still a selfish bitch."

I tore my eyes away from the numbers to glare at him.

"Some things never change," he snarled just as the elevator came to a halt.

Relieved that I could finally escape the oppressiveness of the enclosed box, I waited for the doors to slide open. When they didn't open after a moment, I looked up at the numbers, confused that they were all lit up.

"You have got to be kidding me," Justin said, reaching for the telephone in the elevator's call box.

Dread filled me. "We're stuck?" I asked as panic quickly made its appearance. "We're stuck?" I repeated, since he had ignored me the first time.

"Can I help you?" I heard through the receiver in Justin's hand.

"We stopped moving here. Is something wrong with the elevator?" Justin answered, holding the phone closer to his ear so I could no longer hear her response. Not that anything the mysterious person had to say would have mattered at the moment. I was freaking out, making it hard to hear anything but my own shallow breaths.

I frantically jabbed at the OPEN DOOR button over and over again to no avail. My breaths became short quick pants as I struggled to bring air into my lungs, which were refusing to cooperate. The elevator walls felt like they were closing in on me. I instinctively held out my arms to push them away. Black spots popped up in front of my eyes and I felt myself swaying slightly. I could hear Justin's voice from far off as he hung up with the operator.

"What's the matter with you?" he asked, still sounding like he was talking from the other side of a tunnel.

"I hate closed-in spaces," I mumbled, realizing just as blackness pulled me under that this was another thing he didn't know about me.

Maybe we really never had known each other at all.

4.

November 2010

The crashing of our dorm room door against the wall woke me out of a sound sleep Halloween night. I sat up confused, rubbing my knuckles across my eyes so I could fully comprehend the sight in front of me.

"What the hell happened to you?" I asked, taking in the sight of Melissa standing in the doorway with half-inflated balloons covering her from her neck to her ankles. She looked like a cluster of grapes that had been left on the vine too long and had started to shrivel up.

"I met someone," she squealed, bouncing up and down on my bed, not caring that she was crushing my legs.

"Again?" I asked, tugging at my legs to dislodge them from under her bony butt.

"This one's not like the others. He's different," she said in a dreamy voice as she absently picked at the balloons that covered her body.

"Right," I answered, swinging my legs off the mattress. Glancing at the clock, I grimaced when I saw the time. "Gahhh, Melissa. It's two freaking AM. I have a trig exam in the morning," I complained, heading to the communal bathroom we shared with the room next door. Whoever came up with the brilliant idea that four girls could share a teeny-tiny bathroom must have been smoking crack.

"Oops, sorry. I lost track of time. Rob and I spent hours talking. He's so smart and funny. He's some kind of business major, but he writes this poetry that makes your toes curl," she gushed as she flopped backward on my mattress, popping the few remaining balloons on her back that still had air in them.

"You don't say," I mumbled. I was used to her immediate fascination with something that was new and shiny. I closed the bathroom door behind me, but I could still hear her chattering away like I was in the room.

"So, how did you meet this Rob the Poet character?" I asked once I was back in my bed.

"Bobbing for apples. He tied my hands behind my back," she sighed happily, pulling the balloons off one at a time.

"Honey, I'd watch who I mentioned that to. You know, the whole bondage thing," I teased, stifling a yawn.

"Ha, that's so not funny," she growled, throwing a balloon at me that missed the mark completely as it fluttered harmlessly toward the floor.

"I try. Now shut off the light. I'm exhausted."

"Fine, party pooper," she grumbled before plunging the room into darkness.

I fell asleep to the sound of more deflating balloons and Melissa still chattering on about how fantastic Rob was and how she couldn't wait for me to meet him. She finally quieted down after I chucked a pillow at her, even though I heard her complaining quietly how it would have been easier to take her costume off if she had a little light.

"Hurry, Brittni, we're going to be late," Melissa demanded, hopping impatiently from one foot to the other while I pulled my favorite loosely woven sweater over my head.

"I thought you said it starts at seven," I replied, adding the final touches to my appearance.

"It does, but Rob wanted us to get there early so we can support his friend. So get your ass in gear."

"Fine, but need I remind you I'm the one doing you a favor here? Art shows really aren't my thing."

"I know, I know. How about you mention it another million times? But you agreed to go so Rob's best friend in the world isn't embarrassed if he doesn't get a good turnout."

"So, having me there to witness his misery is a perk, how?" I asked, pulling on my coat.

"Bodies are bodies. Anything that looks like people actually showed is better than nothing."

"If you say so," I said gloomily, wishing I'd stood firm on my original answer, which had been a resounding no. Melissa had worn me down over the last few days using every resource in her arsenal from begging to outright bribery. Her final last-ditch attempt was to offer to bring me morning coffee every day for the next month. That finally sealed the deal. What can I say? I'm a coffee whore.

"You at least have to *act* like you're having fun or you'll be getting decaf delivered in the morning," she said as we made our way across campus huddled together. The brisk November wind was making a good effort at cutting through our jackets.

"You wouldn't dare," I gasped.

"I would. Now show me a smile."

I finally let my lips spread into a smile that came off more as a grimace.

"Whoa, slow down, sister. We don't want to scare them. How about a smile that doesn't look like someone is pulling off your toenails with pliers?"

"How about this?" I asked, flashing an exaggerated smile that was all teeth.

"Better, I guess, but you might want to rethink the piece of spinach you have stuck between your teeth," she chirped, nudging me toward the campus art museum.

"Crap, really?" I griped, using my nail to dislodge the offending leaf.

"At least I told you," she pointed out as we stepped into the warm lobby. "Whew, it is freaking cold out there."

"That's nothing compared to what we get back home this time of year."

"That's insanity," she replied, pulling off her jacket as she scanned the atrium. "Oh, there's Rob," she squealed, smoothing her hair down before dragging me off toward a dark-haired guy standing off to the side of the entryway talking to another guy who had his back to us.

"Melissa," Rob said as he broke off his conversation and dragged Melissa into his arms for a quick hard hug.

"Rob, this is my roomie, aka college bestie, Brittni Mitchell," Melissa said, tugging my hand so I was face to face with her current crush.

"Rob, it's nice to meet you. Melissa thinks quite highly of your poetry," I said, holding out my hand for him to shake.

"I'm more of a hugging kind of person," he said, ignoring my outstretched hand to pull me in. I automatically stiffened since I wasn't much of a hugger. It must be a trait I inherited from my dad because my mom is the exact opposite. She would hug a stranger on the street. Even Tressa and I were more the punch-in-the-arm kind of friends than hugging it out. "I'd like you to meet my friend Justin," Rob finally said, releasing me. I knew by the chuckling behind me that it was too much of a coincidence to pray that his friend was not the same Justin who had hit on me the previous week.

"Brittni, is it? I told you I'd be alone the next time we met," the same voice drawled.

I turned around to acknowledge him after flashing a glare at Melissa, who looked completely mystified.

"You two know each other?" she asked, looking questioningly at Rob, who looked equally confused.

"Yeah, we had the honor of meeting last week," I answered sarcastically. "Did you leave your Playboy bunnies at the mansion, or are they fetching you a drink?" I added, making a production of looking around. I knew I was being an uber bitch. I had no idea what was wrong with me. So he was a flirt. Half the males at UW were flirts. It just rubbed me the wrong way that he had no problem flirting with me while he was with someone else.

"I told you, they're just friends, so sheathe the sword, honey," he answered smoothly, completely unscathed by my biting tone.

"What is the matter with you?" Melissa hissed in my ear.

"Nothing," I mumbled out of the corner of my mouth, feeling slightly abashed at my behavior.

"Well, knock it off. It's rude to insult the artist at his first showing," she said through gritted teeth, looking embarrassed for me.

"This is *your* show?" I asked unbelievingly.

"Surprised again? How could a bad boy have actually left the tattoo parlor and dropped the beer long enough to create something, right?" he quizzed, smirking at me.

"Absolutely," I answered, smiling grudgingly at him for the first time. "Of course, I'll reserve further judgment until I look around."

"I wouldn't expect anything less from you," he answered, with the same smirk on his face. It was clear he was enjoying himself immensely.

"I'm sorry. That wasn't nice of me," I said apologetically, turning toward my friend, who was studying me like I was a creature that had just crawled up from the pits of some swamp. She looked at me with an equal mixture of horror and morbid fascination. I couldn't blame her. In the year and half that we had been roommates, I had never acted like this. Sure, I could be standoffish, but I was never stuck up. It was like I was channeling my inner Mean Girl.

Rob, on the other hand, was openly laughing.

"What's so funny, bro?" Justin asked.

"Did you say 'bad boy'? More like 'dud boy,'" he said, gasping for air.

"Don't be a douche-stick. I could totally be a bad boy," Justin complained, socking Rob in the arm.

"Riiiiight."

"I'm so glad I asked you here tonight to lend some moral support," Justin said dryly.

"Dude, I've got your back on your art, but the bad-boy status is a no-go," Rob said, slinging an arm around Melissa's shoulders. "So, let's show these ladies your kick-ass artwork," he added, leading Melissa into the main room of the building.

"You game?" Justin asked me, nodding toward the room.

"Sure, let's see what you got," I said, following along, but not sure what to expect. Maybe something abstract, like art created from metal or maybe beer bottles. Stepping through the doorway, though, I was completely caught off-guard at what I saw. The art on display in front of me stopped me in my tracks.

"What do you think?" Justin asked, turning to look back at me.

I couldn't speak as I took in the pieces scattered throughout the room. I wasn't even sure if *beautiful* was the right word to describe his art. It deserved a word with more impact, like *breathtaking*, even though that didn't seem quite sufficient either. They literally took my breath away. He didn't use the typical canvas to make his mark. Instead, he used huge slabs of distressed wood that were easily six feet across and five feet high. Each piece of wood was different in shape, but there was no mistaking that every one belonged to him. He didn't do the cutesy landscapes or abstract art that left you scratching your head in confusion. I guess an ignorant person would call what he did portrait art, but to call it that was almost an insult. Each piece depicted a different face. Some were young, while others were older. There was an equal mixture of women and men of all races. Each one was beautiful beyond words. Instead of covering the wood with paint, he had used the paint to enhance the natural coloring in all the different types of woods he used. It was as if he had stamped an image on each piece.

"Insane, right?" Melissa squealed, joining me. I hushed her, not wanting to spoil the mood with mindless chatter.

"So come on. What do you think?" Justin asked earnestly as Melissa melted away into the background. I took a moment to answer as I studied the painting of the elderly woman in front of me. The attention to detail blew my mind as I took in every wrinkle and crease on her face.

"They're amazing. You're going to be famous," I breathed, finally able to speak.

"Did hell just freeze over, or did you just give me a compliment?" he asked, winking at me as he reached for my hand with excitement. "There's hope for us yet."

"Hope? That's an awfully strong word to use," I said, looking down at our linked hands. "I'm not going out on a date with you, even if you're not a typical bad boy," I added, pulling my hand from his. I tried not to think about how warm and inviting it had felt wrapped around my fingers or whether every part of him was equally warm.

"Give me one good reason why not," he coaxed.

"I'll give you two. One, you're a terrible flirt," I said, holding up a finger.

"Hey, I think my flirting skills are top-notch," he interrupted, deliberately being dense.

"Exactly, you'd flirt with anything that has a pair of tits."

"Not true. I've never hit on a cow," he teased.

"Only because there aren't a whole lot of cows walking around the Seattle area," I pointed out.

"I think you're exaggerating the flirting, but that's a doable fix. What's reason number two?"

"I don't date smokers. Ever."

"Again, easy fix," he bragged.

"How so?"

"I'm not really a smoker. I enjoy an occasional cigarette, but that's about all."

"I don't date people in denial who only smoke occasionally," I stated skeptically.

"No, I'm serious. I bet I smoke a cigarette a week, if that."

"Even one a week is a deal breaker for me. I hate the smell and the smoke."

"Done. I won't smoke while we're dating."

"Who said anything about dating? We were talking about one date," I squawked, wondering how he'd gained the upper hand. I wasn't sure how I felt about his persistence.

"Fine. Go out with me once. If you hate it, no harm, no foul."

"I can't go out with you. I don't even like you," I said, less convincingly than I had the last time I'd seen him.

"Sure you do. Otherwise you wouldn't be here," he said confidently. "Come on, one date."

I studied his earnest expression for a few seconds, mentally weighing the pros and cons. "Fine, but I'm going to hate it," I said, caving as he grinned at me.

5.

Present Day
11:20 AM

I came to with Justin hovering over me. My eyes focused on his, and for a moment I thought I saw a flash of concern before his stare hardened again. "I never thought you'd take the damsel-in-distress route," I heard him say as he backed up to the far side of the elevator.

I closed my eyes again to try to get my bearings. Whatever asshole comments he had, coupled with the fact that I was lying on some nasty elevator floor, were the least of my concerns. My biggest problem was that I felt no movement beneath me, meaning I was still stranded in this death trap. I slowly slid myself up until I was sitting against the wall of the elevator.

Feeling no less panicked than when I blacked out, I focused on keeping my breathing steady to move my attention from the elevator walls, which still felt as if they would smother me.

"What did she say?" I asked, indicating the call box.

"Just that there's some kind of power failure and we should sit tight while they call the experts," he barked out. He couldn't even bring himself to look at me as he held his phone in the air. "I'm not getting dick for cell service either. I'm going to kick Rob's ass when we finally get out of here."

His words slowly registered in my brain. *Sit tight?* What the hell did that even mean? Sit tight for the next few seconds? A few minutes? Several hours? Seriously, who tells someone to sit tight while they're trapped with their ex in a small enclosed space hundreds of feet in the air?

"You're not going to pass out again, are you?" he asked sarcastically as he studied me from across the elevator. "I don't remember you being such a pansy."

I ignored his ribbing while I concentrated on my breathing. "Did she guesstimate how long it would take?" I tried to sound unconcerned but knew it was pointless.

"Does it matter? We're stuck together. Talk about irony at its worst," he snapped. "If I didn't know better, I'd say you'd had something to do with this."

"Oh yeah, you got me," I snapped, sitting up straight. "I've missed your winning personality so much that Rob and I worked out this whole plan to hijack an elevator so I could be alone with you and tell you how much I missed you, and how

I can't live another day without you, and how I've tried to get hold of you for the last two years. Oh wait—I haven't."

He eyed me critically for a moment before looking away, almost satisfied. My sudden anger had dissipated any panic I was feeling. Judging by the look on his face, it was as though that had been his intention all along, but I knew better. It would be a cold day in hell before he ever did anything that came close to helping me.

The little bit of adrenaline I felt from my outburst was short-lived. Slumping back against the elevator again, I no longer felt like the walls were closing in on me, but it didn't make the situation any more comfortable. We both sat in stubborn silence, as if the first one to talk would somehow lose the battle. The tension was high and began to feel heavy and oppressive, but I wasn't about to cave.

"Since when are you scared of elevators?" Justin asked, without looking at me.

I silently celebrated my small victory and even debated being petty for a moment and not answering him, but the silence was wearing on me. "Since always."

"Why didn't I know?"

"I don't know. Maybe because we never went on an elevator together—or maybe we just didn't talk about those things.

"Yeah, you're pretty good at keeping secrets."

I sighed loudly. This was why there would be no reconciliation, even after two years. I had made a decision that threw down a gauntlet between us. I clamped my mouth closed, determined not to say another word until we were out of this situation. Pulling my iPhone from my bag, I began to scroll through my apps in search of anything to help pass the time. No bars meant no Facebook or Twitter, so I clicked on Spider Solitaire. I could feel Justin's eyes boring into me, but I wouldn't give him the satisfaction of looking up. By the time I was playing my second hand of solitaire, I had successfully managed to put him somewhat out of my mind. When he finally did speak again, the suddenness of his voice made me jump.

"So, why the hatred of elevators?" he asked.

Glancing up, I weighed his question, wondering if it was even worth it to tell the story. Surely the elevator would start moving at any time. Justin continued to stare at me, waiting for an answer. This was how it had always been with us. He was always asking questions about my life before college, wanting to hear all my stories. I had chalked it up to the artist in him, who seemed to look at life in layers, as if it were a painting or a sculpture. Looking back now, it seemed crazy that I had never shared the elevator story with him since it was such a traumatic moment in my life.

"When I was in seventh grade my hand got crushed in an elevator door," I answered, flexing the fingers on my right hand, which to this day still tended to tighten up and often went numb.

He didn't say anything, waiting instead like he had so many times before for me to continue. It was so achingly familiar that my heart actually hurt. In the two years since our breakup, I had convinced myself that our relationship had been nothing special. That it only seemed that way because it was so intense and new at the time. Now, sitting here, it was painfully clear that I was kidding myself to think I could dismiss what we had shared.

"We were on a field trip to the public library in the big city not far from Woodfalls. It was a yearly tradition for seventh graders and believe it or not, was a pretty big deal for us considering the library in Woodfalls at that time was a joke. We were supposed to be doing research for some class project on influential figures of the twentieth century. Our teacher was old school and wanted us to use actual books for research in lieu of the Internet. Anyway, this library was huge and had two floors with an elevator. Well, for some reason—I don't even remember why anymore—a few of us decided to go for a joyride. Then, that creep Tommy Jones, who knew I was scared anyway, had convinced everyone to run off the elevator just as the door was closing. Afraid of being on the elevator by myself, I stuck out my hand to stop the door, but my hand didn't make it to the rubber sensor that should have caused the doors to bounce back open. Instead, the elevator door closed against my fingers for the entire ride up to the second floor. I screamed bloody murder the entire time and freaked out everyone in the library," I said, grinning wryly. "Especially when they saw my hand," I added, wagging my fingers at him. "I broke all four fingers on my right hand and also sprained my left hand in my frantic attempt to try to pry the elevator door open. By the time I got to the hospital, my fingers were swollen to the size of sausages."

"Did you pound the prick Tommy Jones with your cast?" he asked.

"Nope. I didn't have to. Word spread to his mom, who happened to be the principal of our school. She stuck it to him, made him shadow me for six weeks. He had to do all my writing for me in my classes. I had a cast on one hand and an Ace bandage wrapped around the other, but watching Tommy doing double work was almost worth it."

"I would have still pounded his ass," Justin growled.

"That's because you're quick to overreact in a situation," I said, instantly wishing I could recall the words.

"At least I react in some fashion, like any normal human. I'm not some freaking robot that can't show any emotion," he snarled, turning away from me. My heart dropped. We were never going to get past this. He thought I was emotionless, but he hadn't been there to see what had really happened. I wouldn't allow myself to dwell on how harsh he sounded, because I knew the truth.

6.

November 2010

"Where are we going?" I asked with Justin leading me by the hand from my dorm room. It had been a week since his art show and the day of our first date had finally arrived. I'd had serious doubts and even tried backing out. I pleaded with Melissa to lie and cover for me, but she wouldn't budge.

"What the frick is your deal with this guy?" she asked, placing her hands on her hips for emphasis because somehow that made her point more clearly. "You've never been like this before. You've got your OCD issues when it comes to dating, and whatever that crazy one-date-only rule is, I'll never understand, but usually you give the dude a chance."

"I don't know," I sighed, sinking down on my bed. "Something about him just unsettles me."

"Unsettles? Do you not trust him?" she asked, concerned. "Did he do something?" she added, looking as ferocious as her slight five-foot-one-inch frame would allow.

"Chill, mother hen. No, he just makes me feel weird, kind of jittery. I disliked him on sight, and yeah, maybe that was wrong and a bit presumptuous on my part. Especially considering at his art show I got a glimpse of a side of him I wasn't expecting, but now I'm worried I'll be disappointed because he'll turn out to be the asshole I pegged him for in the first place."

"That's some messed-up logic," she said, hitting me with a pillow. "It sounds to me like you like him and you don't want to admit it."

I shrugged my shoulders since she'd pretty much nailed it on the head.

"In that case then, no, I won't lie for you. It'll do you some good to forget about these preconceived notions of yours and realize that sometimes it takes more than one date to get to know someone. Besides, you've got to give a little to get a little."

"I'm not like you. I don't give anything on the first date," I teased.

"Hey, whatever, slut, that's not what I meant," she squealed, tossing the pillow at my head.

"I'm kidding," I laughed. "Anyway, I disagree. If the first date sucks, then why should I torment myself by going out a second time? Face it, Melissa, college guys are the same duds they were in high school. They're just a little cockier and more persistent here," I pointed out, since her track record wasn't that much better than mine.

"Rob is different, though," she replied. "And maybe Justin will be too."

"So you say. Only time will tell," I said, rising reluctantly from my bed so I could get dressed.

An hour later I wished I were still on my bed instead of heading out on some date, during the day no less, waiting for Justin to answer my question.

"If I tell you where we're going, it'll ruin the surprise, but I think you might like it," he said, grinning confidently as he stopped in front of a beat-up jeep with no roof and no doors.

"You're kidding, right?" I asked.

"What? You don't like jeeps?" he asked, leading me to the passenger side.

"I'm not sure how I feel about them one way or another. I've never ridden in one. It's just—you do realize you live in Seattle?"

"Sure, why?"

"Well, it's not the most practical vehicle for this state, is it? You know the whole 'no roof, no door, lots of rain' thing. Not to mention, I could easily picture one sharp turn sending me tumbling out to become instant roadkill." With those words, I pulled on my seat belt to make sure it was firmly latched.

"Aw, you're not afraid to get a little wet, are you?" He cranked the engine, which started with a loud grumble before idling louder than I was used to. I'm sure the missing windows and roof were partly to blame for some of the noise, but not much.

"Not at all," I answered. "Just tell me you at least have an umbrella."

He laughed as we accelerated down the road. "Don't worry, it has a roof and doors for rainy days and a soft top for the summertime, but when it's cool like this with no rain in the forecast, I like to take it all off," he said conversationally.

I nodded but didn't answer since the wind whipping around us made it difficult to hear. I was glad I'd pulled my hair back before I left my room, since riding like this would have surely turned me into a striking replica of a scarecrow. The breeze was downright cold as we sped along, but surprisingly it felt kind of nice as it chilled my face. My fear of tumbling out the side of the jeep had faded as the exhilaration of the ride took over. There was an odd sense of freedom that came from speeding down the road with nothing boxing me in. I didn't realize I was smiling until Justin commented on it.

"I knew you were a jeep kind of girl," he said, pulling into a half-full parking lot.

"Seattle Aquarium?" I asked.

"It's sort of my muse for a new series I'm working on," he answered, hopping down from the jeep and heading over to my side. He pulled off his gloves and placed his hands on my chilled face. The warmth of his hands and his close proximity set me on edge.

"What are you doing?" I pulled back.

"Oh, sorry. I was just warming up your face. It's beet red from the wind," he answered, taking another step closer. We stared at each other for a moment as if in a trance. I couldn't help focusing on his lips, wondering what they would feel like on mine. Part of me wanted to shove him away, but then I thought about what Melissa had said. My brain was sending me frantic warning messages and I could feel myself leaning in like I had no control of my body.

"Here, let me help you down," he said, reaching for my hands. I sat for a moment, confused about what had just happened. Did he just play me, or had I misread his signals? The look on Justin's face gave me no indication. Either he had a great poker face, or he was oblivious and I was the idiot who thought she was about to be kissed.

"Ready?" he asked.

"Huh, yeah, I guess," I answered, hoping I didn't sound as squirrelly as I felt at the moment. "I thought you only painted people?"

"Most times I do. I was asked to do a series for the hospital, so I'm kinda mixing it up."

"Wow, that's awesome. It must be cool to earn money off your talent while you're still in school." Money was kind of tight for me since I only worked a few hours a week at a local daycare. Working around my school schedule had proven to be much more difficult this semester and I had lost a ton of hours.

"Nah, this isn't a paying gig," he answered as we approached the ticket booth.

"What? That's insanity. Your work is too good to give away."

"It's cool. I just like being able to do what I love. Besides, think about all the people who will get to see it every day."

"I guess, but I still think you should get paid. I know a hospital is a more charitable kind of thing, but I also know they make the bucks too."

He shrugged, making it obvious he wasn't all that crazy about the direction of the conversation. I wanted to say more about the fact that he was being taken advantage of and that he needed to know his value, but I let it drop. It wasn't any of my business to tell him what he should or shouldn't do.

Some of the awkward tension left Justin once we walked through the aquarium doors and he linked his fingers with mine. I could have easily pulled my hand away but became quickly distracted by the large window in front of us with hundreds of fish swimming behind it. We didn't have anything this cool near Woodfalls. My only experience with aquariums was a trip to the Baltimore National Aquarium I had won in a short-story writing contest when I was thirteen. Ten winners got to go. The best part was our English teacher, Ms. Cooper, was our chaperone. The worst part was the twelve-hour van ride to Baltimore. I felt nauseated the entire way, but once we got there it was completely worth it. I enjoyed seeing all the different exhibits and being able to feed the dolphins and touch the stingrays. The Seattle Aquarium was tiny in comparison, but I kinda preferred the intimate feel. Plus, it was a hell of a lot less crowded.

"Oh, wow," I proclaimed, staring into the large enclosure.

"Pretty cool, huh?"

"It's crazy cool."

"I remember you saying how much you liked Puget Sound last week, so I thought you'd enjoy seeing what's beneath the surface," he said, sitting down on a bench. He unzipped an old worn-out backpack that had seen better days and pulled out a sketchpad and a thick pencil.

"So, you're doing fish for the hospital?" I asked, nodding toward the large window.

He ignored my question and focused completely on the sketchpad in his hands. It was as if he had been put under some kind of trance the moment the sketchpad hit his hands. The pencil seemed to have a mind of its own as it moved effortlessly across the page. I turned my attention back to the fish behind the thick glass. It was entertaining to watch the dynamics of life in a world so different from my own. Some of the fish swam lethargically along, like they didn't have a care in the world, while others seemed to be chasing each other as they darted in and around the plants. With my eyes still on the live show in front of me, I settled on the bench next to Justin, who still had not looked up. Minutes faded away and many families came and went. Some gasped over the fish behind the huge glass, while others didn't look impressed at all. Through dozens of screaming and squealing kids, Justin and I remained on the bench. If not for the scratching of the pencil, I would have assumed he had fallen asleep.

It was thirty minutes later when he finally looked up from the page. "Sorry, I wanted to get that down while it was still fresh in my mind," he said, closing the sketchpad.

"Not so fast," I said, holding out my hand. "Let me see."

"It's not done," he answered, stowing it in his bag.

I didn't argue. The intensity he had the entire time he was drawing led me to believe he took his work very seriously.

"So, what do you think?" he asked, indicating the large expanse of windows in front of us. "Pretty cool way to show visitors a glimpse into what it's like beneath Puget Sound?"

"It's breathtaking. I could stay here all day."

"Been there, done that," he said, throwing his head back to laugh. Several preteen girls turned to stare at him, looking completely entranced before dissolving into a heap of giggles. As we left the viewing area, I could still hear them giggling and chattering away.

"I think you have a fan club," I said, throwing a look over my shoulder at the girls.

"You think?" he asked, raising his pierced eyebrow, which naturally drew my attention. Everything about him seemed designed to appeal to the opposite sex. I wasn't the only one to notice as we continued walking through the aquarium. I caught women young and old openly admiring him. There was no denying he was attractive. Obviously, any warm-blooded female would attest to that. Knowing the way the female mind works, I realized I was also being judged by his many admirers as to whether I was worthy to be with some-one with his looks. Not that I felt I was ugly, but feeling inse-cure around guys was never my thing. Being with Justin had a way of making me feel like I was lacking in one capacity or another. It was more my problem than his, and I realized that.

The only problem was I was beginning to find I actually enjoyed his company. He was laid back, good-natured, and very easy to talk to. It was a shame I had to end things before they got started.

We were eating lunch when I mentioned it. "Today has been really fun."

"Why do I sense a *but* coming?" he asked, dipping a French fry in ketchup.

I smiled slightly at his intuitiveness. At least he wasn't dense like the last guy I ended it with before the first date was even over. "But, I just think we're too different."

"Different? How?"

"I'm sure you've noticed I'm not the most open person," I started, glaring at him when he grinned broadly at my words. "Fine, it's obvious," I acknowledged. "The point is you're the exact opposite. You have a way of making someone feel special even if you don't say a word."

"Care to elaborate?" he asked, settling back in his chair with his arms crossed across his chest.

"Like you don't know," I answered, exasperated. "A smile here. A wink there. You're a born flirt. I may have been off on the bad-boy part, but I was dead-on when it comes to your flirty nature."

"Flirty nature? God, could you emasculate me any more?" he joked, leaning forward so we were closer. "So, I'm friendly. No harm, no foul."

"Player," I countered.

"Easygoing," he volleyed.

"Tease."

"Affectionate."

I couldn't help laughing at his persistence. "Whatever way you phrase it, I'm not looking for a relationship."

"What are you looking for?" he asked with a more serious tone.

"I'm not sure," I answered honestly. "I've been here a year and a half and I feel like I'm barely scratching the surface. Take today, for example. I'm not sure I would have ever come here if you hadn't brought me. It's not like this is a place my friends are talking about. There are so many things I want to do that I've never had the opportunity to do before."

"Strict parents?" he questioned.

"No, it's not that. It's just, I'm from a very small town. You know, the kind of place where you sneeze and everyone knows about it. God forbid you actually do something scandalous like make out with Gregory James in Mr. Jacobs's science lab."

"Gregory James? Is he someone I have to worry about?"

"Very funny. My point is I'm enjoying my freedom more than I ever thought I would. I don't feel like bogging it down with a relationship."

"Don't you get lonely?"

"Have you met my roommate?" I joked. "Melissa kinda doesn't allow for loneliness."

He laughed. "She is something else. I like her, though. Her enthusiasm is cool and Rob seems to dig her."

"Oh, don't get me wrong. I love her to death, but she pretty much fills any void I may have."

"I didn't realize you two were those kind of roommates," he teased, his innuendo clear. "Maybe I should come hang out."

"You wish."

"You mean you two don't have pillow fights?" he asked, giving me puppy-dog eyes.

"Strangely, no. We also don't have wet T-shirt contests or play Truth or Dare every night."

"Just on some nights?" he asked hopefully.

"Is it hard-wired in every guy's brain that girl-on-girl is hot?" I asked, popping a fry into my mouth.

"Depends on the girls," he answered.

"Oh boy. Sexist much?"

"Girls just look at it wrong. It's more of a compliment that we'd like to see you hook up at least once."

"Excuse me while I puke," I said, making exaggerated gagging noises.

"Does that mean you're done with lunch?" he asked. He crumpled up his burger wrapper and tossed it into his empty fry container.

"Yeah. Are we leaving?" I asked. I was surprised he'd given in so quickly. Just goes to show my instincts were dead-on.

"Hell no. If I only get one date with you, I'm going to make it worthwhile. We've pretty much seen everything here, so we're going to head out to see one of my favorite things about Seattle. You game?"

I turned his words over in my mind, trying to decide what to do. My intention had been to call it a day once we left the aquarium. I wasn't one to give false hope for something that wasn't going to happen, but he already knew where I stood and seemed to accept it. I didn't see the harm in finishing the day as long as he knew once it was over, that would be it.

"Lead the way," I finally answered, trying to convince myself it didn't mean anything that he smiled broadly at my words.

My second ride in his jeep was as exhilarating as the first. The sun had broken through the cloudy morning haze, making it feel almost warm outside. My face was still red and felt slightly chapped by the time we pulled into the parking spot at our next destination. "Olympic Sculpture Park?" I questioned.

"Have you been here?" he asked, sounding disappointed.

"No, but some guys were talking about it in my psychology class last semester. I've wanted to come out here but kept forgetting about it," I answered, jumping down from the jeep.

"Well, I'm glad I thought to bring you here, then," he said, leading the way.

I could see why this was his favorite place. Even though I wasn't an artist, something about the outdoor museum was tranquil and peaceful. The art was oversized and I knew I was most likely missing the significance of each piece, but I still enjoyed looking at each one. Justin kept up a running commentary, providing all the details of the nine-acre park. He also pointed out the pieces that were permanent and the sections that were there on a temporary basis. I couldn't help eating up his words. His attention to detail and facts about each piece kept me interested.

"What do you think?" he asked as we made our way back to where we had started from.

"Definitely has the cool factor," I answered, buttoning up my jacket to ward off the sudden chill in the air.

"Thanks for bringing me here. Today was fun," I admitted as we left the park.

"Day's not over yet. It's time for some grub."

"Again? We just ate," I said, checking the time on my phone.

"Like four hours ago. Besides, by the time we eat it'll be closer to five hours."

"Where are we going?"

"Another favorite place of mine."

"You seem to have a lot of those."

"When I like something, I don't have any qualms about stating my feelings," he answered in a voice that made me wonder if it held a double meaning.

"Are you cold?" Justin asked as we piled into his jeep.

"Not too bad now, but I'm sure I'll be a Popsicle once we start moving."

"Here," he said, reaching behind my seat and extracting an oversized fleece blanket. "Don't worry, it's clean. I keep it in here for when my kid sister is in the jeep with me."

"Your sister?"

"Yes, my sister. Are you always this distrustful?"

"No, but with your reputation I'm just trying to stay on my toes."

"What reputation?" he asked, popping open the glove compartment and pulling out a skullcap. "You've got some pretty funked-up views about me."

"Please. Melissa told me you've dated enough girls to fill a sorority house."

"Whatever. Talk about people in glass houses."

"Are you insinuating that I've gone out with as many people as you?" I sputtered indignantly.

"Insinuating? Hell no. I'm stating a fact. You're no different than me, sister."

"It's not the same thing," I replied.

"Whatever helps you sleep at night," he said loudly over the wind that was whipping through the vehicle.

I fought the childish urge to stick out my tongue at him. His dating life and mine were worlds apart, considering the fact that I didn't fall into bed with every guy I dated. I kept that piece of information to myself, though. No reason to discuss my sex life with someone I hardly knew. Of course, I wouldn't be surprised if loose-lips Melissa had already filled him in on my stats in that category. Her ass was mine when I got back to the dorm. Revenge would be swift and just.

We drove in silence for close to thirty minutes and despite my misgivings about the blanket on my lap, I ended up burrowing my face in it when the wind became almost painful. With the warm fleece against my sore face, the ride was bearable and I could enjoy it despite my watery eyes.

I began to have misgivings about more than the blanket as the city and businesses faded behind us and were replaced by suburbs. Justin made a left turn, and a right, and a left again. Not that it mattered. All the house-lined streets looked the same. There were no restaurants in sight, which left me with only one sadistic thought. *Please don't let him be a weirdo who is dragging me to his dungeon or something.*

My heart sank when he pulled into a circular driveway and parked behind an oversized SUV that screamed *family vehicle.*

"Please, for the love of all things holy, tell me you're not some crazy stalker. That this isn't your secret residence and you plan on chaining me up in your basement or something," I said, eyeing the brightly lit house with trepidation.

He looked at me like I had sprung an extra head before laughing loudly. "Sorry. I'm fresh out of chains. This is my mom's house."

"Fuck me," I mumbled as he jumped down from the vehicle.

He laughed at my colorful choice of words, but I could have sworn I heard him mutter something along the lines that he'd like to do just that.

7.

Present Day
12:14 PM

"This is bullshit," Justin ranted. He surged to his feet after twenty minutes of uncomfortable silence in our stalled-out tomb.

I remained silent as he paced back and forth, swearing with each step. His outburst was unexpected. The entire time we'd dated he'd always been so laid back, except for the end, of course. I watched him with a heavy heart, wondering where the boy I had fallen in love with had gone. The man pacing in front of me showed little resemblance to the person I once knew. Was this my fault? Did the lies and secrets lead to this?

After a few minutes of watching him tick like a bomb waiting to go off, I finally broke into his rant. "How's your family?" I asked quietly.

The words instantly had the effect I knew they would. Above all else, Justin loved his family. The first night I met them I would have gladly swum with a tank full of hungry flesh-eating piranhas rather than walk into their house. It had taken Justin a full five minutes to talk me out of his jeep. I remember how he had laughed at my apprehension as we made our way up the lighted path to the front door. It was obvious he thought I might bolt, which was completely possible.

"They're all the same," he sighed against the elevator wall. "Crazy, loud, obnoxious at times, but I guess some would call it lovable," he answered with a hint of pride in his voice.

"Some things never change," I mused. I had to admit I missed them.

"They still ask about you," he admitted, studying his knuckles.

"They do?" I asked, although I wasn't surprised. They were sweet people who had welcomed me from the beginning.

"I never told them what happened."

"You didn't?" I asked in a strained voice.

"No. I figured, why ruin the illusion?" he said bitterly. "They all thought you were perfect."

"I never pretended to be perfect," I mumbled, picking invisible lint off my pants. "How's Hollie?" I asked, trying to steer the conversation away from another yell-fest.

"She's great. The same gangly, awkward, but beautiful girl. She started middle school last year and is a total band geek now," he answered like a proud parent. She was his kid sister, but in truth he was probably a better father than her real dad.

"Band? That's great. I guess the tone-deaf gene skipped her, huh?"

"Must have. She definitely has mad skills."

"What about Travis?"

"He's better once we convinced him he wasn't that unique just because he came out of the closet."

"And your dad? Is he still giving him a hard time?" I inquired with an edge in my voice. Out of his whole family, the only one I'd disliked was his father. Since his parents were divorced, I'd had the misfortune of meeting him once. He was a total monkey-douche. How Justin's sweet, loving, and a bit hare-brained mother wound up with such an ass was beyond me. He was unyielding and opinionated and gave all new meaning to the word *dictator*.

The ringing of the elevator's emergency phone interrupted our conversation. "Finally," I shouted, jumping to my feet as Justin grabbed the receiver.

"Yeah," he answered. "We're fine, just ready to get out of here." I wished I could hear the voice on the other end. With all my nervous energy, I almost ripped the phone from his hand.

"Oh, come on. You can't be serious," he replied, looking deflated. "Can you at least contact Rob Froch on the fifty-second floor and let him know we're in here? He's expecting us." His words immediately took the wind from my sails also.

I slid back down against the elevator wall, waiting for the inevitable bad news.

"It may be a couple hours at least before they can get someone here to fix it," Justin complained as he hung up the receiver.

8.

....

November 2010

Meeting Justin's family was as awkward as I thought it would be. His mother was pleasant during the introductions, but judging by the surprised look on her face, my visit was as unexpected for her as it was for me. I kept a smile plastered to my face as we exchanged pleasantries, while I plotted Justin's demise the entire time in my mind. Things became more comfortable after his brother and sister joined us, and I watched how they interacted together. He teased his little sister, Hollie, mercifully, but she ate it up. It became glaringly obvious Justin was her hero. His younger brother, Travis, instantly drew me in with his intuitiveness and tender but humorous insight. During dinner he regaled us with stories that I'm sure Justin would rather have remained family secrets. My stomach ached from laughing so hard. It turned out Justin's mother was a teacher, which made for smooth conversation also. We talked about my majoring in education and how things had changed in public schools during her twenty-five years of teaching. Things had gone so well at that point that I was in the process of silently patting myself on the back, when of course the inevitable happened, and I dropped a stack of dishes as I was helping clear the table. Justin, Travis, and Hollie had all responded by applauding at me standing among the pile of broken dishes. Suddenly, Justin's demise became an option again.

"I'm really sorry about the dishes," I apologized for the hundredth time as Trish, Justin's mom, walked us to the front door.

"Honey, it's really no big deal. They were a gift from my former in-laws, so you actually did me a favor," she said, patting me on the back.

I returned her smile, even though I felt like a complete heel.

"Come back and break dishes soon," Hollie teased from the couch, where she was reading a book.

I grimaced at her words as everyone else laughed at my expense.

"Are you ready, or was there something else you'd like to drop?" Justin joked before opening the door and guiding me out.

"I should kill you for that," I complained as we made our way back to his jeep.

"Who are you trying to kid? I saw the way you were smiling. You enjoyed yourself. Admit it," Justin chided me as he opened the door to the jeep. He and Travis had reinstalled the roof and doors after dinner. His mom had chastised him about trying to freeze me out. I tried to reassure her it wasn't all that bad, but she'd played the mother card and gave the guys no choice in the matter. The nighttime drop in temperature made me silently thankful for her insight. I would have frozen my butt off.

"Fine. It wasn't as bad as getting the skin on my face melted off," I declared, buckling my seat belt. "Though I could have done without the dish disaster."

"Well, I would hope not."

"They were cool," I admitted, trying to keep things in perspective.

"They thought you were 'cool' too," he said dryly, seeing through my nonchalant façade.

"So, you don't live on campus?" I asked as he cranked the engine.

"No. I moved back home when my dad decided to make an example out of Travis. He moved out and I moved in."

"What do you mean 'make an example out of Travis'?" I couldn't picture anyone having a problem with the sweet, lovable teenager I had just met.

"My dad didn't take too kindly to Travis coming out. He put Travis through the wall in our dining room when he found out," Justin bit out as he clenched the steering wheel tightly in his hands.

"Seriously? No offense, but how could he not have known?" I asked. After having a simple conversation with Travis, I was able to figure it out. Not because he wore it like a badge or anything, but his mannerisms and soft-spoken nature had been a dead giveaway.

"Yeah, well, my dad is famous for ignoring what's right in front of his face. He doesn't like it when things stray from the path he's set. God forbid his little soldiers have a mind of their own or move to a different beat."

"So, what beat do you move to?" I asked, sensing so much more to his story.

"Just put it this way: My dad is in the frame of mind that art is for pansies. He had some crazy notion that I would grow up to be a lawyer or some crazy shit like that. When he found out I was majoring in art, he gave me an ultimatum. Pick a real major or get out. I got out. Of course, I made it hard for him to ignore my art," Justin said.

Suddenly, his words from a couple of weeks ago clicked through my head. "Your tattoos are your designs," I stated as understanding dawned on me. "You got them so your father would have to face it," I said with awe, wondering where that kind of belief and strength came from. It made me think about my relationship with my own mom. It wasn't until I turned fifteen that her notorious busybody ways really began to bother me. I wanted to tell her but could never think of a way to do it without hurting her feelings. Instead, I made it my goal to hold my secrets close and away from her eagle eyes. It was that desire that had prompted me to apply to a school as far from home as I could get.

"Yeah, I got my first tattoo when I moved out. The second and third followed quickly after that."

"Did it work?" I asked, wondering if his father was finally accepting his dreams.

"Silent treatment for two months," Justin answered proudly.

"Mature much?" I said sarcastically.

Justin's laugh had a bit of an edge to it. "Two months is nothing. He hasn't spoken to Travis in like a year."

"What a dick," I said, not caring that I was talking about his parent.

"That about sums it up," Justin said, shooting me a real grin this time. "Let's talk about something else. We've wasted enough of our one and only date talking about him."

"Hmmm, I don't know. You might be able to score another date if you play your cards right," I answered in my most blasé tone.

"I knew the ole meet-the-family trick would seal the deal," he said triumphantly, slapping the steering wheel with enthusiasm.

"Are you telling me you played me?" I asked with mock indignation.

"Hell yeah, I did."

"Maybe I'll change my mind."

"Not going to happen. Admit it. You were wrong about me," he said, placing his hand on my knee.

I narrowed my eyes on his hand, wondering exactly how I felt about it on my knee. I was by no means a prude, but by allowing it I was sending a signal that I was interested. Moments stretched into seconds and seconds into minutes as I allowed his hand to stay. It was neither ignored nor forgotten as each minute slowly passed and the warmth of his hand heated my leg beneath it. I felt like a preteen on my first date with a guy I was crushing on. Back when each brush of his skin against yours would send your pulse racing and make your palms sweaty. Each time he removed it to shift gears on the jeep he would return to the original position on my knee, distracting me all over again.

"Ready?" he asked, breaking into my knee trance.

"What?" I asked confused, pulling my mind back to reality. "Oh, we're back," I said as I spotted my dorm.

"You okay?" he asked, cutting the engine.

"Just tired, I guess," I answered lamely.

He looked disappointed at my words, but nodded like he understood and climbed from the vehicle. I mentally kicked myself for my uncouth response as he made his way around the vehicle and opened my door. His chivalry didn't go unnoticed, especially since the last guy I dated not only didn't open doors for me, but actually let a door slam in my face as he walked through ahead of me. Melissa didn't even try to reason with me on that one. "Only a dickhead would allow a door to slam in the face of his date." Her words, not mine.

"You don't have to walk me all the way up," I told him, trying to regain some of my common sense as I climbed down from the vehicle.

He looked at me incredulously. "Do you really think I'd just drop you off?"

"It's not as foreign a thought as you would think. I figured it was the whole I'm-a-college-guy-and-chicks-are-lucky-to-be-with-me mentality."

He mumbled something about missing out, but I couldn't quite catch it. I thought I caught *kiss* and *dumb-ass losers*, but I couldn't be sure.

"I had a lot of fun today," I surprised myself by admitting as we reached the front door of my building.

"Was there ever any doubt?" he teased, lightly tugging at my hand until I was standing in the embrace of his arms.

I snorted out an unattractive laugh. "Have you missed my track record? There's always doubt when it comes to dates and me," I joked, trying to appear casual even though his face was suddenly inches from mine. I could make out each line and curve that made his lips look so delectable. I wanted to kiss him and yet I was scared. Kissing was hit-or-miss for me and everything seemed to hinge on it. Today had been pretty close to perfect, but what if he turned out to be one of those kinds of kissers. The ones who tried to eat your entire face and felt it was their job to slather you in saliva—or he could be one of those kissers who used his tongue like a weapon, and not in a good way. In my mind, kissing was an art form, not an assault. Lips should be soft and gentle at first, while the tongue cautiously introduces itself. Only after they've met and hit it off should they become more commanding and take charge.

"Hey, where did you go?" Justin asked, breaking into my lip-trance.

"Uh, what?" I asked, dragging my mind away from his lips.

"You totally seemed to fog out there."

"Sorry. I was thinking about an assignment I should probably work on tonight," I lied, meeting his eyes.

"Really?" he asked. He called my bluff as his own eyes wandered down to my lips.

"Yes," I said with bated breath as he moved closer.

"Because it sure looked like you were focused on something else," he teased, leaning in so his mouth was a hair away from mine. "You sure you weren't thinking of something else?" he asked as his warm breath fanned across my face.

"Like what?" I asked, unwilling to give him the satisfaction.

"Like maybe this," he said, placing his lips firmly on mine.

The instant our lips touched, any doubts about what kind of kisser he would be flew from my mind like a kite caught in a sudden gust of wind. His lips were every bit as lush and soft as they looked. I responded to his touch like I had never been touched before. My lips felt desirable and special as he treated them like a rare delicacy. His hands found my hips and he pulled me in closer. My own hands crept up his chest until they were gripping his jacket in knotted fists. Without breaking the kiss, he slowly backed us into the shadows of the building. The small part of my brain that could form a rational thought was thankful for his foresight, only to be quickly shut off as he coaxed my lips open. His tongue slowly found mine as he seduced my mouth and my senses. Everything faded away as I lost myself in the slow burn of desire that was multiplying through every cell in my body.

After a moment, he pulled away as I tried to catch my breath.

"I knew kissing you would be hot," he said, resting his forehead against mine.

"I'm glad it wasn't one-sided," I admitted, still gripping his jacket.

He chuckled. "I've wanted to kiss you since you gave me attitude the first time we met. I've been dying to know what those bossy lips felt like."

"Bossy?" I said, shoving at his chest halfheartedly.

He captured my hands in his, pulling me close. "I like that you were bossy. The girls who normally want to hang around me always turn into giggling bobbleheads."

"That's because you have a way of reducing girls to blithering idiots," I admitted.

"You're not a blithering idiot."

"I've had my moments. It's those damn lips and pierced eyebrow. They wilt away our senses."

"You think my lips are sexy?" he asked huskily, running said lips across my cheek. They left a trail of heat across my skin as they made their way to my ear.

"Did I say 'sexy'?" I asked in a shaky voice as his hot breath breathed into my ear.

"Well, you said 'damn lips,' which I happily translated into 'sexy lips.' Can I see you tomorrow?" Justin asked, switching gears.

"I have to study for a World History exam on Monday."

"How about after?" he persisted.

"Um," I hem-hawed, trying to decide if two dates in a row was a wise idea. I wasn't sure how fast I wanted things to go.

"Come on, you know you want to."

"Oh, I do, do I, Mr. Know It All?"

"Are you saying you don't want to see me tomorrow?" he asked, placing his lips back on mine.

All thoughts of taking it slow and casual fled from my mind like they were being chased by demons. I'd been right all along. He was definitely dangerous.

"Fine, but I get to pick the place," I caved.

"Deal," he said, finding my lips one more time. "Now get your cute butt inside before you freeze it off," he said, taking in the shivers I'd been unsuccessfully trying to suppress.

"Who's bossy now?" I griped, pulling open the door.

His chuckles followed me as I made my way into the building with a goofy smile on my face.

"I'd be careful with that one. He's nothing but a player." A voice startled me from behind.

"What?" I said. I turned around to face the one girl in our building who drove me absolutely batshit crazy. It had taken less than one day last year to see right through her act. Kara put on a good Southern charm show, but after one conversation, it was obvious she was as venomous as a poisonous snake. My instincts had proven to be true. Somehow, she managed to be the root cause of any drama that happened in our dorm. She had an uncanny knack of making people think they were special just as she placed her well-sharpened knife in their backs. Her lies and half-truths had backfired in her face, and by the end of last year everyone was wise to her routine. I'd hoped I wouldn't get stuck being in the same dorm with her again, or that maybe she'd live off campus somewhere, but I wasn't that lucky. For the most part, I'd been able to escape her web of drama. Melissa wasn't as lucky, which would have been enough for me to hate Kara if I hadn't already come to that conclusion on my own. I had a strict rule: Don't fuck with my friends. No ifs, ands, or buts about it. You hurt someone I loved and that was it.

"Justin. He's a player. He uses and moves on. Just thought you should know," she said, fluffing her hair.

"Thanks for the news flash. Don't you have a 'woe is me' Facebook status update to make or a picture to upload on Instagram?" I asked.

"You don't have to be a bitch. I never would have pegged you as the type to go out with a playboy. I was just trying to help. Trust me. I know from personal experience what a bastard he can be."

"Yeah, well go 'help' someone else. Any so-called advice you have to offer is neither needed nor asked for. Got me?" I said, making my point clear.

"We'll see if you're still saying that when he leaves you high and dry for the next set of tits that catches his eye," she snipped, all honey gone from her voice.

"Duly noted," I muttered, taking the steps two at a time to the second floor. My kiss-induced elation had dissipated by the time I made my way to my room.

"Crap, it was that bad?" Melissa asked, looking up from her nails she was painting.

Without answering, I threw myself back on my bed, mulling Kara's venomous words through my head. It wasn't like she had delivered earth-shattering news. I knew he had a colorful dating track record, but playing sloppy seconds to that bitch Kara made me want to dry-heave. Anyone else I could overlook, but a hookup with that twat was a different story.

"Brittni, tell me. Was he a complete dud?" Melissa asked, throwing the stuffed turtle she kept on her bed at me.

"No. He was effing great, but I can't see him anymore," I said, feeling sick as I uttered the words aloud.

"Why not? If he was so fantastic, why can't you see him anymore?" Melissa demanded, throwing a pillow at me this time when I didn't answer her right away.

"Because, he went out with Twat-Waffle Kara," I moaned against her pillow that I had pulled over my face. I couldn't decide if I wanted to scream or smother myself.

"Oh shit. Please tell me you're joking?" Melissa asked, making gagging noises.

"I wish. I ran into her downstairs, where she tried to warn me about him. As if she'd ever try to help anyone. I think she was just looking for a way to tell me they had hooked up," I wailed. What a disappointing end to an otherwise perfect date. I wouldn't even allow myself to think about the kiss. The idea that his lips had kissed hers made me seriously consider taking a stiff bristle brush to my own lips.

"Monkey asses. I was hoping he was the guy for you," Melissa huffed, returning to her nails.

"You and me both," I grunted, heaving myself off the bed so I could drown myself in the shower. This would be why I set such high guidelines when it came to dating.

By the next morning I was able to successfully put Justin in the same category with all the other guys who didn't matter. I blocked out the insistent voice that kept trying to convince me otherwise. I took the wimp's way out and sent him a text, telling him I would need the whole day and evening to study for my made-up exam. He never returned my text, which showed he had the attention span of a gnat. I patted myself on the back, convincing myself I had dodged a bullet.

The day turned out to be long and tedious anyway as I really did try to get schoolwork done. It proved to be difficult as my brain highlighted moments from the day before. The way he had warmed my face when we had arrived at the aquarium or the way his younger sister's eyes had shined when he told her he was taking her to see her favorite play. By two o'clock, I gave up studying. It seemed futile at the moment. I tossed my schoolbooks on my desk and lay back on my bed with the book I'd bought a few days prior. Even recreational reading proved to hold little appeal as my mind continued to focus on Justin. Finally giving up, I tossed the book aside and picked up my iPhone. The relief I felt after I had sent him my lame text earlier turned to irritation as I pondered why I hadn't heard from him. Bypassing the text messages, I went to my standby Spider Solitaire game that always did the trick when I needed something to occupy my mind.

Several hours later, I'm embarrassed to say, I was still lying on my bed playing the mindless game when Melissa returned to our room.

"Hey, you want to get some dinner?" I asked.

"Don't be mad, okay?" she said, stepping into the room, but leaving the door open behind her.

"Why would I be ma . . . Oh God, please tell me you didn't," I mumbled as Rob and Justin strolled into our room. Our room that was the size of a closet to begin with. With two extra people we were packed like sardines.

"So, Rob and I will be back in a minute," Melissa said, dragging a confused Rob from our room as she ignored the daggers she knew I was glaring at her.

I swung my legs around and sat up on my bed, trying not to dwell on the fact that Justin wasn't exactly catching me at my best. My hair probably looked like a bird's nest and I was wearing an oversized UW T-shirt with no bra and my favorite Victoria's Secret sweats.

"What are you doing here?" I demanded, taking out my discomfort from the situation on him.

"We have a date," he replied. He plopped down on Melissa's bed, looking unfazed by my tone.

"We *had* a date. I sent you a text," I stated, holding up my phone for emphasis.

"That's right, and if I remember correctly, you broke it off so you could study," he said pointedly, looking at the game that was still open on my phone.

"I was giving my fried brain a break," I lied.

"What's the deal, Brittni? I like you. A lot. I've made that clear, but I can't keep chasing you if you don't want to be caught," he huffed, running his hand across the light layer of scruff that covered the bottom half of his face. "I mean, what do you want from me? Are you really not interested?"

I sighed heavily. How could I articulate my feelings without sounding like a jealous half-wit? "It's not you . . ." I started.

"Oh, please. Tell me you're not trying to feed me the 'it's not you, it's me' crap. I'm not sure I'll be able to stomach that."

"Fine. It *is* you. Well, not you exactly. It's who you've banged," I snapped, jumping to my feet so I could pace the room.

"Who I've banged? Are we at that point in this relationship where we're handing over our lists?"

"No," I said, shaking my head. "You want to think it's ridiculous, that's your problem, but did you really have to sleep with Kara the Twat-Face?" I sank back down on my bed and dropped my face to my hands.

"Kara the Twat-Face?" he questioned, prying my fingers from my face.

"Fine, that's not her real name."

"That's a relief, but I'm still drawing a blank here."

"It still doesn't change the fact that you dated the one girl I can't stand, Kara Bellmont," I said, wanting to puke.

"Kara Bellmont? In that bitch's dreams," he shuddered.

"You didn't date her?" I asked. What a relief if he was telling the truth.

"Hell no. She was in my Bio Chem class last year. She tried, believe me. Always talking about how she 'can't keep any of the formulas straight,' and 'could we get together to study.' Study, my ass," he said.

"And you never fell for her sweet-Southern-girl bullshit?" I asked skeptically.

"Look. I've dated lots of girls. You know this, but that chick is bad news. Too much damn fake drama for me."

"Give me a break. The Barbie twins you were with the first day I met you were about as fake as they come."

"Fair enough. I never said I was perfect. Besides, who really caught my attention that day? Oh yeah, that's right, it was you. I told you, I'm not a player, Brittni. You're going to have to believe me or this thing between us is never going to work," he said, putting the ball in my court. "And you have to stop jumping to conclusions about me."

He was right, of course. From day one I'd been too harsh where it concerned him. "I'm just scared," I finally admitted.

"Why would you be scared?" he asked, reaching for my hands.

"Because I suck at this whole relationship thing."

"So do I. We can learn how to be good at it together," he said, pulling me to my feet. "I think we should practice with kissing," he added.

"Kissing sounds like a good place to start," I whispered as his lips claimed mine.

9.

Present Day
12:55 PM

"I'm starving," I grumbled, checking my iPhone for the millionth time.

"Yeah, me too. I wonder if that asshole Rob even knows we're stuck in here. He's probably eating lunch as we speak," Justin complained, glancing at his phone. "Still no damn signal. I freaking hate elevators!"

"Now you sound like me," I said, digging through my purse in a vain effort to find something edible. I struck gold when my hand closed around the cereal bar I had gotten at the airport earlier. Digging farther, I found the small bag of nuts they gave me on the plane. "You wanna eat my nuts?" I asked in an attempt to lighten the mood. He sat for a moment without looking up. "Come on. You know you want to eat my nuts," I said, pulling the small bag from my purse and holding it out. "That's it. Grab my nuts," I teased, causing the corners of his mouth to rise into a smile.

"Thanks," he said grudgingly.

"Sure," I smiled, remembering how much he loved peanuts.

"How did Rob talk you into coming to his office if you hate elevators so much?"

"He told me he wanted to talk about an engagement surprise he had planned for Melissa. He swore me to secrecy. As far as Melissa is concerned, my plane isn't supposed to land for several more hours," I sighed. I still wasn't pleased that a trusted friend had lied and tricked me.

"I bet she's excited you'll be here for the party," he said in a voice absent from the earlier hostility.

"Yeah, she was happy when I finally caved," I answered. I instantly regretted my words, knowing I had given too much away.

"Caved? You mean you didn't want to come to your best friend's engagement party?" he asked, raising the eyebrow that had once been pierced.

"When did you take out your eyebrow ring?" I asked, avoiding his question.

"Two years ago. I decided it was time for a change," he answered as the hostility returned to his voice. That was definitely another dagger meant for me.

I kept my head down rather than take the bait. Of course

his words hurt, but I'd be damned if I was going to let him see that.

"Well? You said 'caved.' Does that mean I was almost spared the pleasure of seeing you again?" he asked sarcastically.

"I can't remember; were you always such a dick?" I asked, matching his tone.

"Honey, I didn't become a dick until you lied to me and took something from me without even giving it a second thought. You and your goddamn secrets!" he snapped in a raised voice.

"They were my secrets—MINE," I yelled. I was sick of fighting a battle with him I would never win.

"That's horseshit. I deserved to know. God, the fact you don't get that makes me sick. I wish I had never talked to you that day," he snarled, turning away in disgust.

"That makes two of us," I lied as my weakly mended heart broke into pieces.

10.

November 2010

"So, this is your rodeo. Where to?" Justin asked as we climbed into his jeep.

"Well, since this is a second date and I'm not entirely sure how those are supposed to go, I thought we'd hit one of my favorite places."

"Puget Sound?" he asked, merging into traffic.

"You definitely win brownie points for paying attention," I commented. "No wonder all the girls like you."

"You can thank my mom for that. I think she was afraid I'd turn out like my dad, so she preached the whole respecting-women thing. She has nothing to fear, though. Travis and I would never turn out like him. Travis is too soft-spoken to ever raise his voice to anyone, let alone a girl. And, me—I don't know, I think maybe growing up and seeing the way my dad treated my mom, I always felt in my gut it was wrong. That girls shouldn't be treated that way. Does that sound weird?"

"What if the girl was a total bitch?" I inquired, messing with him.

"I wouldn't rise to the bait. I'm a lover, not a fighter."

"What if she keyed your jeep and slept with your best friend?"

"You have a thing for Rob?" he asked, raising his eyebrow suggestively.

"Are you avoiding the question?"

"Truth? I'd probably pound my friend for sleeping with my woman, but if she's going to cheat, she's not the girl for me. As for keying this beauty, it would probably add character," he said, patting the dashboard of his jeep. "What about you?"

"I don't go out with guys long enough to cheat, so you should be safe."

He laughed at my words as he searched for a parking spot. "Food first, or would you rather walk?"

"How about we walk for a while? Once the sun goes down it might be too chilly outside for a stroll."

Nodding his approval, Justin laced his fingers through mine as we made our way to a path that ran along the water. He kept up a steady stream of questions as we walked. At first I felt weird divulging so much about myself, but he steadily chipped away at my defenses. He asked me all kinds of questions about Woodfalls, intrigued by the dynamics of such a small town. I thought he was going to pass out when he heard the closest art museum and Starbucks were forty-five minutes away. For whatever reason, I found it difficult to open up about my mom. I did confess how much it bothered me that she was considered the town busybody and was often ridiculed for it.

"I think we're both natural people-watchers, but she takes it a step further. I've tried to explain it to her, but she laughs it off and reassures me that everyone likes that about her. I don't have the heart to tell her how I really feel. It's now a game in Woodfalls to see how long everyone can keep Pam from finding out something," I sighed. "Despite what I think her flaws are, I know she loves me and I love her. At the end of the day, that's all that matters."

"It must be rough," he said sympathetically. He draped his arm around me as a sudden gust of wind blew off the water.

"Sometimes," I answered. I felt guilty painting such a bleak picture of my life in Woodfalls, but no one seemed to realize how hurtful all the remarks about my mom were to me. I learned early on to use dry humor and sarcasm as a shield. "What about you? Do you ever wish things were different with your father?"

"Sure, all the time when I was younger. Especially when I hung out at Rob's house, or with some of my other friends. I used to get jealous when I'd see them interacting with their dads, who treated them like they actually mattered. My dad was like a drill sergeant. Follow orders or suffer his wrath. It was usually only verbal, at least. Me and my brother and sister all learned at a young age to avoid those moments as much as possible. He used to proudly brag that we were all so well behaved because he ran a tight ship. Truthfully, it was because he scared the shit out of us. Eventually, as I got older, he didn't look nearly as intimidating as he did when I was five and six."

"How did your mom even fall for him? She seems so different."

"They were high school sweethearts. He proposed to her before he joined the Army, and they got married after he came home from basic training. Mom said she got pregnant right away, but my dad didn't have the best experience in the service. He hated it, becoming bitter and angry. I don't know if leaving him back then was ever a consideration. I think maybe she always hoped he would somehow change back into the man she originally fell for."

"I'm sure she's grateful she has you," I pointed out. "That was a pretty solid thing you did, moving back home."

"See, I told you I was a good guy."

"We shall see."

"Man, you're tough, but I'm confident I'll win you over. Are you ready to eat yet?"

"Sure. There's a great little pizza place not far from here," I answered. "That's if you like pizza," I joked, although I had yet to meet a guy who didn't like pizza.

"This is your day. You call the shots," he declared. "Lead the way."

The topics of conversation during dinner were far more

lighthearted. We chatted about my job at the daycare and his ideas for the job at the hospital. Feeling more comfortable with him than I had the day before, I broached the subject of whether he should charge the hospital for his work. I pointed out they were lucky to have someone with his artistic abilities and he at least deserved some kind of compensation. After he changed the subject to a story about his brother and sister, it became obvious the hospital job was still a subject he wasn't comfortable discussing, so I let it go. Instead, he regaled me with stories about Travis and Hollie when they were younger, and I told him horror stories about working with small children at the daycare.

As the evening progressed, I was finally able to identify what made Justin stand out from every other guy I had ever dated. He had a mature way about him and seemed to have a firm grasp on what he wanted out of life. You would never expect it from looking at him, which had been my initial mistake, but he had shown his maturity by confronting his father and stepping in to help take care of his family. Since I arrived at college, I seemed to date one of two types of guys: Either they were wishy-washy about their futures and wanted to party all the time, or they were so fanatical about their goals that they didn't care who they crushed along the way. Justin seemed to be the happy medium. He was laid back and funny, but at the same time he had a seriousness that matched my own.

"I'm not going to beat around the bush here, Brittni. Like I told you before, I like you," Justin said as we were leaving the restaurant. "And I would really like to take you out again."

"By 'like,' do you mean you want to go steady and I need to start drawing hearts with our initials in them?" I teased.

"Exactly, and I'm going to get matching T-shirts that say 'I'm with her' and one that says 'He's with me' for you."

"You don't think that's pushing it?" I said.

"Hell yeah, it is," he laughed. "So, are you ready to give this whole dating thing a try?"

"Do we have to say we're going steady?" I asked, scrunching my nose.

"How about we stick with 'we're dating' instead?"

"Dating. I guess I can do that. Melissa will be so proud."

"Rob too," he said, parking the jeep in an empty lot several blocks from the campus.

I looked at him questioningly as he yanked the emergency brake.

"I figured we should seal it with a kiss, and since I don't relish the idea of kissing you in front of your dorm again with everyone looking, I thought a little privacy was in order."

"Hey, can I trust you to be a gentleman?" I asked as he cupped my face with his gloved hands.

"Definitely not," he replied before his lips captured mine.

I sighed with satisfaction as his lips slowly moved against mine. His tongue was gentle and naughty at the same time as it coaxed my mouth to open for more. His hands drifted from my face and down my neck as they slowly began to explore my body. The gentleness of his touch ignited a fire inside me and I strained to get closer to him, loathing the gearshift that was proving to be a hindrance. After a few minutes of trying to work around it, we were forced to give up.

"I'm now wondering if this is why my mom was so into the idea of me getting this jeep, because she knew this would be a pain in the ass," Justin complained, thumping the long stick with the side of his fist.

"I sense a conspiracy," I said, sliding back into my own seat while I got my breathing under control.

11.

Present Day
1:37 PM

Justin had remained stoically silent since his last outburst. I acted like I didn't care and felt my indifference was well played by the way he would glare at me every few minutes. While he sat contemplating my demise, I played the "if only" game in my head.

If only I hadn't stopped to stare at the building when I first arrived, I might have wound up on a different elevator. If only I'd stayed in the bathroom a few seconds longer, I could have missed the ride in Elevator Hell all together. If only I had stayed out of Seattle, I wouldn't be sitting here playing the damn "if only" game.

Eventually I realized the game only made matters worse. It wasn't like I had a time machine and could go back and fix any of this mess. Justin was still avoiding my eyes, so I took my time studying him. Two years ago, he was already pretty much a man, but I noticed subtle changes that showed he had completely outgrown boyhood. His shoulders seemed wider and his face looked leaner and more defined. Everything else about him was the same. Like the way he ran his hand over his scruff-covered face when he was frustrated or trying to make a point. I was sad the eyebrow ring was gone, but truthfully, its absence only enhanced his looks. With it gone, you were able to appreciate the golden specks in his brown eyes without interruption. My eyes moved from his face, down his arms, and to his hands. His hands were my favorite thing about him. They were large with rough calluses like a man's hands should be but gentle enough to create beautiful works of art. The idea that he was so creative always enchanted me.

I forced myself to pull my eyes away from him. It was almost painful to remember how those hands had felt on me.

12.

November 2010

"Don't be silly. Of course you'll join us for dinner," Trish, Justin's mom, chastised as she hustled around the kitchen, putting the finishing touches on the pasta feast she'd been preparing all day.

"Thanksgiving is a family holiday, Mrs. Avery. It would be tacky if I showed up," I countered, ignoring the smirk Justin was throwing my way.

"Trish," she reminded me.

"Fine. Trish, it's not necessary for you to feel obligated to invite me to a holiday dinner because a certain manipulator strong-armed you into it," I said, glaring at Justin.

"As if that lightweight could strong-arm anyone," Hollie,

Justin's precocious ten-year-old sister piped in from her perch at the counter, where she was shredding lettuce for our salad.

"Who you calling lightweight, short stuff?" Justin demanded, pointing the knife he was using to dice tomatoes.

"Don't point that thing at your sister," Trish admonished, handing me a cucumber to slice. "And, sweetie, Hollie is right. Justin didn't tell me to invite you. We all want you here."

"It just seems fast," I replied. "Justin and I have only been dating for a couple of weeks," I reminded them. I refrained from mentioning that the last few weeks had been the best weeks of my life. Once I'd let my guard down and agreed to let my misgivings about him go, I quickly realized Justin was different from any other guy I had ever dated. We traded the traditional dates of dinner and a movie for more walks around Puget Sound and afternoons strolling through the Seattle Art Museum. Justin was an attentive date and made sure that he never dominated the conversation. Girls still checked him out wherever we went, but I was able to ignore it. He never returned the attention and instead focused solely on me. It was a heady experience to be treated with such devotion. Any ideas I might have entertained at keeping it casual were long gone. He was becoming like a drug I couldn't get enough of.

"Two weeks? That's like a year by Justin's standards," Hollie giggled, ducking as Justin reached over to mess up her hair.

"Don't think Brittni's track record is any more pristine. She goes through guys like most girls go through hair products."

"Wow, what a way to throw me under the bus," I griped.

"It's every man and woman for themselves," he teased,

dropping a kiss on my lips, despite the fact that his mom and sister were looking on. I flushed, still not used to such open affection in front of others.

"Say you'll come," Hollie begged, pushing the serving bowl of lettuce toward me so I could add my sliced cucumbers to the salad. "Please," she added with wide eyes.

I contemplated my options. I could stick to my plan of eating a frozen meal in my dorm room, or I could have a real meal. It seemed like a no-brainer. I just wasn't sure it was a smart no-brainer. "Okay, I'll come," I caved as the three of them beamed at me.

"Well played, kid," Justin said, reaching into his wallet and extracting a five-dollar bill. "I think the puppy-dog eyes sealed the deal."

"I figured those would work. Did you like how they were even watering a little? I was pinching my hand for that effect. I should charge you extra," Hollie said, grinning at me as she shoved the five-dollar bill into the back pocket of her jeans.

"You bribed your sister to talk me into coming over?" I sputtered out, glaring at the guilty duo that had just played me.

"Just covering my bases," he answered, dragging me from the counter and leading me toward his small but functional apartment in the basement.

"Dinner will be ready in twenty," Trish called as Justin closed the basement door behind us.

"Your mom's going to think we're coming down here to make out," I commented as I sat on the small leather sofa in the living room of the basement. I'd been down in his apartment one other time, but Hollie had been excitedly chattering away at my side as she gave me the tour. Justin's bedroom was at the far end of the large space. The bathroom was beside it and could be accessed through the bedroom or the large living room. A full-size kitchen sat at the other end of the living room with an island that separated the two spaces. Justin had confessed to me that he had yet to use the kitchen. He felt guilty about it, but the kitchen had been his mom's idea. She had told him when he moved back home that he deserved his own space. My favorite part about his mock apartment was the door that led outside. It wasn't like I planned on sneaking in or out, but having a separate entrance offered up a small measure of privacy.

"If she's going to think we're down here doing something, then why hide it?" Justin said, pulling me to my feet. He wrapped his arms around me and lowered his mouth to my neck.

"It doesn't make you uncomfortable that she knows what we're doing?" I asked. It came out as more of a sigh as his lips found the sensitive skin behind my right earlobe.

"We're both adults and she respects that. I'm just glad we're alone," he said, trailing his lips over my cheek until they settled fully on my own lips. I whimpered with pleasure as his tongue parted my lips. I had made the startling realization on our second date that I was a fan of kissing him. I mean, I absolutely loved kissing him. It had become my favorite pastime, making me feel like a crazed hormone-driven teenager.

Justin eased us toward the full-sized sofa, never taking his lips from mine. I felt the sofa against the back of my knees and smiled as he slowly lowered me to the cushions below. I pulled him down with me so that his body was flush against mine. With only twenty minutes until his sister came barreling down the stairs to get us for dinner, we were playing with fire. Over the last two weeks, we'd had our share of heavy make-out sessions in his jeep, but that was as far as we'd taken things. The couch, unlike the jeep, had no obstacles, allowing me to feel every inch of him against me. I enjoyed his weight on top of me and I couldn't help shifting beneath him as he deepened the kiss. He groaned against my lips as our bodies settled fully together. Feeling powerful from the effect I was having on him, I shifted again, grinding my hips against his. Fire spread through me as his body reacted to my movement.

The sound of Hollie calling our names only seconds before she clamored down the stairs had us springing apart like two guilty teenagers. Justin was busy hiding the sudden bulge in his jeans, while I pulled down my shirt that had somehow crept all the way up to my neck.

"What are you two doing?" Hollie asked, bouncing onto the couch between us.

"Uh, watching TV?" Justin answered, reaching for a throw pillow and setting it on his lap. I chuckled at the look on his face.

"How can you watch TV when it's not on?" Hollie asked. "I think you were watching *Kissing 101*," she added, smirking at us.

"You do, do you?" Justin asked, ruffling her hair. "You're too smart for your own good. Now beat it, squirt. Tell Mom we're on our way."

"Fine, but hurry. I want Brittni to sit by me at dinner," she said. "Hey, Mom, they said they'll be up as soon as they finish making out," she called prior to racing up the stairs before Justin could hit her with a pillow.

"Having trouble there?" I joked, looking at his obvious problem the pillow had been covering.

"Are you offering to help?" He winked.

"If only we had time."

"Tease," he said, helping me rise from the couch.

"Hey, you're the one who started this. I distinctly remember mentioning we only had twenty minutes. You know what they say about those who play with fire getting burned."

"True, and in Hollie's world, that's closer to five minutes. Someday we're not going to have a gearshift to stop us or my kid sister."

"Promises, promises," I said, stepping on my tiptoes so I could place my lips on the back of his neck as we headed for the stairs.

"Who's playing with fire now?" he asked, turning so abruptly I almost fell down the few stairs we had started climbing. He reached out to steady me before dropping a hard kiss that was filled with promise and need on my lips.

"Can you two ple-e-e-ease stop kissing so we can eat dinner?" Hollie demanded at the top of the stairs.

"I need to muzzle her," Justin mumbled against my lips, making me giggle.

We could here Trish chastising Hollie to leave us alone. She stomped away from the door, complaining that she didn't get the big deal about kissing and that she personally found it gross.

"One day you won't," Trish said as we entered the kitchen, handing Hollie a stack of plates to add to the table. "Hopefully that day is way down the road," she added under her breath, shooting Justin and me a wry look.

"Years and years," Justin clarified, looking green at the thought of his little sister lip-locking with anyone.

"Boy, I pity the first guy who asks Hollie out," I remarked, carrying drinks to the table.

"Don't drop those," Justin mocked, making a production of helping me with the glasses.

I stuck my tongue out at his reminder of my previous clumsiness.

"Why?" Hollie asked inquisitively.

Justin grimaced, making Trish and me laugh and only confusing Hollie more.

"Why do you pity the boys?" she demanded this time, afraid that she was the butt of the joke.

"Because, honey. Your brother is just a wee bit protective over you. I'm afraid it'll make the Spanish Inquisition look like a walk in the park," Trish laughed.

"What's the Spanish Inquisition?" Hollie asked. She was easily distracted.

"It was the way they handled certain religions back in the fifteenth century. I remember hearing about it in a history lecture years ago, but more notably, it was a Monty Python skit I saw years back, before you or your brothers were even thought of."

"What's Monty Py—"

"Why don't you go see if Travis is ready for dinner," Trish interrupted, dropping a quick kiss on top of Hollie's head.

"How's the play going?" I asked at the mention of Travis as I sat in what had become my normal seat at their dinner table.

"Good, if the new bounce in his step is any indication," Trish said, smiling broadly. I had learned on my first visit to their house two weeks ago that Travis had landed the role of Ebenezer Scrooge in his high school's production of *A Christmas Carol*.

"Yeah, except he's taking his role a little seriously," Justin complained. "He tried to con me into giving him extra dough so he'd know what it would feel like to have some wealth. Those were his words."

"Hey, can't blame a guy for trying," Travis said, entering the kitchen. "Brittni," he smiled widely, happily pulling me up for a bear hug. Travis was a hugger. I was slowly adjusting to it. Slowly.

"Hey, Travis," I said, returning his smile. When Travis was around, you couldn't help responding to his enthusiasm and personality. "How goes the showbiz?"

"Well, it's tough to be a star, but I'm adjusting to all the fame and paparazzi," he joked, taking his own seat.

"Oh boy. You better get the contractors out here, Mom. Looks like we'll need to have the doors widened to fit Travis's head and ass if he doesn't stop eating all the bread," Justin growled, moving the bread from his brother's reach before he could add a third roll to his plate.

"I can't be blamed for being a growing boy," Travis answered, unfazed by the ribbing. Justin held the bread basket out to me so I could claim my own roll.

"Key word there being 'boy,'" Justin joked. Travis retaliated by throwing a piece of the rolls in question at Justin, who deflected it, where it ended up landing in Hollie's glass.

"Ew, gross. Can you two please act your age?" she huffed, stomping to the kitchen to get a new drink.

"Boys, behave," Trish said, looking up from a stack of papers from school she was grading while we ate.

I still liked the fact that Trish was a teacher, which is what I wanted to be for as long as I could remember. My friend Tressa said it was because I was born bossy, which was probably true. I liked the idea of teaching others. I wasn't the most affectionate or easygoing person, but I really did like kids. Even if I did gripe about the ones I worked with at the daycare. It was just the way I was. I put on an air of gruffness, but working with kids was my passion.

"Yes, Mom," Justin and Travis answered in unison. They both exchanged silent death threats once her head was bent down again.

Hollie and I laughed at their antics, which made Trish's head shoot up again as she mockingly glared at both of them. "I mean it, or I'll put you both on dish detail for a week without the dishwasher."

Her words had the desired effect, as both guys instantly grimaced at the idea of a week of hard labor.

"Harsh, Mom," Hollie quipped, taking a large bite of her salad.

"Sometimes the dish card is necessary," Trish laughed, pulling her reading glasses off and placing them on top of the stack of papers. "Now, tell me about your day."

"Molly threatened to cut my braid off if I wouldn't let her cheat off my paper today," Hollie piped in while helping herself to a serving of the big bowl of spaghetti at the table.

"What the hel—" Justin started to say as Trish sent him a warning look for his language. "What the heck?" he clarified.

"You can say 'hell.' Ms. Johnson says it all the time," Hollie said nonchalantly as she took a hearty bite.

"I thought you said this charter school would be a good experience for her," Justin said, shooting his mom a look.

"It is a good school. Hollie, what did you do when Molly threatened you?"

"Nothing. Mr. Davis was right behind her and heard the whole thing. You should have seen her face."

"I bet. What did Mr. Davis do?" Trish asked, holding up a hand so Justin wouldn't interrupt again.

I smiled and patted his leg as he clamped his lips closed.

"He sent her to Principal Rhodes. She didn't return to class, so I'm pretty sure she got suspended, which is too bad since we took the test and she wasn't there for it." She grinned mischievously.

"Okay, that's good. Now what is this about Ms. Johnson?"

"Well, a couple of kids in my class have been cussing lately.

Not me," she added quickly when everyone pivoted to look at her. "Anyway, Ms. Johnson told us that chances are we were all going to be exposed to swearing and most likely do it ourselves. She made us think of all the swear words we could and she wrote them on the board. The only curse word she wouldn't write was the F-word because she said that's just vulgar," Hollie continued around a bite of her roll. "She said as long as we use them in context, she was fine with us using them, but if we use them out of context, we have to write a five-hundred-word essay on the origins of swear words. None of the boys want to write the essay, so the cussing has stopped. I guess they were using them wrong."

"I guess so," Trish answered dryly. "Sounds like Ms. Johnson knows what she's doing."

"Yeah, she sure tricked them," Hollie said, obviously not fooled by her teacher's ploy. "Anyways, Justin can say 'hell' because it seemed like he was using it in context, since that was my response when Molly threatened to cut my braid off."

"Thanks for your permission, squirt," Justin replied as the rest of us laughed.

"What about your day?" Trish asked, turning her attention to Travis.

"It was good, except I don't know why girls come to me about clothing or costume questions now that they know I'm gay. It's not some kind of prerequisite that all gay guys are into fashion and clothes," he griped.

"Welcome to stereotypes," Justin said. "Remember when I was in high school and everyone assumed my friend Mitch would be an excellent basketball player because he was like a six-foot-three giant? He couldn't run and dribble at the same time if his life depended on it. Hey, even Brittni has been known to put people in stereotypical bubbles," he added, smirking at me.

"Guilty," I shrugged.

"Like what?" Travis asked, looking at me with interest.

"I assumed that a guy who is tattooed up and was flirting outrageously with two girls at once must be a player," I answered dryly.

"Seriously, bro? Two chicks at once? That's so not cool," Travis said, polishing off his spaghetti.

"Shame on you, son," Trish said, clucking her tongue.

"Not cool at all," Hollie added, shaking her head.

"Hey, put down your pitchforks. What makes you think she's talking about me?" Justin asked, trying to look innocent as he held up his palms.

"Um, gee, I don't know who she could be talking about—duh. Besides, she's got you on the one thing. You are a terrible flirt," Travis mocked.

"See, like I said," I crowed triumphantly.

"I'm so glad I have my own family on my side. Thanks for the love," Justin said, standing up from the table.

"Don't leave mad, just leave," Travis joked.

"You're hilarious," Justin said, holding out a hand for me.

"Thank you for dinner, Mrs. Avery, I mean, Trish," I said, standing also.

"Anytime, Brittni. It's nice to see Justin with someone who

has her own mind," she answered warmly. "Now, we'll be seeing you Thursday for Thanksgiving, right?"

"Are you sure?" I asked. I wasn't overly excited about crashing their family holiday.

"I won't take no for an answer. Justin will pick you up by noon," she said, leaving no room for argument.

"Yes, ma'am," I said, surrendering.

13.

Present Day

1:48 PM

It was official. They were deliberately toying with us. More than two hours had passed and we were still stuck. Since his last outburst forty-five minutes ago, the only words Justin had spoken were through the elevator phone.

"How much longer are we going to have to cool our heels in here while you dick around with this elevator?"

I could hear the woman's unruffled voice, assuring him that it was being worked on as quickly as possible. She'd inquired about our health and well-being, and once Justin informed her we were still alive, we got the same advice we'd received for the past two hours—to sit tight.

Justin slammed down the phone and resumed his stony silence. My iPhone was clinging to life with less than ten percent battery left. I couldn't decide if my phone dying would be a blessing or a curse. I was driving myself nuts checking the slow-moving time so often. Then again, with nothing but Mr. Stone Wall over there, I might go stir-crazy.

Unable to handle sitting there doing nothing, I emptied the contents of my oversized bag onto the floor. It had been ages since my purse had a good purge. A bottle of water rolled across the floor, stopping near Justin's foot. Ignoring his stare, I grabbed the bottle and set it on end so it wouldn't roll away again. I methodically sorted through months of old movie ticket stubs, receipts, and loose change that for some reason never made it to the small change purse that I also found among the other items. I hit the jackpot when I discovered a mini package of peanut M&Ms one of my students had given me before I left and a handful of peppermints I had snagged from my boss's office last week. At the bottom of my bag, I also found a couple of ideas that I had jotted down on a Post-it for my friend Ashton. She was relatively new to Woodfalls, but Tressa and I had hit it off with her right away. Her only quirk was the crazy bucket list of things she wanted to do. It seemed odd, but she said it was research for a thesis paper. Tressa and I suspected there was more to it than that. Of course, Tressa's idea that maybe Ashton was some kind of closet adrenaline junkie was different from my theory. My suspicion was that the list was because of something much more serious. I hoped to God I was wrong.

"Why do girls carry so much shit in their bags?" Justin asked, taking in the piles of stuff I had sorted in front of me.

"Oh, hi. Are you talking to me again?" I asked sarcastically. I was sick of him treating me like a yo-yo. One minute he was cordial enough to hold a conversation with, and the next he was a raving lunatic.

"I don't know. I'm trying here, okay?" he said, running his hand through his hair.

"Yeah, well, so am I. So if you could hold off using me like a verbal punching bag until I can escape from this hellhole, I'd appreciate it. You're not the only one who was hurt." It bothered me that he seemed to forget everything that had transpired.

His teeth came together with a snap, but he didn't comment. While he mulled over my words, I continued cleaning out my bag.

"What's in those little bottles?" he finally asked, eyeing the seven mini bottles of hand sanitizer I had unearthed.

"Hand sanitizer," I admitted, seeing the proof of my OCD.

"And you need seven bottles, why?" he asked.

I shrugged my shoulders. "Beats the heck out of me. I guess I'm always afraid of not having one when I need it, so I buy a new one every time I go to the mall. I guess I have enough." I smiled, even though it felt slightly forced. I didn't offer up the fact that I also had a basket of them sitting on the dresser in my room.

"Mint?" I asked, tossing him one of the cellophane-wrapped candies.

"Old mints from the depths of your purse. What are you, my grandma? Thanks," he said, pulling off the wrapper and popping the mint into his mouth.

"Hey, they have like a hundred-year shelf life. How's the art?" I finally asked, since we seemed to be on a tentative truce.

"It's good. I do a lot of freelance stuff. That job at the hospital that you convinced me I should charge for snowballed into more jobs than I could handle. I guess I owe you a thanks," he said, looking dismayed at the idea of giving me credit for anything.

"I'm glad it worked out. You're an amazing artist and should be treated as such."

"What about you? Did you get your degree in elementary education?"

"Yep. I'm working part-time at the school in Woodfalls, mostly subbing until a full-time opening becomes available."

"Still scaring the kids?" he asked, making me chuckle that he remembered.

"It's not like it's intentional. My boss teases me about the tight ship I run, but I like things orderly. At least elementary-aged kids don't scare as easily as the kids at the daycare," I mused, thinking back to the days when he and I had dated. I was working part-time at the daycare on campus and it had become a long-standing joke with my co-workers how the babies all seemed scared of me. It wasn't like I ever yelled or anything, but I guess a serious tone of voice was just as frightening. Anytime the other teachers lost control of their classes, I was the one they called. Justin and my friends had found the whole thing hilarious and nicknamed me "Drill Sergeant." The only kid who ever seemed immune to my voice was Justin's sister, Hollie.

"You're lucky. You seem like you've been able to put it out of your mind and move on," he said in a voice that was hard to distinguish. I couldn't tell if he was being sarcastic or cordial.

For a moment, I considered punching him. A quick punch to the jaw or maybe to the gut. It was awfully presumptuous of him to think I could erase it from my mind. In the beginning, it consumed my every thought. Eventually, time heals, I guess, because the pain tapered off to where I would only think of it a handful of times a day. Now, if I was lucky, I could go a whole day without thinking about it. He was an asshole to think I'd ever be able to forget. Let alone move on.

14.

Thanksgiving 2010

"I changed my mind," I said, sinking down on my bed as Justin paced the narrow floor in front of me.

"You can't change your mind. It's all Hollie has been talking about. She's looking forward to seeing you."

"I'm sure I'll be over there in the next few days. Just not today."

"Why not today?" Justin implored, running his hand over his hair in frustration.

"Because."

"Because? What the hell kind of answer is because? Because why?"

"Because . . ." I dragged out. "Spending the holidays with

your family seems too fast, too soon. It's something a couple does when they've been dating for a couple of years, not weeks. For God's sake, we haven't even made it past third base."

"Third base? Does anyone still use that term?" he laughed.

"Shut up, jerk. You know what I mean."

"Okay. Let's fix that right now," he answered, sweeping his eyes around my room. Melissa had left the night before to spend the four-day holiday with her folks. She wanted me to come with her, but I was too broke to buy a plane ticket, so I lied and told her I'd be spending the holiday with Justin and his family.

"Gee, how can I resist such a romantic gesture? Besides, your family is expecting you," I said weakly as he approached me.

"They're expecting both of us," he murmured, stepping between my parted legs that were hanging off the side of the bed. His hands gently cupped my face, tipping my head back until our eyes met. Everything inside me came to life as he slowly lowered me back on my bed. He moaned with desire as his lips found my neck. I felt his hand making its way beneath my shirt, sending shudders rippling through my body.

"Do you like that?" he whispered against my lips.

"Mmm-hmm," was my only answer as I shifted so he could lie fully on top of me. It had been a while since I had been with a guy whose every touch left me yearning for more.

"What about this?" he asked, moving his hand slightly lower so his fingers slipped just inside the band of my jeans.

I nodded, unable to speak as the sensations from his touch muddled my brain. I wanted his hands everywhere. His callused palm against the sensitive skin of my lower stomach made my body arch in a silent plea for more.

"Brittni, you keep moving like that and I'm going to skip third base and slide into home," he said, pulling his lips from mine. I could tell by his glassy-eyed stare that he wanted me as badly as I wanted him.

"And that's a problem, why?" I asked, looping my legs around him so he was intimately pressed against me. My eyes fluttered closed as he crushed his lips to mine. The desire in me raged out of control. I pulled at his clothes, wanting the last barrier gone that separated fooling around from sheer ecstasy. He had his shirt halfway off when a familiar ringtone blared from the pocket of his jeans.

"Damn," he said, showing me the phone, which displayed "Home" on the Caller ID.

"Yes?" he answered in a strained voice.

"Are you on your way back?" I could clearly hear his mom thanks to our close proximity.

"Almost. Brittni needed to finish a few things," he answered, grinning devilishly. I pinched his arm and pushed at him, trying to get him to move off me. Even though she couldn't see us, it felt weird to be getting it on with her on the phone.

"That's fine, but I need you guys to pick up a can of cranberry sauce from the grocery store. You know how your grandpa insists that the canned version is the only good kind."

"No problem, Mom. We're heading out now," Justin said, finally rising off me.

"Thanks, son. Love you."

"Love you too," he answered, ending the call. "You ready?" he asked, looking down at me where I was still sprawled out on the bed.

"What part of 'I'm not going' did you not understand?"

"You have to. Hollie made you a place card thingy and everything. You wouldn't want to crush my poor kid sister's heart, would you?" he asked, reaching a hand down and hauling me to my feet.

"Why does she like me anyway? Most kids hate me," I said, sliding my feet into my favorite boots.

"You sure education is the right career choice for you?"

"Yeah, ironic, right?" I answered. "Believe it or not, I enjoy it. I like the idea of teaching our next generation. Technically, kids are not scared of me. They just listen really well when I'm around."

"I could see that. You've got that drill sergeant voice nailed."

"Is that your way of telling me I'm bossy?"

"Not necessarily bossy. I'd say assertive."

"Ha, that's just a nice way of saying *bossy as hell*," I said, grabbing my bag as we left. I wasn't as sad as I thought I would be leaving my room behind. Even though I fought the dinner invitation, the idea of being alone on Thanksgiving was a real downer. Who cares if we were mixing up the steps in the relationship? It wasn't like there was some rule book that said you couldn't join your boyfriend for a major holiday after only a few weeks of dating.

"Oh, you still have the roof on?" I asked, tamping my disappointment at the fully enclosed jeep.

"Disappointed?" he asked, opening my door.

"Sort of. It's cold as hell, but I liked the freedom of no doors or roof."

"It's only until spring. You'll appreciate it more when it's not so frigid."

His words hit me like a bucket of water had been dumped on me. Spring was months away. Did he really think with our dating track records that we'd still be together by then? Sure, we were getting along well at the moment, but up until now, my longest relationship was in the eighth grade when Garrett Blinn and I decided we were a couple after a rousing game of Spin the Bottle in Tressa's basement. We lasted four whole weeks. The first week was bliss as I added his name to every square inch of my notebooks. By week two, I was wishing I had saved a little space for other doodling. By the third week, his wet lips on mine no longer held the same appeal they had during Spin the Bottle, and by the fourth week into our relationship, I was busy plotting different ways to break it off with him. In the end, he wound up with a bloody nose and a busted lip when I punched him for trying to stick his hand down my pants during a make-out session. The tale of how he had acquired his busted lip spread like wildfire through our small school. Needless to say, my next relationship was two years later. After Garrett, I was pretty much a two- to three-week kind of dater. Experience taught me that most guys showed their true colors four weeks in. Considering Justin and I were just shy of three weeks into our relationship, he was probably banking on a fairy tale to think we would make it to spring.

"I can't wait," I answered, deciding now was not the time to get into the logistics of failed dating.

The grocery store was packed with harried shoppers who were frantically searching for the last few items they needed. Buggies with crying children and women arguing over the last bag of russet potatoes were just a few of the obstacles we had to maneuver around in our search for cranberry sauce. We were about ready to declare the trip a failure when a helpful bag boy found us a dented can behind one of the registers. Justin hurried and paid and we hustled out of the store.

"Damn. Women get scary when it comes to shopping," Justin said, hopping into the jeep and slamming the door quickly, as if the insanity of the shoppers were an airborne virus.

"You're not kidding. Life lesson here: Never visit a store on a holiday," I added, relieved we had made it out alive. "They were like vultures in there."

"I sure hope Grandpa appreciates this," he said, tossing the bag with the single can inside into the backseat.

"He better do backflips when you show it to him," I added, fastening my seat belt.

"That would be funny as shit," Justin laughed.

"Truth." The fact that he had the same dry sense of humor as me was definitely a perk.

My good mood dissipated when Justin pulled into his over-crowded driveway behind four cars I didn't recognize.

"How many people did you guys invite?" I asked, slinking down in my seat.

"Relax, it's all family," he said, climbing out of the driver's seat.

"Swell. That helps so much," I grumbled.

"Hey, Uncle Fred," Justin warmly greeted a good-looking distinguished gentleman. He appeared to be roughly the age of my mom.

"Justin, how's the art?" his uncle replied, pulling Justin in for a massive bear hug.

"Not bad. How's the insurance business?" Justin countered.

"Not bad," his uncle Fred returned, laughing. "And who is this lovely lady?" he added, turning to smile at me.

"This is my girlfriend, Brittni," Justin said proudly. He pulled me closely against him like I was a coveted possession. I fought the urge to elbow him for his possessiveness.

"Girlfriend? That's terrific. We'd all pretty much given up hope that my nephew here would find a nice young lady," Fred said, shaking my hand with both of his.

"Oh, I'm not nice," I answered.

He threw his head back and roared with laughter. "You are my kind of lady," he said, putting an arm around me and leading me toward the house. Maybe it was the warm way he smiled or the twinkle in his eyes, but my natural instincts to stiffen up from a stranger's touch never manifested. "So, how long have you been making my nephew a better man?" he asked, guiding me up the porch steps to the front door.

"Only a few weeks," I answered, laughing uncomfortably.

This was what I had been afraid of. By coming to dinner, I was giving the impression that we had a history.

"A beneficial few weeks, if the grin on my nephew's face is any indication," he professed, opening the front door for me.

The noise inside the house was overwhelming as we stepped into the entryway. Everywhere I looked there were people. An elderly couple sat on the sofa while adults stood around the room chatting. Children of various ages darted through the living room, dining room, and kitchen like they were on a racetrack. Every few seconds one of the adults would tell them to stop running.

"Everyone, this is Justin's girl, Brittni," Fred announced, nudging me into the middle of the chaos. I looked back at the door longingly, feeling like I had been thrown into a shark tank. Just when I thought Fred was a good guy. Suddenly everyone's conversations became less important as a dozen eyes pivoted to look at me. With a gentle push from Fred, I was introduced to another uncle, whose name escaped me; Fred's wife, Adriane; and his aunt Holly, who turned out to be Justin's sister's namesake, just with a different spelling. The three teenage boys playing the Xbox in the family room with Travis belonged to Fred and Adriane. The four younger kids running around with Hollie belonged to Justin's aunt Holly and the uncle whose name I couldn't remember. The adults all seemed nice enough, and the teenage boys were typical teen-agers. They eyed me appraisingly before returning to their game. Hollie greeted me by giving my waist a crushing hug before racing back down the hall after her cousins.

After a few initial questions about my major and where I was from, the other adults quickly returned to their respective conversations. All the comments I had expected about how long we had known each other or how serious we were never surfaced. It wasn't like they shunned me. They just accepted that I was there without question.

Justin and I stood around chatting with his grandpa and mother, who both had questions about the job he was doing for the hospital. I was distracted from the conversation by Justin's uncle, the one whose name I couldn't remember. He looked like he was watching the football game on TV, but every time my eyes drifted his direction, he was staring at me instead. If his wife hadn't been sitting two feet from him, I would have said he was checking me out. It was completely creep-fest and grossed me out. His stares didn't get better during dinner, and I made an effort to try to ignore him as he downed several beers. If the others noticed his behavior, they ignored it.

"What's with your creeper uncle?" I asked Justin when we headed down to his apartment with our desserts in hand.

"Uncle George?" he asked.

"Yeah. He was looking at me all through dinner," I answered, seeing no reason to beat around the bush.

"He's a dick," Justin answered, placing our drinks on the coffee table. "He lost his job last year and pretty much decided that was his ticket to become a complete deadbeat."

"Oh, I didn't realize that. Losing a job has to be tough."

"He was an ass before that. I think Aunt Holly was on the verge of divorcing him, but then felt bad once he lost his job.

Maybe she thought that would be like kicking a man while he's down or some shit. He drives my mom nuts, and almost everyone else for that matter. I guess every family has to have one. The oddball who annoys everyone."

I nodded. I knew where he was coming from. Of course, I refrained from mentioning that the oddball in my family was my mother. In her defense, though, she wasn't nearly as bad as his uncle George. And definitely not creepy. She just made everyone's business her own. My only other relatives were a distant aunt and uncle who lived in Arizona. They were a lot older than Mom. Mom had been a surprise baby when she came along. Her sister was planning for college and already had one foot out the door when my mom showed up. Over the years, I'd seen them less than a handful of times, mostly due to a death in the family. Although I didn't see them much, they did make a point of sending me cash every holiday, including Thanksgiving, which always seemed odd, but who was I to argue with free cash.

"If he makes you uncomfortable, let me know," Justin added as he took a bite of the pumpkin pie on his plate.

"It's all good. I just thought I was imagining it."

"Nah, everyone knows he's a total douche. He's a lot of fun when he has a couple more beers in him," he answered sarcastically.

"At least he's up there and we're down here," I pointed out, not realizing until the words left my mouth how suggestive they sounded.

"Good point," Justin answered with a wide smile as he

placed his plate on the table and leaned toward me. His intentions were halted by the sound of multiple feet trotting down the stairs with Hollie's voice calling us.

"I need to learn to lock that door," Justin groaned before placing a quick kiss on my lips.

"One of these days . . ." I trailed off, running my hand over his chest as four preteens invaded our quiet place.

As the day progressed, those few minutes of quiet were the only ones we had. Hollie and her cousins convinced Justin and me to play a game of Monopoly. The game turned out to be one of those marathon games that stretched on for several hours. Hollie took the game seriously and analyzed each move before she made it. Two of the cousins went bankrupt fairly early and made it their mission to create the perfect playlist for our game on Justin's stereo. We took a break after a few hours to head back upstairs for seconds. Turkey sandwiches, stuffing, and leftover mashed potatoes were loaded up on heavy-duty paper plates that Trish had left out on the counter. Eventually, Monopoly came to a draw when Hollie and Justin owned the majority of the cash and properties. The game was stowed away and blankets and pillows were dragged downstairs and laid out on the floor, while Justin loaded one of the DVDs he had picked up the day before. Shooting me an apologetic look, he maneuvered around the bodies on the floor and crawled onto the couch beside me.

"Sorry," he whispered.

"For what?" I asked, scooting closer to him on the sofa.

"The movie party. It's kind of a ritual."

"Right. You're just afraid to be alone," I whispered, snuggling into his arms.

He chuckled lightly, tightening his arm around me. "Very afraid," he breathed into my ear, making my pulse race. His hand trailed down my side, gently tugging my shirt up until my rib cage was exposed. Every nerve inside me seemed to come alive as his fingers brushed across my skin.

"Be good," I hissed, trying to control the shudder that rippled through me from his heated touch. I tugged my shirt down and rested my head against his chest. His quiet laughter clued me in that he was well aware of what his touch was doing to me. Feeling all was fair in foreplay, I placed my hand on his knee and smiled with satisfaction when I heard his intake of air in the dark room. I slowly caressed his leg, letting my fingers creep up to his inner thigh before moving back down and then back up again. With each pass, my fingers would move just a little higher. The effect of my touch was evident by the rapid racing of his heart against my ear and the slight bulge that was difficult to hide even in his jeans. His response was enough to make even my own breath come out quick and fast, as if I were sprinting to finish a race. Eventually, Justin had enough of the sweet torture. He removed my hand from his leg and held it firmly in his own hand. I doubted it would douse the desire that crackled like a live wire between us. I closed my eyes, enjoying the feel of his arms around me and the noise of the movie playing in the background. I felt so relaxed I drifted off to sleep.

15.

Present Day
2:13 PM

"I was just thinking about that Thanksgiving weekend we spent together," Justin said, changing the subject before I gave in to the impulse to punch him.

I acknowledged his words by meeting his eyes. I was still pissed at his previous statement, but a small part of my heart melted at his words.

"That was the day I started to really fall for you. Did you know that?"

I shook my head, but it shouldn't have surprised me. After all, Thanksgiving was pretty much the beginning for me too. Our relationship was not the kind of whirlwind love story you read about. It didn't start with insta-love or even insta-lust. It was a slow build that progressed with each new detail we discovered about each other. Maybe it was our past failures at dating, or maybe we had somehow sensed that our relationship would be different from all the rest. He used to say we worked because I was immune to his powers of flirtation and he was the looseness to my uptightness. He claimed we brought out the best in each other. He was right until he was wrong. Eventually, we would get to the point where we absolutely brought out the worst in each other.

"Is your aunt Holly still with creeper George?" I asked, pulling my mind from the one place I didn't want it to go. The place I couldn't allow it to go.

"Nope. She filed for divorce that following summer. Turns out he was a mean-ass drunk. Aunt Holly could overlook his faults until he turned his fists on her and the kids. He's on his fifth or sixth stint in rehab. I've lost track."

"I know it's probably wrong to say I'm glad, but I really am. Your aunt deserves way better."

"Don't apologize. That feeling is unanimous, but I'll pass your sentiments along."

"So, why Thanksgiving? Was it because of that night?" I asked as his eyes bore into mine.

"That was a part of it, but it was all the before too," he answered.

"You mean you fell for me because of my mad Monopoly skills?" I smiled.

"Among other things," he answered, grinning wryly.

That grin. It had always been my downfall. If I pinpointed all my favorite memories that involved him, that grin could be found at each and every one. It held the power to melt my insides, make my pulse quicken, and make certain other areas ache with need. I loved that grin until I hated that grin.

16.

Thanksgiving 2010

I woke up disoriented. I knew I was in Justin's bed. I was just unsure how I had gotten there when the last thing I remembered was dozing off on the sofa. It was pitch black in his room, but I could feel I wasn't alone. Reaching out a hand, I tentatively touched Justin's arm, wondering if he was awake. The mattress shifted as he turned over. I could sense he was now facing me. He didn't speak as he reached over and gently caressed my cheek. I turned my face so I could place a kiss on the palm of his hand. Excitement raced through me at the thought that we were finally alone. He ran his hand around my head until it was cupping my neck. Holding my head in place, he leaned in close and placed his lips on mine. His lips were soft but sure as they slowly began to seduce me. My desire became stronger with each touch of his tongue and every sigh he elicited from me. As if he knew my body even better than I did, Justin rolled on top of me when the kisses were no longer enough. I could feel just how much he wanted me as he pressed his pelvis against mine, feeling harder than should be possible. My body had a mind of its own as it ground and begged for something more.

Justin's hands moved away from my face to the hem of my shirt. Lifting my torso slightly, I helped him remove my shirt and bra. His hands moved up my ribs until they cupped my breasts, causing my breath to labor as he gently rubbed my nipples, which were almost as hard as he was. His lips pulled away from mine. I protested by lacing my hands behind his head to pull him back to me. He chuckled lightly but fought my urges and captured my nipple in his mouth. I arched my back, trembling with desire as he sucked my nipple fully into his mouth. My body no longer belonged to me. I frantically moved against him, trying to ease the fire that was raging uncontrollably through me. Justin's needs matched my own as he jumped up, tugged off his shirt, and kicked his jeans across the floor. He reached for my jeans and pulled them off my body in one swift movement before dropping hot seductive kisses on my stomach.

His hands momentarily left my body as he tore open the condom wrapper. Once he had it in place, he knelt between my legs and hooked my right leg over his shoulder so he could place a kiss on the inside of my thigh. My legs trembled with need as I felt him pressed against my opening. With one sure and quick thrust, he was completely buried inside me. His mouth found mine again as he moved inside me. I was already too far gone to hold back the orgasm that ripped through me. I locked my legs around his waist as I rode it out. Justin increased his tempo as he raced toward his own release. With one final thrust, he collapsed on top of me.

It took several minutes for our breathing to return to normal. Justin remained on top of me. His weight was heavy but still comfortable. Everything about it felt right. Usually after sex I was quick to push the guy away once we finished. My rules had always been set in stone. Once I got what I wanted, my desire would disappear in a flash and I would look for the nearest exit. All my past rules were forgotten with Justin. My hands moved to his back, where I relished the feeling of stroking him on top of me.

"Am I too heavy?" He broke the silence as he propped himself on one elbow.

"Is a Mack truck heavy?" I teased. "Kidding," I added, looping my hands around his neck to hold him in place once he tried to lift himself off me.

"Let me take care of a few things," he said, placing a kiss on my lips before pulling away. My body felt oddly bereft without his weight on me. Light flooded the room when he flipped on the switch in the bathroom. Feeling self-conscious, I dragged the blanket over me. After a few minutes, he turned the light off, plunging the room back into darkness. I heard the clicking of his bedroom lock before the bed dipped down when he climbed in.

"I should move to your couch," I murmured as he tucked me back into his embrace.

"Hell no," he said, tightening his arm around me.

"What will your mom say?" I asked, feeling like a teenager who was contemplating how to sneak out of her boyfriend's house without getting caught.

"Brittni, she's not going to say anything. I'm an adult. When I moved back home we set up boundaries, and this was one of them. That's why the basement was redone into an apartment. I respect my mom, but I'm not going to apologize for being a man and desiring the comfort of a woman in my bed."

"So, I'm being silly that I feel like a teenager who's expecting her boyfriend's parents to crash in at any moment."

"Yeah, I would say so. Besides, if sex had been that mind-blowing when I was a teenager, I would have been chasing after girls nonstop."

"Who are you trying to kid? You know you chased them anyway."

"True, but I would have put more effort into it."

"It was good, though?" I asked groggily as my eyes drifted closed.

"*Good* is the understatement of the year."

Thumping on the floor above woke us both the next morning. Sunlight streamed into the room from the small window near the ceiling, making everything appear just a little more stark. In the cloak of darkness, being naked didn't seem nearly as illicit as it did in broad daylight.

"Oh God, your mom is going to hate me," I mumbled, hiding my head under my pillow.

"Are you always so dramatic the morning after?" Justin chuckled, pulling the pillow from my face.

"I wouldn't know. I've never had a morning after," I confessed.

"What? How is that possible?" he asked incredulously.

"It's not that big a deal. I just usually leave after."

"So this is a first for you?" he asked, sounding gleeful.

"Don't let it go to your head. Once your mom bans me from the house, this will be the last time."

"Ye of little faith. It's all good. Now come take a shower with me," he said, dragging the covers off. I blinked in the light, taking in his naked torso for the first time. Tattoos spanned his entire chest as they wove around his lean muscles. I had never given tattoos much thought, but his were a work of art. Reaching a finger up, I slowly traced the lines covering his toned skin.

"Do you like them?" he asked in a husky voice.

"If I say yes, is it going to inflate your ego more?" I asked.

"Babe, it won't be anything I haven't heard."

"Don't be an ass," I said, swatting his shoulder, which made the sheet slip off me, exposing my chest. His eyes zeroed in on my breasts, making my nipples tighten under his stare.

"Do you like them?" I asked in a hitched voice, stealing his previous question.

"Very much so," he answered, running a thumb over one

of them. "Come on. Take a shower with me," he said, gently tugging on my hand.

Ignoring my misgivings, I allowed him to lead us to his adjoining bathroom. We were entering new territory here. Showering with a man was definitely a first for me. Justin took it upon himself to show me just how pleasurable it was to be washed from head to toe by strong masculine hands. By the time we were hastily toweling off, we were both anxious to finish what we had started.

Our second time together was quick and hot. Our releases came seconds apart and left us spent as we collapsed on his bed.

"Hmmm, who knew a shower could be so fun?" I sighed.

"Told you," he said, beaming down at me.

"I don't even want to know how you knew it would be so enjoyable," I said, giving his shoulder a push so I could get up and get dressed.

"A gentleman never tells," he answered, tossing a clean UW shirt my way as I pulled on my jeans from yesterday.

"Gahhh," I said, chucking my boot at him, which he easily ducked.

"Let's go get breakfast," he said, handing my boot back to me. "There's a great diner not too far from here, and after that I have a surprise."

Unable to stay mad, I finished getting dressed, willing myself not to dwell on his past conquests. We left the house through his private entrance and headed out for the day. The diner turned out to be every bit as good as he said it was, and even though we'd both eaten our weight in food the day before, we were famished from our nighttime and morning activities. We lingered over our meal, trying to one-up each other discussing past holiday disasters. Over a second cup of coffee, I won the contest when I showed him the spiral-looking scar on the palm of my hand. It had taken thirty stitches when I stuck my hand in the sink to remove a steak knife from the garbage disposal that happened to be running at the time.

"What the hell were you thinking? Man, your poor hand," he said, tracing the scar on the palm of my hand.

"It was a total brain-dead moment," I joked, downing the last of my coffee. "So, where are we going?" I asked as we shrugged into our jackets.

"You'll have to wait and see."

His surprise turned out to be an hour-long ferryboat ride to Bremerton. It was a tranquil experience as we stood against the rail, watching the water and taking in the wildlife we passed on the way. Once we arrived, we strolled around window-shopping the quaint shops that sat along the water-way before ending up at the Navy Museum. Finally, we ate a late lunch at a café on Puget Sound before heading back to the ferryboat for the ride back to the mainland. We decided to stay the rest of the weekend at my dorm since Justin had scored tickets to a Seattle Seahawks game on Sunday. I didn't admit it, but I was relieved I wouldn't have to face his mom for at least a few days. Like our shower together, the weekend continued to hold many firsts for me. My first ferryboat ride, my first professional football game, and the first time I spent a solid four days in the company of a male. More astonishing than all the firsts of the weekend was the fact that each day with Justin was as enjoyable as the day before. Our nights were spent wrapped in each other's arms. That was the weekend I began to fall for the one guy I never expected to.

17.

Present Day

2:41 PM

"This is seriously getting ridiculous," I ranted, stomping my foot in frustration. We were past hour three of being stuck and I was regretting my decision to not use the restroom when I had the chance. Of course, if I had taken the few extra minutes to go to the bathroom, I wouldn't be stuck on the elevator from hell. That's the thing with hindsight. You had no way of changing anything. It was just a way of highlighting your mistakes and getting pissed off about it.

"I can see your temper is still intact," Justin observed as I stomped my foot again.

"I don't have a temper."

He raised his eyebrows skeptically, calling my bluff.

"Fine. Normally, I don't have a temper," I ground out, which was partially true. Justin always had the knack of igniting the anger in me. It wasn't like we fought all the time, but when we did, a temper I never knew I had would emerge.

"Admit it. You're really a closet redhead."

"Maybe I have Irish blood in me."

"Tell me about your job," he said, changing the subject. "Is teaching as fulfilling as you thought it would be?

"My job? Do you really want to know whether I find my work fulfilling?"

"It'll help pass the time."

"Talking about work and whether I find it fulfilling would lead some to believe we're friends," I pointed out.

He looked uncomfortable with my assessment, obviously not sure he was ready to call that much of a truce. I wasn't surprised by his reluctance to wave the white flag. If you had told me that morning that Justin and I would be talking cordially to each other, I would have laughed in your face.

"It's good. I've been subbing since I graduated last spring, but a full-time position will be opening up after Christmas."

"Are you living with your mom?"

"No. I have a small apartment above the hardware store in Woodfalls. It's more of a loft than anything else. Kinda reminds me of your apartment in your mom's house."

"How did your mom feel about you not living at home?"

I laughed at his question. He had a good memory. "She fought it at first, but in the end she didn't have a choice. We get along much better without her checking to see what I'm doing twenty-four-seven. She's still meddling all the time and worries about me, but we make it work. Tressa thankfully still takes a lot of heat off me. Mom is so busy wondering who Tressa is corrupting that most times I'm able to skate under the radar."

"Do you miss the city?" he asked, showing how well he knew me again.

"Every day, but it's not as acute as I thought it would be. Tressa was glad to have me back in Woodfalls, and I've made a few other friends."

"Guy friends?" he asked, stepping into no-man's-land.

"Really? Are we talking about my sex life now?"

"Never mind. It's none of my business," he muttered, looking a little green in the face.

"Are you seeing anyone?" I asked, unable to stop the words even if I had clamped a hand over my mouth.

After what felt like a full minute had passed, I began to think he wouldn't answer the question. "I just ended a relationship," he admitted. "You?" he asked.

I shrugged my shoulders "You know me. My track record is the same as it always was. In my defense, it's not like there are a lot of choices back home," I answered as he smirked at me. "Why did you end your relationship?" I asked, not liking the knowing look on his face. It wasn't like he was some chick whisperer when it came to relationships.

"She wanted things from me I wasn't willing to give."

"Commitment?" I asked. This time it was my turn to smirk.

"No," he snapped before smiling somewhat sheepishly. "Okay, yeah, maybe. It's not like you have any room to talk."

"I never said I did. We might as well face it. We suffer from commitment-a-phobia," I said, making him chuckle at my terminology. "Maybe that's why we worked," I mused.

His chuckles died midway through and his eyes clouded over. "We didn't work," he answered simply.

I stifled a sigh. Welcome back to no-man's-land.

18.

....

December 2010

"You're being irrational," Justin argued, pacing in front of me with a light drizzle of rain dripping down his face.

"Right. It's all my fault. I'm the irrational one," I yelled, glaring at him with my hands on my hips.

"You think you saw something you didn't see," he countered, stopping in front of me. "You can't break up with me without listening to my side."

"Your side? Your side! She was in your goddamn arms. Let me guess. She slipped and just happened to land in your arms with your mouths inches apart. If I wouldn't have shown up, you would have been lip-locked."

"No, we wouldn't have been. She's an old friend."

"I bet she is."

"She just found out she got into the master's program she was hoping for. She was happy and wanted to share it with me."

"She certainly did," I said sarcastically. I sank down on the rain-covered bench in front of my dorm. The fact that it was raining seemed fitting and matched my mood. Dark and brooding. Earlier, my mood had been the exact opposite. Melissa had labeled it as "downright chipper," claiming I was a different person now that I was dating Justin. I didn't even try to argue. She was right. Being in a relationship with Justin had changed my outlook on life. Of course, that was before I saw his arms wrapped around another woman. The arms that I was growing quite partial to were wrapped around a blond girl with legs practically up to her armpits. I wanted to snatch her by that long shiny hair and tie it in knots. Most of all, I wanted to punch Justin to make him hurt as much as he had hurt me, but I did neither of those things. Instead, I stomped away, trudging through the puddles and belittling myself for being so stupid for falling for him. Melissa found me on the bench in front of our building an hour later. My raincoat had kept my clothes relatively dry, but my hair was a mess of dripping curls. Justin arrived ten minutes later. It didn't take an Einstein to deduce that Melissa was behind his arrival. Twenty minutes after he showed up, we were still arguing.

"Nothing happened," Justin said loudly.

"I know what I saw. She wanted you."

"But I didn't want her. I only want you, you idiot."

"Don't call me an idiot, you cheating jerk," I said, surging to my feet as a new wave of anger roared through me.

"I'm not a cheater. If you could get past your narrow-minded prejudiced views, you would see that."

"I am not narrow-minded or prejudiced," I shouted, thrusting my balled-up fists into my jacket pockets so I wouldn't punch him. Two girls from my dorm stopped to stare at us but scurried on when I glared at them.

"You are. You've assumed from day one that I was a cheater. You are prejudiced. I have never cheated on a girl and I never will. So for the love of God, will you stop expecting me to?" he pleaded, gripping me by my shoulders as if he wanted to shake some sense into me.

I wasn't sure if it was the actual words or his pleading tone, but all my anger began to leak away. "Okay," I finally whispered, sagging beneath his hands.

"Okay?" he asked.

"Okay, I believe you."

"You should," he said, tucking me under his arm and leading me out of the rain and into the building.

"Did we kiss and make up?" Melissa chirped as we entered the room.

I stuck my tongue out at her in a completely childish way.

"Does that mean we're still going to see that new indie band tonight?" she asked, ignoring my childishness.

"Eight o'clock?" Justin asked, looking at me questioningly.

I nodded, giving him a small smile. All the anger was gone, but embarrassment and confusion had replaced it.

"See you then," he said, placing a tentative kiss on my lips.

"Okay," I said, shrugging out of my raincoat as he left the room.

"How goes it?" Melissa asked once the door had closed behind him.

I shrugged, flopping back on my bed. "I swear he'll ruin me. Never in my whole life have I ever shouted at another person like that. He brings out the inner monster in me," I said, feeling sick now that all the anger was gone.

"Not anger, passion," Melissa piped in.

"What?"

"You feel passionately about him," she said, proud of her diagnosis.

"I'm pretty sure what I felt was anger," I said wryly.

"Anger and passion are basically the same thing. If you truly were angry, you would have walked away. Instead, you faced the problem. You embraced it passionately," she said insightfully as she stood up and stretched. "Now, I need to take a shower before the person I feel passionately about shows up," she said, flouncing off to the bathroom.

I contemplated her words. Was she right? Did I feel passionately about Justin? She had to be wrong. People felt passionately for each other months into a relationship, not after one month. I knew what I had felt in the courtyard when I spotted him with the other girl wrapped around him like some serpent or something. It was jealousy and hurt that waged a battle inside me as I tried to comprehend the scene. For a moment, every insecurity I'd ever felt surfaced. He made me feel that way, whether accidental or not. He made me face the reasons why I tried to avoid relationships.

I was still on my bed studying the ceiling and contemplating the doom of my sanity when Melissa exited the bathroom with a towel wrapped around her torso. "Are you okay?" she asked, taking in my expression.

"No. I'm a weak, nimble-minded female who's letting some guy lead me around like I'm his bitch or something," I grumbled. "Why did you have to introduce me to him? I was fine without some guy clouding the water."

"Yeah, but think how boring that would be. Cloudy water is good for everyone. It's the people who have the crystal-clear water who scare the crap out of me. So stop taking everything so seriously and enjoy your swim in this crazy murky water," she said, grabbing a change of clothes and heading back to the bathroom.

I watched the door shut behind her and felt slightly better. That was the beauty or at times the horror of living with someone who was all rainbows and unicorns. Maybe she was right. Maybe murky wasn't bad. So what if I had dived into water that was impossible to see through? Maybe just once I would let myself go.

Maybe I could put my faith and trust in one person.

19.

Present Day
2:53 PM

"I'm hungry," Justin complained, checking his phone for the millionth time.

"We've covered that," I said, shifting my position to help ease the numbness that had set in.

"I know, but I'm now thinking about food like it's a lover or something. Like how juicy and delicious a cheeseburger loaded with bacon and all the fixings would be at the moment."

My stomach rumbled loudly at his words. "Not nice," I said, placing a hand on my stomach to quiet the gurgling.

"Or a large pepperoni pizza with extra cheese," he continued, ignoring me.

"No, a tender steak cooked to perfection with a side salad and a loaded baked potato." I added my two cents in.

He groaned at my words. "With a hot fudge brownie sundae," he added, looking pained but eager at the same time.

"We're gluttons for misery," I pointed out as my stomach growled its displeasure.

"We have to do something to pass the time."

"I have a deck of cards," I offered up.

"What? Why are you just now mentioning this?" he asked, scooting across the floor until he was sitting less than a foot and a half from me.

My heart stuttered for a fraction of a moment before kicking into warp speed at his close proximity. The tantalizing smell of his cologne, which I had spent the last three hours trying to ignore, swirled around me like a blanket woven from countless memories. It was his scent. It didn't matter that millions of men probably owned the same cologne. On him it smelled different. I knew this because back in my pain-filled road to recovery, I had made the forty-five-minute drive to the mall outside Woodfalls and purchased a bottle of it. Unable to wait until I got home, I had sprayed my jacket, wanting that small part of him. I was bitterly disappointed that it wasn't the same. Sitting across from him on the elevator floor, I couldn't help breathing in, trying to brand the smell to my memory so maybe this time it wouldn't leave me.

"What do you want to play?" Justin asked, shuffling the cards like he was a blackjack dealer in Vegas.

"Go Fish," I teased, laughing outright at his look of dismay.

"Not funny," he claimed. "If I never play another hand of Go Fish, I'll die a happy person."

"Oh, that's right. You don't like Go Fish," I commented in a voice laced with false innocence.

"You'd feel the same way if you were me. I swear Hollie made me play a million hands the week she was recovering from getting her appendix out when she was seven. Mom threw out all the decks of cards after that."

"I remember you telling me. You always were a great big brother. Travis and Hollie are lucky to have you."

"They're good kids. Well, I guess they're really not kids anymore. Hollie would have my head if she heard me referring to her in that capacity. I haven't seen a whole lot of them these past six months," he said, shuffling the cards again.

"You don't still live at home with them?" I asked, surprised. I just assumed nothing had changed in my absence, which was silly of course. Just because I was no longer there didn't mean time had stood still."

"Nah, once Mom married Paul I was no longer needed at home."

"What? When? Your mom married Paul." I said the last part as a statement. I'd met Paul only once, since he and Trish had just started seeing each other right before our relationship had gone to crap. He was the new single parent who had moved in next door right after Christmas. Hollie had been ecstatic when she found out he had two kids, including a daughter her age.

"Yeah, right after Christmas last year. Exactly one year after their first date."

"Oh boy," I muttered, snickering at how cliché it seemed.

"You never were one to overromanticize things," Justin commented as a smirk spread across his face.

"I'm not the only one. If memory serves, you mocked such rituals yourself."

"Can you blame a guy? I'm not against romantic gestures, but if you're going to do something, do it right. Go big or go home," he said. "Anyway, once Paul moved in with Brady and Andrea, the house became pretty crowded. Travis took over my basement and I moved out."

His words faded as I focused on his previous romantic gestures comment. *Go big or go home.* He had done that once. One grand romantic gesture that had stolen my heart completely and left me breathless. I wondered if that moment crossed his mind as he told the story of Paul and his mother. Only in my loneliest self-pitying moods did I allow myself to ever think about it.

20.

Christmas 2010

"I'm going to miss you," Melissa cried, wrapping me in a tight hug.

"Mel, it's only three and a half weeks." I focused on breathing since she had her arms around my neck like a drowning victim.

"Almost four weeks," she sniffled.

"Oh my. You are very dramatic today. What's the real issue? Are you sad you're leaving Rob for the next few weeks?

"Yes," she wailed.

At least I had gotten to the root of the problem. "Why didn't you ask him to go with you?"

"I didn't want to appear needy and clingy," she replied, sniffing loudly.

"Honey, I think that ship has sailed," I told her, pointing to the *I Love Rob* shrine on the bulletin board above her desk.

"Hey, I like to save everything," she protested, looking at her board with misty eyes.

"Sweets, you're a mess. Maybe you should compromise and see if he wants to spend New Year's with you," I said cheerfully.

"You're only so cheerful because you get to spend all four weeks with your boyfriend," she said wistfully.

"Three and a half weeks," I corrected, trying not to smile. She was right, though. I was over the moon about spending the next few weeks with Justin without any interference. No studying, no exams, no classes, and no deadlines. My classes over the last few weeks had consumed every waking hour, including the majority of my sleeping hours. Every second was spent preparing for finals. The last exam had ended sixteen hours ago. I celebrated by stumbling across campus in a fog before crashing into my bed for fifteen hours of much-needed sleep. Finally, I no longer resembled a zombie and could be accepted back into humanity. More importantly, I was ready to spend time with Justin. Seeing him for only a handful of hours during the last few weeks had sucked. If I didn't miss him so much, I might have been concerned at my growing codependency on him. Either way, I was shocked at how well our relationship had been progressing. Since our blowup three weeks ago, we had grown even closer. Now, almost two months into my longest relationship ever, I couldn't help feeling almost giddy.

"You don't think it's too forward?" Melissa asked.

"Not at all. Asking him to come for New Year's is the best of both worlds. You'll get to spend Christmas with your family and New Year's with your boyfriend."

"Good point," she squealed, pulling her phone from her pocket. Her tears dried up as she hastily called Rob. I had done my job.

Shaking my head at her quick rebound, I headed to the bathroom to get ready before Justin arrived to pick me up. I could hear Melissa's excited chatter through the door. By the sounds of it, Rob was obviously receptive to her invitation. Pleased with my good deed, I switched on the shower, grabbing the cashmere-scented gel from the Bath & Body Works gift basket Melissa had given me for Christmas. *She knows me so well*, I thought as I inhaled the heavenly scent.

By the time I returned, our room was empty. I found a note from Melissa on my desk wishing me a happy holiday and instructing me to text or call if I needed anything. She was sweet. I pulled out my suitcase from under my bed. After many back-and-forth texts, Justin had convinced me to spend the holidays at his house since my building would be closed to students for the break. My original plan was to sublet a room off campus from a friend who was going home for the holidays. It was a win-win situation for her. Spend the holidays at home, while she earned a little spending cash by renting her room for a few weeks. It would have put a strain on my cash surplus, but spending the entire three weeks with Justin and his family bordered on crazy. Eventually, he wore me down. I couldn't deny I was happy about my decision. Honestly, the idea of rooming with some other poor sap who didn't have the funds to go home for the holidays held little appeal.

It took less than an hour to finish packing. Knowing I needed to eat a little crow, I decided to call my mom before Justin arrived to try to make amends for not coming home for the holidays.

She picked up the phone after one ring, like she had been waiting for my call.

"Hey, Mom."

"Brittni, why did it take this long for you to call me?" she said shortly.

"I know, I'm sorry. I just had a lot of loose ends to tie up before they lock this place down," I said, pacing the floor.

"Sorry enough to fly home to your poor lonely mom?" she sniffed.

"I would if I could, Mom, but we discussed this, right? I'm seriously behind in some of my classes. If I want to keep my grades up, I need to buckle down."

"Why are you behind? Have you met someone?" she probed.

I closed my eyes, counting to five before answering. "No, Mom, I haven't met anyone," I lied. "The classes I'm taking are just very time-consuming."

"I just don't see why you can't work here. Honey, it's Christmas and I haven't seen you since summer break."

"I know, Mom, but that would mean me lugging all my textbooks home and all my study materials. I have everything I need here, including the library if I need anything else."

I could hear her long sigh of acceptance. I felt guilty lying to her and almost changed my mind.

"Besides, Mom, I wouldn't be any fun holed up in my room the whole time. I'd just wind up feeling guilty."

"I would understand," she said halfheartedly.

"No, you wouldn't, and I wouldn't blame you. That's why it's best if I just stay here." She remained silent for a moment. I couldn't tell if she was crying or just trying to think of something else to say to try to convince me to come. "Look, Mom. It's not like college will last forever. Maybe I can come home for spring break."

"No maybes about it. You *will* come home for spring break," she insisted. "I guess maybe I could go see Suzie and Steve in Arizona," she finally conceded.

"I think that's a great idea. Why don't you give Suzie a call now?" I said, relieved we had reached a compromise.

"Are you sure you'll be okay all alone during the holiday? I feel bad at the idea of my baby alone on Christmas."

"I'll be fine, Mom. I'll be so brain-fried from schoolwork I probably won't even notice. If I get lonely, I'll see if a few of the other students sticking around want to see a movie or something," I said.

"You're sure?"

"Positive. Now call Suzie," I ordered.

"Fine, but I expect calls from you nightly."

"Mom," I warned.

"Fine. Every couple of days, so I know you're okay."

"Fair enough. I love you, Mom."

"I love you too, sweetie. Be safe."

"You too," I said, ending the call. I felt guilty for lying about Justin, but that was a subject I didn't have the time or patience to tackle right now.

By the time Justin arrived, I was lying on my bed trying to read. Unfortunately, the effects of talking to my mom tended to linger for a while, making it hard to concentrate.

"Look at you," he commented. "I thought you'd be done with books for a while."

"Not this kind of book," I said, holding up the racy cover for him to see.

"Hey now. Maybe I need to borrow that."

"I don't know if it's appropriate for your virgin eyes. It's pretty steamy," I teased.

"Well, bring it along anyway. There may be some stuff in there I can use."

Justin hauled my bags into the hallway while I gave my room the once-over to make sure I had everything I needed. The building was eerily quiet as we made our way down to the first floor.

"Man, it's like a ghost town here," Justin commented, holding the entryway door open for me.

"Yeah. I think Melissa and I were the last to leave. It was like the school announced the building had the bubonic plague or something with the way everyone scattered after exams ended."

"Is your mom still mad you decided not to come home?"

"No. I think she bought my excuse that I needed to be here."

"You know, I would have helped buy your plane ticket so you could have gone home," Justin said, stowing my suitcase in the back of the jeep.

"It wasn't the money. Mom would have bought my ticket if I had asked. It's just—when I made the decision to attend UW, I didn't want to fly home for every break. I went last year, but you heard how much she and I aggravated each other. It's better to save the six hundred dollars for a plane ticket and we can video chat on the phone instead. Besides, I kinda got the vibe after talking to her a little while ago that she's thinking of flying to Arizona to see my aunt and uncle," I said, fastening my seat belt. "It'll be good for her if she does. I think a few weeks away from Woodfalls is just what she needs." I smiled.

"She can't be nearly as bad as you make her sound," Justin chuckled as we headed out of the city.

"Well, her nicknames are: Creeper, Stalker, Enquirer, Lurker, Peeping Pam, and many more."

"Peeping Pam? That one's pretty funny," he laughed.

"Yeah, that one is courtesy of Tressa."

"Now that's a girl I want to meet."

"She's one-of-a-kind, that's for sure. So, how was your humanities exam?" I asked, changing the subject. Just the mention of Tressa made me feel terribly homesick. Facebook and texting didn't suffice when it came to best friends.

"Like seagulls were pecking my eyeballs out."

"That bad?"

"Mr. Rucker is such a windbag. We spent months taking notes on every dribble of crap that left his mouth since he warned us at the beginning of the term that notes were the key to success in his class. I spent hours with my study group going over all that crap, and would you believe only two questions out of fifty were in our notes? Two! Who does that?" Justin said, holding up two fingers in frustration.

"That sucks. Do you think you failed?"

"God, I hope not. If I have to take an extra semester of humanities, I'll jump off a ferryboat and hope another one runs me over," he said, shuddering at the thought. "What about you?"

"I think I did okay on all of mine. I might have screwed up some of the equations in statistics, but seriously, they were ridiculous. I'll eat my entire textbook the day I actually use any of that kind of math," I grumbled. "I plan on teaching third grade, for crap's sake."

"Well, at least they're behind us now," he said.

"Truth. Is Hollie excited about Christmas?" I asked, pulling the conversation away from school.

"You have no idea. She's channeling Tigger at the moment, bouncing around everywhere."

"Tigger?" I asked confused.

"Yeah. You know, from *Winnie the Pooh*," he said at my puzzled expression. "You don't know who Tigger is?" he asked, like I'd just told him I didn't know who the president was.

"I wasn't a big *Winnie the Pooh* person when I was little," I confessed.

"Yeah, but you had to have watched it at least once."

I shook my head.

"I think I'm having a stroke," he said, placing his hand on his heart.

"Dramatic much?" I quizzed at his antics.

"I'm just in shock. How could your mom let this happen? Next, you'll tell me you didn't watch *Sesame Street* either."

I looked out my window so he wouldn't see my lips quirking.

"Shut up. No *Sesame Street* either?"

"Nope," I answered. "Tressa and I were into other cartoons," I admitted.

"Please tell me it wasn't *SpongeBob*."

"No, not *SpongeBob*," I hem-hawed.

"Spill it," he demanded, tickling my leg until I gasped out the answer.

"Fine. We were *Johnny Bravo* and *Batman Beyond* fans."

"Seriously? Those were the shows I watched."

"Probably not for the same reasons as us," I said.

He looked at me questioningly as he pulled into the driveway beside Trish's minivan.

"We sort of watched them because we thought Johnny Bravo and Bruce Wayne were cute," I muttered, grabbing my bag and hopping from the jeep.

"Ha, and you call me the flirt," he teased, grabbing my suitcase and leading me to the stairs to his apartment.

"You are a flirt."

"Brittni," Hollie squealed, barreling down the basement stairs as we entered Justin's apartment. She threw her arms around my waist, making me stagger to keep my balance.

"Hollie, what did I tell you?" Justin chastised.

"That I have to knock before I come down here," Hollie answered petulantly.

"Knock and what else?" he asked, placing my suitcase on the coffee table.

"And wait until you answer," she added reluctantly.

"Exactly. If I were in a regular apartment, you wouldn't be able to barge in anytime you want. I like seeing you every day, but you have to respect my privacy. Now, go back upstairs and knock," he said, steering her toward the stairs.

"Sheesh, it's not like you two were lip-locked or anything," she muttered, stomping up the stairs.

"Tough love?" I asked, turning to Justin.

"I just want her to know her boundaries. I don't want to have to worry about her interrupting us all the time for the next three weeks."

"And what exactly do you think she'll be interrupting?" I teased, wrapping my arms around him and placing a kiss on his neck. "Maybe this?" I added, running the tip of my tongue along his jaw. "Or this?" I asked, trailing my lips to his ear and gently tugging on his earlobe with my teeth.

"You are evil and need to be punished," he growled, dragging me against his pelvis to emphasize his point. I moaned my approval as I felt his enthusiasm against my stomach. "Your punishment will have to wait, though," he said, dropping a quick kiss on my lips as Hollie pounded on the basement door.

"I'm holding you to that," I taunted, trailing him up the stairs.

"Hi, Mom," Justin said, giving her a one-armed hug. She was busy mixing a bowl of chocolate chip cookie dough.

"Son, Brittni," Trish greeted us. Her voice seemed slightly strained when she said my name.

"Yum, cookie dough," Justin said, scooping some of the dough from the side of the bowl with his finger.

"Gross," Hollie piped in, taking the time to grab a spoon for her own stolen bite. "Can Justin and I bring the decorations down now?" she asked with puppy-dog eyes.

"As long as your bedroom is clean," Trish answered, spooning the cookie dough onto a cookie sheet.

"It is," Hollie claimed. She jumped up and down with excitement and grabbed Justin's hand to drag him from the kitchen.

"Do you need help?" I asked, rising from the bar stool I was perched on.

"No, we got it. Sit and relax. I bet Mom would even be willing to share her coffee," he said, indicating the coffeepot on the counter.

"Cups are in the cabinet over the microwave," Trish said shortly.

Feeling uncomfortable, I walked around the counter and grabbed a large mug. Awkward silence filled the room as I doctored up my coffee to my taste preference before heading back to my seat.

Trish kept her eyes on the task at hand, while I contemplated broaching the subject that was most likely bothering her. Finally, after several minutes had passed, I decided to take the plunge. It was like removing a Band-Aid. If you did it slowly, it hurt way more than one quick pull.

"Um, Trish," I started, wondering if I should have fallen back on formality and used her last name instead.

"Yes," she said finally, looking troubled.

"Are you upset that I'm staying here for Christmas break?" I asked, pulling the Band-Aid off in one swift motion.

She waited several heartbeats before answering. "I'm not upset. I'm just having a hard time accepting the fact that my baby is old enough to have a live-in girlfriend."

"It's just temporary," I answered weakly.

"I know, dear. I also know that you're both adults. It just seems a bit seedy that I'm allowing my son to sleep with his girlfriend under my roof," she huffed out, looking relieved that she was finally able to get it off her chest.

"Would it help if I slept on the couch?" I offered.

"No, dear, that's not necessary. I keep reminding myself that if Justin were in his own apartment, he would be free to have whomever he wants over."

"I'm sorry it makes you uncomfortable," I said sincerely. "I can still rent a room off campus," I volunteered.

"Honey, that's not necessary. I'm just acting like an old

fuddy-duddy. Who would have ever thought I'd turn into my mother?" she said, chuckling ruefully. "Just tell me you two are being safe. I'm definitely not ready to be a grandma yet."

"We are," I said, shifting uncomfortably in my seat. Safe sex wasn't high on the list of things I wanted to talk about with a parental figure.

"That's all I ask," she said, flashing a genuine smile.

Hollie and Justin entered the kitchen, halting any further sex conversation. Their arms were loaded with clear plastic tubs filled with Christmas decorations. The three of us spent the rest of the day decorating while Trish baked enough cookies to feed an army, filling the house with a sinfully mouthwatering aroma. By the time darkness fell, the house looked like an elf had puked up the North Pole everywhere. Hollie kept up her usual steady stream of chatter, clamming up only when Travis threatened to buy her a muzzle as a Christmas gift.

It was almost midnight before Justin and I finally found ourselves alone in his apartment.

"Alone as last," he said, sitting on the edge of his bed. He grabbed my hand and maneuvered me until I was standing between his legs. "I've been fantasizing about this all day," he added, deftly unfastening the buttons of my shirt.

"Do tell," I said, placing my hands on his shoulders since my legs felt unusually weak.

"It's been a long two weeks. I think we need to move in together before we have to take exams next time," he said, placing his lips right below my belly button.

"That ought to go over well with your mom," I murmured,

gripping his shoulders harder as his lips left a fiery trail across my abdomen.

"What do you mean?" he asked as I crawled on top of his lap to straddle him.

"Nothing." I was pretty sure his mom wanted our earlier conversation to stay between us.

"Just think how nice it would be to do this in between studying," Justin said, gripping my hips in his hands as he moved against me.

"It would definitely make math just a little easier to digest," I said. I reached a hand down to stroke him through his jeans.

He moaned loudly, straining against my hand as his lips found mine.

"You're right. Two weeks is way too long," I said, pushing his shoulders back until we were both lying on his bed.

"Never again," he answered, capturing my lips.

"Never," I agreed as we removed the rest of our clothing. He flipped me over in one fluid movement until I was beneath him. I sighed with pleasure as I felt him seeking the wetness between my legs, bringing our bodies together.

21.

Present Day

3:11 PM

"Hit me."

"Are you sure?" Justin asked in disbelief.

"Absolutely. Now, hit me," I demanded.

"It's your funeral," he said, raising his hand.

I slammed my eyes shut, unable to look.

"Twenty-three," he crowed loudly, making me groan with frustration.

Opening my eyes, I looked down at the three cards in front of me with dismay. Damn, he was right.

"You jinxed me," I complained as he snatched up the peppermint candy I had bet.

"Not everyone can play blackjack like me," he bragged, scooping up the cards.

"We'll see about that. Let me deal," I said, holding my hand out for the deck of cards.

"As long as you promise not to weep as I continue to rack up the wins."

"I'm surprised this elevator is big enough for your ego," I observed as he reached over to hand me the cards. My hand grazed his, making my heart stutter. For two years I'd willed myself to forget how his touch felt. I told myself that I'd romanticized it, that all we'd shared was a typical college fling. Now, as I looked down at our hands apprehensively touching, a flood of memories washed over me. There was a time when that same hand had skimmed over my body, cherishing it like a work of art.

I looked at Justin with confusion, wondering why he didn't pull away. He'd once proclaimed for the world to hear that he would rather cut off his own hand and feed it to an alligator than touch me again. Without looking up, Justin moved his pinkie minutely to stroke mine. I sat without moving a muscle as the forgotten playing cards slowly cascaded from my hand. He laced his fingers through mine, looking as thunderstruck as I felt. My grip instinctively closed around his like a clam claiming a piece of sand.

"How could you do that to us?" Justin asked raggedly, finally meeting my eyes. "Why do I still want you after everything you did?" he added harshly, tightening his grip around my hand until it was almost painful.

I didn't answer his question. I could not speak for him. I was having a hard enough time sorting through my own feelings.

"Why?" he repeated.

"I don't know," I finally answered.

"Neither do I," he said with disgust. He released my hand abruptly and scooted back to his side of the elevator. I watched with grief as he dropped his face to his hands. We had done this to each other. We took and took until we were stretched so thin that we became brittle and eventually shattered.

22.

New Year's Eve 2010

"Oh, Brittni, you look beautiful," Hollie breathed as I put the final touches on my appearance.

"Why thank you, sweets," I said, giving her a squirt of my favorite perfume.

"I love your dress. The material is so silky smooth."

"You should. You helped pick it out," I reminded her.

"I know, but it looks even better fully accessorized," she said, indicating the matching shoes and my hair, which was styled on top of my head in a mess of curls.

"Justin is going to flip when he sees you," she added, flopping down on Justin's bed while I added a few essentials to the small beaded evening bag I'd splurged on.

"He'd better. I spent a month's salary on this getup," I joked.

"I wish I could go," Hollie said wistfully.

"One day soon we'll take you somewhere special, okay?" I said, giving her a quick hug before joining Justin in his living room.

Justin was in the process of sending a text when I entered the room. I smiled when he looked up and gaped at me. Hollie giggled behind me.

"I think that means he likes it," she said, skipping toward the stairs. "Have fun," she called behind her.

"You look amazing," Justin said, standing up to join me.

"You like?" I pirouetted around so he could get the full effect of the dress.

"Very much. Makes me second-guess my decision to take you out tonight," he answered, placing his warm lips on mine.

"Too late for that, buddy. This dress cost a small fortune and demands to be seen," I said, stepping out of his embrace. "Although looking at you should make me rethink that. Girls will be dropping their panties wherever we go tonight when they see you in this suit," I added, running my hand over the smooth material of his charcoal-colored blazer. I felt no jealousy, though. Somewhere along the way I realized that he wasn't going anywhere. Truly believing that made all the difference in the world.

"I only want one pair of panties dropped tonight," he said, tugging me back into his arms for another hard kiss. "Let's do this before I change my mind."

"Where are we going?" I asked while Justin helped gather my dress into the jeep.

"Wouldn't you like to know?" he answered.

"Yes, I would."

"Soon," he answered, pulling out of the driveway.

"Whatever." I pretended to sulk, even though in reality I was touched he was going to so much trouble to make tonight a surprise. "I can't believe classes start next week," I complained.

"At least we still have a week. Besides, before we know it, it'll be summer break. Did you tell your mom you decided to stay in Seattle for the summer?"

"God no," I answered evasively, shifting in my seat.

"Chicken?"

"Absolutely. I just need to catch her on a good day."

"Well, good luck when you finally do it. That's if you still want to?" he asked, looking uncertain.

"Of course I do. I'm afraid it's a little fast, and I'm scared about what your mom will think," I admitted.

"I already told her."

"You told her?" I asked incredulously. "What did you say? What did she say?" I fired at him in a rush.

"I told her that I asked you to move in with me during the summer. I asked her if that was going to be a problem."

"What did she say?"

"She said it was my decision to make."

"She didn't say it was too soon? That we were making a mistake?" I asked, admitting my own fears.

"I know you think it's fast, but by summer you'll feel differently," he reassured me, patting my leg.

"How can you be so sure?" I asked. I already had butterflies filling my belly and it was months away.

"Because, after the last few weeks together, I know I want that all the time. I like having you with me."

"What if you get sick of me? What if I get sick of you?"

"Then we'll cross that bridge if it happens. Have you gotten sick of me these past few weeks?"

"Well, no, but that's because we're like in the honeymoon stage," I answered, regretting my words instantly.

"Honeymoon? Who's rushing things now?" he teased.

"You know what I mean."

"Trust me. It'll be okay," he said, pulling into a parking garage. "We have to hike a little to get there, but parking near the restaurant is almost nonexistent. This parking garage is as close as we will get."

"That's fine," I answered, looking down at my delicate heels. They looked cute, but walking in them more than a few steps would turn them into medieval torture devices.

Justin offered me his arm as we left the garage and headed across the street.

"You okay?" he asked as I stumbled for the third time in less than two minutes.

"Yeah, except these damn heels hate me," I said, glaring down at the traitors on my feet.

"Can you make it? The restaurant is less than a block away."

"Sure. I may have to murder the maker of these shoes, but I'll make it. As long as you promise to visit me in prison, we're good to go. Of course, I'm sure some butch chick will make me her bitch within the first day."

"Homicide of uncomfortable shoemakers is accepted, not that I wouldn't be interested in seeing you with another girl," he teased.

"You're such a guy," I said, swinging at him with my hand. I almost biffed it for the fourth time. It seemed the heels wouldn't be satisfied until I was a smear on the pavement.

"Here we are," he chuckled, stopping in front of the restaurant.

"Pink Door? Oh yeah, I've heard of this place."

"Live music, romance. It's the perfect destination for a New Year's Eve date," he said, guiding me into the restaurant.

We stepped inside and the first thing I saw was a woman swinging from a trapeze hanging from the ceiling. There was light jazz music coming from a band onstage. Taking in my surroundings, I was glad I had gone the extra distance on my appearance. Everyone seemed to be dressed to the nines to celebrate the evening.

Justin approached the hostess, who found our reservation and signaled another girl to show us to our table.

"This is amazing," I commented, removing my jacket and placing it on the back of my chair.

"A buddy of mine came here a couple months ago for his girlfriend's birthday. He said the food is really good."

His friend's assessment proved to be an understatement.

Every dish that was brought out seemed to top the one before it. The ambiance of the restaurant was just as intoxicating. The interior was cute and chic. I felt like I was in a bistro in Paris or something.

"That was incredible," I said as we slowly strolled back to the parking garage. *Slow* being the key word since my shoes weren't done tormenting me. By the time we made it to the jeep, I was cursing my shoes with every step.

Justin was chuckling as he helped tuck me into the jeep before climbing in himself.

"What's so funny?" I asked, pulling off my shoes to rub my sore feet.

"You. Your temper is downright cute. I'm not even sure a frat boy cusses as much as you just did."

"Sorry, swearing is my downfall. I try to curb it, but when my body parts are screaming in agony, it gets the best of me."

"No apologies necessary. I admire the fact that you were able to make it as far as you did," he said, pulling in front of the art gallery at UW where I had first agreed to go out with him. "We're here."

I raised my eyebrows. "You missed school so much you had to return during break?"

"It's all part of the evening's festivities," he said, climbing from the vehicle and coming to my side. "Here, put your arms around my neck."

Following his orders, I placed my arms around his neck as he swooped me into his arms.

"Wait, you can't carry me. I'm too heavy," I protested as he carried me effortlessly to the front of the building.

"Seriously? You weigh nothing," he said, pulling me tightly against his chest as he unlocked the front door of the building with a set of keys he pulled from his suit pocket. "Now, the wooden planks I use for my artwork, they're heavy," he stated, placing me down once we were inside the building.

"Are we going to get in trouble for being in here?" I whispered.

"Mr. Smith knows I'm here. That's how I got these," he said, dangling the keys.

"If you say so. I feel I should point out that it would be a huge bummer if I got kicked out of UW and had to return home with my head hung in shame," I pointed out.

"Never fear, it's all cool. Trust me."

"Said the fox to the hen," I mumbled. I trailed behind him toward the only source of light on the far side of the large room.

He laughed and linked his fingers through mine. We were still ten feet or so away when the painting on the wall came into focus. The familiar face staring back at me stopped me in my tracks. Stepping closer, I studied the painting intently. It was me, but it wasn't. It was far too beautiful to be me. I mean, I felt I was cute, but never beautiful, not like this. Justin had taken every feature about myself that I saw as a flaw and somehow made them appear beautiful, almost exotic.

"How?" I whispered, tracing a finger over the image as I fought to keep my tears at bay.

"I did the outline the day we went to the aquarium. You were so beautiful seeing the fish for the first time. You took my breath away. I wasn't sure I would be able to capture it."

"This is how you saw me?" I whispered.

"This is how I see you. This is how everyone sees you. I'm not sure where this low self-image you have came from, but trust me. You are the only one who sees it," he clarified, turning me to face him. "I love you, Brittni."

"What? Wait. You love me?"

"I love you," he said, crushing his lips to mine. He loved me. He thought I was beautiful. Me. He loved me.

"I love you too," I said as the truth roared from me like a freight train. I wasn't sure when it happened, but somewhere along the way he had captured my heart.

23.

Present Day
3:27 PM

"I hate that your touch still affects me," Justin admitted after a few minutes had passed.

"Join the club. It's not like I'm doing cartwheels here," I muttered, slowly picking up the cards we had dropped.

"You don't seem to understand what I'm going through here."

"What you're going through?" I shook my head at his arrogance. "You think you somehow hold the market on hate?"

"You have no reason to hate me," he said, shaking with barely suppressed rage.

"Really? What about the fact that you left me and refused

to listen? That you never considered my feelings or how hard it was on me. I hate to break it to you, but you betrayed me long before I betrayed you. So get off your high horse. Contrary to what you believe, the world does not revolve around you."

"I did not cheat on you with Shelly," he said, jumping to his feet so he could pace again. "I told you that."

"I'm not talking about cheating."

"Then what do you mean?" he yelled.

I cringed as his voice vibrated off every corner of the small enclosed space.

"I'm talking about my heart," I said, surging to my feet. I stood directly in front of him with rage cloaking us like a blanket. "You betrayed my heart. You left me broken and alone in front of everyone," I added, jabbing him in the chest with my finger. "You left me alone holding all the shattered pieces," I whispered as the dam holding my sobs at bay finally crumbled.

24.

February 2011

"Brittni, you're going to be late," Melissa said, nudging my shoulder.

"What?" I said groggily, squinting in the bright daylight streaming through the window above our desks.

"I said you're going to be late. Don't you have biology at ten?" she asked, pulling on her jacket while she crammed her feet into the cute pair of flats she had gotten for Christmas.

"Yeah," I answered, placing the pillow over my eyes to block out the unwanted light.

"Well, unless you get your ass in gear, you're going to miss it."

"What time is it?" I mumbled. My heavy eyes tried enticing me to stay in my nice comfortable bed for the rest of the day.

"It's nine forty-five. Unless you're skipping for the second time this week, you have to get up now," she said, pulling the pillow off my face.

"Nine forty-five?" I repeated, trying to make sense of the time in my head, which seemed to be in permanent foggy mode lately.

"Yes, so get up," she said, grabbing her shoulder bag.

"Yes, Mom," I snipped, dragging my legs around so I was sitting up. The room spun slightly, making me feel queasy.

"Are you okay?" Melissa asked with her hand on the doorknob.

"Yeah, just a little light-headed. I didn't eat much yesterday. I think I have a dumb stomach bug," I mumbled.

"Maybe you should stay in bed. You look like hell," Melissa replied, looking concerned.

"Thanks for the compliment. Philips would have my head. We're covering mitosis phases versus meiosis phases this week. She's hinted that they'll be important facts to know for the midterm." I struggled to pull on my favorite yoga pants at the same time that I was yanking my UW hooded sweatshirt over my head.

"Yeah, but if you're sick," Melissa said, taking in my lethargic movements.

"I'll be fine. Once I finish biology, I'll come back here and go to bed," I said as I shoved my hair into a clip to secure it.

"Don't you have a date with Justin tonight?"

"No, he's studying with some guys from his humanities

class tonight. His teacher is being a complete asshat," I said, grabbing my bag and following her out of the room.

"I've heard horror stories about that guy. Thank God we steered clear of him," Melissa said before we parted ways. "Make sure you go back to bed after class," she added sternly.

"Yes, Mom," I teased, feeling slightly better now that I was moving around.

"Good girl, and if you're lucky, maybe I'll bring you some soup tonight."

"From Mia's Diner?" I asked hopefully.

"You'll have to wait and see. Now go before you make both of us late," she said, shooing me off.

Heeding her warning, I increased my pace, although my body wasn't happy about it, but at least I reached biology with two minutes to spare. Five minutes later, I was wishing I'd just stayed in bed. To add insult to injury, I discovered that Professor Philips wouldn't be teaching today when one of the research assistants who had previously covered her class came strolling in. The worst part was he had a heavy foreign accent that no one seemed to be able to understand. You could hear multiple grumbles throughout the room as he hooked up his laptop to the overhead screen at the front of the classroom. The best you could do was write down as much information as possible from his PowerPoint presentation and hope that Professor Philips would cover the topic again on another day. I did my best to keep up, but the minutes trickled by at an alarmingly slow rate as I imagined my warm bed back in my room.

"What a joke," Stan, one of my friends, said as we walked out of the building together after class. "I know he's speaking English, but I'll be damned if I understood five words of what he said in there."

"Tell me about it," I said. "I got 'Hello, class,' but everything after that sounded like gibberish."

"Do you want to go grab some coffee? I have an inordinate amount of time left before my next class."

"Can't. I think I'm fighting off some kind of bug. It was all I could do to drag my ass out of bed for this joke of a class."

"That sucks. I hope you feel better," he said, backing away before he could catch any of my germs.

I told him thanks, although I was tempted to lick his face or something, the big baby. The walk back to my dorm seemed endless as the last of my energy surplus melted away. By the time I stumbled back to my room, I didn't even bother to remove my clothes. Before I succumbed to sleep, I sent Justin a text telling him I was sick and that I would call him later when I woke. He replied quickly, telling me to rest and drink plenty of fluids.

Later turned into the next morning as I woke up after nearly twenty hours of sleep. I felt marginally better and relieved that the queasy stomach that had been plaguing me for the last week or so seemed to have disappeared.

"Look who's finally awake," Melissa said, placing a hand on my forehead. "How do you feel?"

"A little better. My stomach isn't as bad." I checked my phone to see several text messages and missed calls from Justin.

"I already told him you weren't feeling well and that you

were crashing," Melissa said when she saw my reaction to my phone.

"Thanks. I'll call him in a few minutes. I need to get moving."

Tuesdays and Thursdays were the two days that I worked at the daycare since I had no classes. Melissa tried to talk me into calling in sick so I wouldn't expose the kids to my germs.

"How do you think I got those germs?" I pointed out, pulling on my last clean pair of pants, which happened to be another pair of yoga pants. I badly needed a trip to the laundry.

"I guess you're right. Maybe that's why you've been so sickly these last few weeks."

"Don't be silly. It's days, not weeks," I chastised, pulling on my boots.

"Weeks," she emphasized. "You've been complaining about feeling puny since the last week of January. Valentine's Day is on Monday. I know my math skills are shaky, but I can read a calendar, and that means you've felt bad for more than two weeks. Maybe you're anemic," she pointed out.

"Maybe," I answered, grabbing my purse.

"You should visit the clinic," she said as I headed for the door.

"Maybe," I said, flashing a fake smile as I closed the door behind me.

The smile faded before the door had closed completely behind me. Two weeks? Could she be right? Two weeks of sickness and five and a half weeks since my last period. For a week and a half I had been trying in vain to ignore the fact that for the first time in my life I was late. It couldn't be possible. I was a Period Clock. Somewhere in the back of my mind I knew something was wrong. I pushed it to the far recesses of my brain and buried it beneath mundane school-related junk, but suddenly the truth hit me like a brick wall, making me gasp for air. I detoured from my usual route to the daycare and sank down on one of the benches along the way. A lack of air made my vision blur and my stomach turn. Leaning forward, I placed my head between my knees. My world was falling apart at the seams.

After a few minutes of trying to calm my breathing, I was finally able to lift my head. The analytical part of my brain told me I needed to get up and go to work. That I needed to restore my life to some semblance of normalcy until it was ready to digest the news I had been avoiding. At the moment, I could not deal with the fact that my body no longer belonged to me alone.

Staggering to my feet, I gripped the back of the bench until the last of the light-headedness completely faded. I began the short hike to work, knowing that once I made it there I would be too busy to think about anything else. With each step I took, the band of despair that was encircling my chest loosened slightly so I was able to breathe a little bit easier.

Breathe, step, breathe, step, breathe.

Seemingly meaningless words when taken out of the context of this moment, but for now they served their purpose as they rolled through my head.

Breathe.

Step.

Breathe.

Step.

Breathe.

I plastered a smile on my face as I greeted the kind elderly receptionist who sat at the entrance of the daycare. Fellow teachers called out their own greetings as I made my way to the lounge and the locker where I stored my belongings. I returned their greetings, keeping the same brittle smile firmly in place. If they saw through my façade, they refrained from commenting.

Once I hit the classroom where I co-taught four-year-olds, my smile became a little less brittle and almost appeared normal if you didn't know any better. The letter Q and number twenty became my best friends for the day as I worked one-on-one with each student. The monotony of the assignment allowed me to shut down the bothersome side of my brain. "Draw a circle and add a tail," I instructed one student after another. I learned to love those words. After all sixteen of the students made their attempt at a capital Q, I moved to watching them count out twenty Goldfish crackers. Once their counting challenge was accomplished, I would hand them a cup so they could munch on their reward. The morning passed quickly and before I knew it, I was folding mats and stowing blankets and pillows in cubbies after naptime. Every task was completed with my mind occupied only on what I was doing. For a moment, a second, a minute, I convinced myself nothing was wrong.

Leaving the distractions of work behind allowed the dormant

thoughts to once again rear their ugly heads. In order to make it
back to the dorm, I focused again on what I could control.

Breathe. Step. Breathe. Step.

"Holy shit, Brittni. You still look terrible," Melissa stated
as I staggered into our room.

I ignored her observation. What did it matter if I looked
like hell or felt like hell? Did any of that matter when I was
living in hell? Collapsing on my bed, I kicked off my boots
and dragged my comforter over my head with one goal: to
block out the world. I could hear Melissa asking if I was still
sick. I gave her a grunt of confirmation, wanting to be left
alone. She went into motherly mode again, giving me advice
on what I needed to do. Ready for her to hush, I agreed to go
to the campus clinic the next day even though I had no intention of doing it. I didn't need a doctor to tell me I was pregnant. Peeing on a stick would make it official. I wasn't ready
to make it official.

During the next few days, I forced myself to pretend everything was okay so Melissa would get off my back. I canceled
two dates with Justin, claiming I wanted to catch up on
schoolwork. My days took on a surreal feeling as I went
through the motions of being a normal person. It began to feel
like I was acting in a play that only paused to take an inter-
mission when I was finally able to succumb to sleep. Through
it all, I continued to hope I would get my period, putting my
fears to rest. Each night I went to bed bitterly disappointed.

25.

Present Day
3:55 PM

Turning away from Justin, I sank down to the elevator floor, exhausted that we were back where we had started. I brushed away the tears from my eyes. It's not like they could rewind time or change the past, and they certainly couldn't undo the harsh words.

"You should have told me," Justin accused.

"It was my body," I countered.

"That's bullshit. It was my baby too."

I cringed at the word. *Baby.* I never allowed myself to think of it that way. It was the only way to ease the pain. Hearing him say it now was like a sword being rammed through my chest.

We were entering territory I had not forged into. Not with Melissa when she begged me to tell Justin everything. Not with Justin, who refused to hear my side when I needed support. And definitely not with my mom, who could never have handled the truth. Only one person knew all the sordid details. Tressa had met me at the airport more than two years ago and, with one look at me, detoured to the airport bar, where she ordered us several drinks in a row. Somehow we avoided being carded. Maybe the bartender, who was also a woman, could sense the grief I was experiencing. Maybe it would have been obvious to anyone. Either way, I was grateful. With the alcohol coursing through my bloodstream, my tongue loosened and my tears fell hot and fast as I poured my heart out to my best friend. She listened as I explained how Justin had ripped my guts out in front of everyone. How he'd refused to listen. At times Tressa's face twisted with anger, but through it all she held my hand, giving me what I needed, someone to hear my side. As the last words left my mouth, I vowed to never utter them again. The pain was too unbearable. Tressa offered the support I needed with no judgment. She was loyal to the core, even offering to fly to Seattle to make Justin suffer.

Now, two years later, Justin and I were stuck together in this elevator, like two dogs forced to fight each other in some illegal backyard brawl. I couldn't fault him for his anger any more than I could fault myself for the choices I had made. I could have pushed harder two years ago, forcing him to hear me. Even through all his resistance, I could have provided evidence that would have explained everything. At the time,

I'd been so hurt by how quickly he had turned on me that I couldn't find the will to do any more than walk away with the small amount of dignity I had left. Maybe if things hadn't gotten so screwed up, so ugly, they could have been different. We would never know that outcome, though.

26.

February 2011

"Is there something wrong with your chicken?" Justin asked, looking at the mangled uneaten mess on my plate.

"No. I'm just not hungry," I said shortly. I was afraid if I said more, the secret I was holding would leak from my mouth, and I wasn't ready to tell him. I was still trying to come to grips with the situation myself. A situation that had been confirmed in the bathroom just a few hours before Justin picked me up. The pee stick delivered the news in seconds. For whatever reason, I thought it would take longer. Instead, I glared at the offending stick, which had instantly stolen any last bit of denial I had left.

"Are you done? I really have to pee," Stephanie, from the

room we shared the communal bathroom with, called through the door.

"Yeah, give me a sec," I answered, washing my hands after hastily wrapping the test stick in toilet paper. Before exiting the bathroom, I unlocked the door adjacent to Stephanie's room so she could get in. I was already exiting the door to my room when she called out a greeting. I pretended I didn't hear her, not sure I could stomach a conversation centering on who was hooking up with who. I liked Stephanie a lot, and most days her idle chitchat was entertaining. She had a way of spinning every story into a mock standup comedy act. It was all in good fun and everyone found it worth bragging about when she decided to add you into her act. At the moment, though, laughing was not on my agenda.

"I can order you something else," Justin asked, sounding aggravated.

"No. I'm really not that hungry," I answered. I wasn't surprised he was losing patience with me. My end of our conversations over the past week had been reduced to one-word answers. I told myself I was waiting to tell him the truth until I knew for sure. Now that the life-changing stick had verified the news, I couldn't find the courage to speak up. He was obviously confused over my sudden standoffishness and broken dates, but I couldn't seem to bring myself to fix it.

"You haven't been in the mood to talk either. What's with you lately?" he probed.

"What is that supposed to mean?"

"I mean, you've been pretty self-involved for days now. Is

this your way of telling me you want out of this relationship? Because if that's the case, all you have to do is say the word," he said, expressionless.

"Are you serious?" I stewed. "Are you trying to break up with me?"

"Is that what you want?" he asked nonchalantly.

"Is it what *you* want?" I asked, throwing his words back at him. The nausea that plagued my body swirled inside me until it lodged in my throat.

"Hey, I'm not here to force you to stay in a relationship if you've lost interest. Last week you broke all our dates, claiming to be sick or busy. This week, every time we're together, you've got a vacant look on your face. Obviously, I'm boring you. If that's the case, there are plenty of other chicks I can hook up with."

His words made me feel like I was being dragged under water with no way to return to the surface. How had we gotten to this point so quickly? I had been moody and a little vacant recently, I got that. Was that really all it took for him to throw in the towel? How could he handle the responsibility of a pregnancy when he couldn't handle a week of not being the center of attention?

"Hook up? Did you really just say that to me?" I asked. I didn't care that my voice carried across the restaurant. He had pushed the wrong button and was being unfair. I was trying to deal with a life-changing event and he was thinking about who he could hook up with next. I clenched my fist, wanting to punch the snarky look right off his face.

"Chill," Justin said in a lower voice, looking uncomfortably at the other patrons sitting near us.

"Chill? You want me to chill? How about you chill," I said, picking up my glass of water and throwing it in his face. The other diners chuckled at the free show, but I paid no attention. "You go hook up with those other girls. I need nothing from you anymore," I said as my voice shook with rage and hurt.

I was halfway home before the tears finally made it past the rage and into sorrow. As they poured down my cheeks with no end in sight, everything inside me turned to burned ash. Why should I be so surprised that it would end this way? Justin wasn't the type to stick to a relationship. Hell, neither was I. Could I really blame him for getting bored with me, especially after my behavior these last few weeks? We were both anticommitment.

"Holy crap, Brittni. What happened to you?" Melissa jumped up as I burst into our room. "You've been crying," she stated, unsure how to handle this anomaly.

I nodded, sinking down on my bed. Scooting back, I picked up my pillow and clutched it against my chest, hoping it would help the pain.

"What happened?" Melissa asked, joining me on my bed. "Did you and Justin have a fight?"

I nodded again. I wasn't sure I would be able to talk around the new wave of tears I was trying to keep from flowing.

Melissa patted my hand. "I'm sure it'll be okay," she said confidently. "By morning, I bet he'll be calling you, wanting to make up."

"We broke up and I'm pregnant," I said in a rush as tears coursed down my cheeks.

"Pregnant?" Melissa whispered, looking horrified.

I nodded through my tears, relieved to finally confess to someone.

"And that asshole dumped you when you told him?" she asked disgusted, snatching up her cell phone. "Rob is going to kick his ass."

"I didn't get to tell him about the baby," I said, stalling her hands before she could text Rob. "Things fell apart before I could tell him, and now it's too late."

"Brittni, you have to tell him. He'll change his mind. I know he'll stick with you through this."

I looked at her incredulously. She had to be kidding. "Melissa, he couldn't even stick it out because I wasn't quite myself lately. He was ready to call it quits because of a few broken dates and my moodiness this week. What in God's name makes you think he'd stick with me over the next nine months and all the decisions we'd have to make afterward? He threw away what we had when it was no longer fun for him."

"He's going to find out, honey. It's not like you're going to be able to hide it," she said, patting my hand.

I looked at her without saying anything as mixed thoughts continued to race around my head.

"Brittni?" she asked, taking in my silence. "Are you going to have it?"

I couldn't answer her. I had no idea how I'd ended up here. I didn't believe in abortion, but it wasn't something I'd thought

I would ever have to face. My views had always been black or white. If you were dumb enough to get pregnant, then you sucked it up and had the baby. If you couldn't handle the responsibility, there were thousands of couples out there dying to adopt. Suddenly, nothing appeared black and white anymore. Everything was gray and cloudy with no right answer. If I decided to have the baby, it would come after my junior year started. There was no way I could attend classes. I would lose my scholarship and everything else I had worked for, but the alternative made me ill.

"I'll support you no matter what you decide," Melissa said, placing an arm around my shaking shoulders. I wasn't even aware I was sobbing until I felt her arm around me.

Melissa sat up with me the entire night as I alternated between tears and staring off into space. She was uncharacteristically quiet with none of her usual glee anywhere to be found. My bleakness seemed to have sucked everything out of us both.

By the next morning I had no more tears left to cry. I moved lethargically through the day from a lack of sleep. Melissa's promise that Justin would come to his senses never surfaced. My phone remained silent as one day trickled into two and then bled into three days.

Melissa stopped asking if I'd heard from him by the end of the second day. I made her promise not to tell Rob, which I knew was selfish. Rob was Justin's best friend. By forcing her silence, I was making her compromise her own relationship. She never complained, even though I could see it was wearing on her judging by her lack of typical enthusiasm.

A full week after Justin and I broke up, I finally went to a walk-in clinic. I took a bus to the other side of town so no one would know me. The doctor was kind and understanding as she confirmed what I already knew. She gave me literature on my diet and sample packs of prenatal vitamins that she said were important for the baby. Discussing it with a doctor made everything seem much more real. My head spun as she continued on about stretch marks and birthing plans and the delivery. Through it all, I nodded like I was listening, but my mind was elsewhere. When I was ready to leave, she gave me a list of doctors to choose from that all took my insurance. Thrusting everything she handed me into my bag, I thanked her and fled from the clinic.

It took several blocks before I was able to digest everything the doctor had mentioned. It all seemed so final, like I had no choices. I began to feel caged in. Pulling my phone out, I reluctantly typed the one thing I never thought I would into the search engine. The map indicated the planned pregnancy clinic was two miles away. During the walk, I didn't allow myself to think about where I was headed. Instead, I filled my head with mundane thoughts as if this were any other day.

When I finally arrived at my destination, I stared at the nondescript building in front of me with morbid fascination. It was a far cry from what I would have pictured. Somewhere in the back of my mind, I had been expecting a seedy, drab building that could only be accessed through an equally dark and dreary alleyway. Not a place that could have housed something as normal as a real estate office. As a matter of fact, I checked the address one last time to make sure I was in the right spot. Pulling the door open, I nearly gasped when I saw the crowded waiting area. At least everyone inside seemed to have the same idea of remaining as inconspicuous as possible. I kept my eyes averted as I approached the long counter with one small window.

"Can I help you?" the middle-aged woman beyond the glass asked without looking up.

"I'd like to speak with someone," I said nervously.

"Sign in and we'll call you back in a while," she replied as she continued to type on her computer. "Make sure you have payment ready."

"Uh-huh," I stammered, unsure of what I was doing here. I wasn't ready for this yet. I'd just needed to make sure there were other options. "Can I just have a pamphlet or something?" I asked, finally able to form a coherent sentence.

"On the far wall between the bathrooms is all the literature you'll need," she said, still not looking up.

Thanking her for her limited help, I made my way to the wall of brochures. Without bothering to read any of their titles, I shoved one of each into my purse, not caring whether they were about STDs, safe sex, or options beyond abortion. The safe sex literature seemed a little like hindsight considering that if anyone in this room had practiced safe sex, none of us would be here now. Cramming the last of the brochures into my bag, I hurried from the building like a bank robber fleeing the scene of a crime. The anxiety I felt haunted me for several blocks as I moved as fast as my legs could muster. I wanted as much distance between the abortion clinic and me as possible. One thing I learned was that returning would be nearly impossible.

27.

Present Day

4:17 PM

"Did you ever consider the possibility that I would want to know?" Justin asked.

"Of course I did," I sighed, pulling my bag to my lap. I held it tightly as if it could shield me from his questions.

"But you decided my opinion wasn't important enough, or maybe you knew I would talk you out of it."

"I was going to tell you. That last date we had, when you accused me of being vacant, I'd just taken the pregnancy test. I was going to tell you and then you were suddenly breaking up with me."

My eyes met his without flinching. I had provided one of the pieces from the puzzle of confusion. I could see him mentally sliding it into place. Because I knew him as well as I did, the remorse hidden behind his handsome features was evident, even if for a moment.

"You had plenty of time to tell me after that day," he said stubbornly, not wanting to own up to his part in the blame game.

"Really? When exactly would that have been? The week after you broke up with me and never even bothered to call? I know you can't possibly be talking about Jacob's beer-pong party, where you spent half the night with Shelly sitting in your lap with her tongue crammed down your throat."

"I didn't call because I was fucking torn up. Your sudden disinterest in me felt like someone had reached into my chest and pulled out my heart."

"Oh, boo-hoo. So you didn't even bother trying to call? It had to be just about you, right? I wasn't disinterested. I was freaking out because I was pregnant, you moron."

"I didn't know," he stated quietly.

"It shouldn't have mattered. You should have stood by me. We'd been dating for three months. You told me you loved me," I said, hating the way my voice cracked.

"I was afraid you were getting ready to dump me. I was trying to save face."

"Well, there you go. All you cared about was yourself. Are you kidding me?"

"Look, the relationship thing was still new to me. Just like you. I was scared that you seemed to hold all the power."

"None of it changes anything. You wanted to know why I never told you; well, now you see. You took yourself out of the equation the moment you tried to 'save face,'" I said, throwing his words back at him.

28.

March 2011

"What are these?" Melissa asked, holding up the stack of brochures I'd cleaned out of my bag after a week of ignoring them.

"Just some stuff I picked up," I answered, taking them from her and shoving them in my bag.

Melissa looked troubled as she continued to study me. "Brittni, what are you going to do? Are you going to get an abortion?"

I didn't want to answer her question. For almost a week I'd been able to pretend everything was okay. I just needed time to sort through my feelings, and by ignoring the pamphlets I was almost successful. "I don't know, Mel. It's too much for me to think about right now," I answered, shoving my books into my bag for my afternoon classes.

"You have to make a decision soon, otherwise you won't have a decision to make," she logically pointed out.

"I know. I have a few weeks to make up my mind. I just need a little more time," I said, ignoring her doubtful look as I headed for the door. "I'll see you later."

"Bye," she muttered, looking unhappy.

Her words repeated themselves on a continuous loop in my head. I knew she was right. A decision had to be made. The idea of returning to the cold forbidding abortion clinic made my stomach turn. I just needed more time.

Classes passed much as they had for the last month. I meticulously took notes in each of them, since it was the only thing that seemed to distract my thoughts.

"Hey, Brittni, wait up," a masculine voice called out as I headed back to my dorm later that afternoon.

Turning around, I saw Jacob Miller hurrying toward me.

"Damn, you're fast," he said, jogging over to me. "Hot date?"

An ironic bubble of laughter erupted out of me in one quick gasp. "Hot date? Not unless you consider math equations hot," I answered, holding up my book.

Jacob laughed along with me before swallowing hard. "I kinda heard through the rumor mill that you and Justin Avery called it quits."

My eyes widened as I willed myself not to react to hearing Justin's name. "I didn't realize you and Justin knew each other," I commented, digging my nails into my hand so I would remain focused.

"Sure, we all go back. Anyway, I'm throwing a party tonight and wanted to know if you'd come?"

"Um, I'm not really in the party mood," I hedged.

"Come on. It'll do you good to let off some steam."

"I'm not ready to start dating again," I interjected, trying to let him down easy.

"Hey, that's cool. You can come hang out."

I racked my brain for another excuse but came up empty. Partying was the last thing on my mind, but the idea of submerging myself in a loud environment had its perks. "Okay, maybe I'll come."

"No maybes. Say you'll be there," Jacob persisted.

"Fine. I'll be there for sure. Here, plug your address into my phone," I said, handing my cell over.

He grinned happily. I felt a twinge of guilt that he thought he stood a chance, but I'd been honest with him. What else could I do?

"See you at eight," he said, handing my phone back before heading in the opposite direction.

"Sounds good," I answered, although I was lying. I was already second-guessing my impulsiveness. I had no business going to a party in my current state.

The rest of my afternoon was spent weighing the pros and cons of going to the party. One moment, I would decide not to go, and five minutes later, I would rationalize that although I was pregnant, that didn't mean I was dead. It was only after

Melissa showed up to our room and accidentally let it slip that Justin had a date that I finally made up my mind. She apologized profusely for telling me, but I reassured her it was fine. It was just clarification that he wasn't there for me and probably never would be.

With my mind now made up, I grabbed my clothes and headed to the bathroom to get ready for Jacob's party. I was in the shower when Melissa knocked on the door.

"Come in," I called out.

"Hey, so Rob and I are going to see that new scary movie that's supposed to be pretty decent. Do you want to go with us?"

"Can't. I'm going to a party."

"You are?" she asked, sounding pleased.

"Yeah. You know Jacob Miller? It's his party."

"That's good. You've been cooped up in our room for weeks."

"I haven't felt like getting out much," I said, stating the obvious.

"Maybe Rob can set you up . . ." She trailed off as I pulled the shower curtain aside to reveal my incredulous look.

"Um, Mel, have you forgotten that I'm pregnant?" I asked.

"Yeah," she said, looking sheepish. "I'm such a ditz sometimes. I forgot."

"I wish I could," I said wistfully, closing the shower curtain.

I could hear Melissa muttering under her breath about being an airhead before she closed the bathroom door behind her.

By the time I was finished in the bathroom, Melissa was already gone. I found another of her famous sticky notes on my dresser, apologizing for her "airheadiness." I laughed at her made-up word. Despite everything going on in my life at the moment, I had to love Melissa. She was the one constant that kept me grounded. I didn't know what I would have done if I didn't have her to lean on.

Grabbing a pen, I scrawled a short return message, telling her not to be a dork, that I loved her "airheadiness" and all. I lugged my heavy book bag off the floor and dug around inside, trying to find my wallet. The pamphlets I had collected from the clinics made it damn near impossible to find anything, so I pulled them out. Sorting through them, I tossed anything dealing with STDs and safe sex into the trash can. In the end, I only kept three: one that provided a breakdown of the nine months of pregnancy, one that discussed adoption, and one about abortion. I couldn't help grimacing at the captions and pictures of the pregnancy pamphlet. I wasn't a wimp, but the idea of pushing a watermelon-sized human out of my body didn't sit well. The one picture that really twisted my guts into knots showed a glowing woman holding her newborn baby in her arms. For weeks I'd refused to think about what was actually happening in my body and what I would have if I went through all nine months of pregnancy. Looking at the picture of the mother holding her baby, everything suddenly got real. In seven and a half months, that could be me. The idea frightened me to the core, but a small part of me couldn't help feeling awestruck at the idea. My life would never be the same if I kept the baby. Everything I had worked for would change in the blink of an eye.

Next, I opened the pamphlet dealing with adoption. It was nothing but testimonials by couples who claimed my child could be the miracle they so desperately wanted. I studied their faces critically. I could go that route. I could make a difference in someone's life. Maybe I could work it out with the school and not lose my scholarship. If I took summer classes, I could lighten my load in the fall when the baby would be due. It was at least worth checking into.

Feeling more in control than I had in weeks, I placed the pregnancy and abortion pamphlets in my bag. I debated pitching the abortion pamphlet but instead tossed it on my desk. I wasn't completely sure which route I would choose, and I could at least read over it when I got home.

I headed out for the party, ready to escape all the heavy decisions that seemed to be saturating the room. The walk to Jacob's apartment off campus was relatively short, and the place was easy enough to find by the noise level throbbing out of the building. I felt sympathetic to any of his neighbors who weren't invited to the party, although judging by the number of people littered throughout the hallway and into his apartment, it looked like the whole building was there.

Loud music made the floor beneath my feet vibrate as I looked around for Jacob. Pushing into his apartment through the wall of bodies was almost overwhelming. Someone I didn't even know handed me a red Solo cup filled to the brim with beer. My stomach turned as the smell of the beer wafted up. Trying not to breathe through my nose, I handed the cup to a willing stranger, who sucked it down like a parched survivor on a deserted island. To avoid any other alcohol handouts, I shoved my hands in my jacket pockets as I continued in vain to search for Jacob.

"Hey, aren't you in my sex education class?" some guy slurred in my face. He grinned at me, obviously pleased with what he thought was a clever pickup line. Of course, all his charm left when he clutched my arm so he could remain upright.

"Nope," I said, prying his fingers away from my bicep. I turned my back on him as I heard him use the same line on another girl, who giggled.

A new wave of bodies entered the apartment, making it harder to move. I was already beginning to regret my rash decision to attend the party. I hated tight spaces and I was beginning to reach my limit. A few of the faces around me looked vaguely familiar, but in truth, I really didn't know anyone here. Inching toward the door, I decided maybe I'd crash Rob and Melissa's date since I wasn't in the mood to return to the dorm. I was scanning the room one last time for Jacob so I could tell him I was leaving when my eyes landed on a couple on the far side of the room.

My heart stuttered as I took in the leggy blonde perched on the lap of the only guy to whom I had ever said *I love you.* I wanted to look away and yet, my eyes refused to move. I watched as Justin ran his hand up the back of her shirt, urging her closer so he could claim her lips. Stomach bile churned its way up my throat as I watched them play tonsil hockey for the world to see. No longer able to be in the same vicinity with him, I backed toward the door, not caring who I bumped along the way. My eyes never left the train wreck in front of me. It was as if I were witnessing a crime that I couldn't look away from. I was almost home free when the inevitable happened.

Maybe he sensed my presence, or maybe God just felt I needed to suffer a little more.

I was almost out the door when Justin broke the kiss and looked my way. Dozens of memories flooded me as my eyes clashed with the guy who had stolen my heart so completely. A flash of something I couldn't discern crossed his face before it was replaced by the cocky grin that had always driven me nuts. He wrapped his arms tightly around the leggy blonde, making it clear I had been replaced.

Flashing him a brittle smile to show I didn't care, I left the apartment without a backward glance. Each step I took was painful, like I was walking across broken pieces of my own heart.

I made my way through the crowd in the hallway, toward the stairs that led to the first floor. My mind was on autopilot as I willed back my tears. Crying in front of a bunch of strangers was not an option. The stairs were almost as busy as the hallway and I had to push past several jocks who were blocking the way. I was halfway down when they decided to show off their testosterone and started shoving each other. Before I could react, someone stumbled into me, making me pitch forward. Drunken hands reached out to steady me, but they grasped uselessly at thin air as the force of the shove sent me the rest of the way down the stairs.

I hit the pavement hard, feeling all the pain to match. Several people gasped while more laughed as I landed in a heap at the bottom of the stairs.

"Holy shit, you totally fell down the stairs," a girl said, stating the obvious.

"No shit," I muttered, sitting up embarrassed. Was there no end to my shame? I straightened my legs, fighting a string of curses as they protested. "Great," I said, grimacing at the holes in the knees of my jeans. From the few lights around the apartment building, I could see both knees were glossy with blood.

"Are you okay?" the same girl asked, reaching a hand down to help me up.

"I'll live," I answered, grunting with pain when my scraped hand made contact with hers.

"Do you need to go the hospital?" she asked, looking concerned.

"No, I'm fine. Thanks for helping me up since the asshole who pushed me down the stairs doesn't seem to care," I said in the direction of the offending idiot, who was still screwing around with his buddies.

"Grant pushed you? What a dick."

"Truth," I said. "Thanks for your help," I added as I started to shuffle away.

"Hey, wait. Are you sure you're okay?" she called.

"I'm fine," I reassured her, even though each step I took made everything hurt. My knees seemed to have taken the brunt of my fall, but my left side felt tender to the touch, cluing me that I must have landed there also. Reflecting back on my fall at least got me home without any thoughts of Justin. It was only after I had maneuvered out of my ripped jeans and took stock of the large bruise on my left side that I finally allowed Justin to enter my mind again. I stepped into a hot shower, letting the water cascade over my stinging raw skin. Everything ran through my mind at once. Justin, the baby inside me, and the decisions I needed to make. My earlier optimism had faded and I was once again indecisive about what I wanted to do.

Switching off the water, I grabbed my towel and was in the process of drying when a sharp pain speared across my abdomen, making me gasp in pain. I clutched my stomach, and a moment later the pain was gone as fast as it had come on. For the first time since my fall, I thought about the baby. I rubbed my hand possessively over my stomach, which had only recently started to bulge. Nothing noticeable when my clothes were on, but something I could feel when I tried to button my jeans, which had gotten a little snug. I sat on the toilet seat lid for several moments, making sure the pain was truly gone and not coming back. After several pain-free minutes had passed, I carefully pulled on my yoga pants and shrugged into an oversized sweatshirt. Limping out of the bathroom, I climbed onto my bed and pulled my comforter up to my chin, placing my hands on my belly as if I could protect the fetus from any more harm.

Before I fell asleep, I reflected on what this sudden possessiveness meant for the life inside me. Did it mean I had ruled out abortion? Was I committing to carry the baby for another seven months? My hands on my belly made it clear I was already starting to care. I wondered if that was a good thing. Maybe I had waited too long to make my decision. I drifted asleep to the mental picture of a baby swaddled in blankets and cradled in my arms.

My thoughts carried through to my dreams, as they were filled with images of me carrying the baby to term and preparing for birth. In the dream I could sense my excitement as I lay in a hospital bed awaiting the baby's arrival. The scene abruptly changed and I was no longer in the same bed. Instead, I was on a sterile table with a doctor telling me they would take care of my problem. I tried to fight him, telling him I had changed my mind and wanted to have the baby. He ignored my pleas as two burly guys stepped in to restrain me. The doctor disappeared between my covered legs. I screamed in agony as his hands reached inside me.

I woke screaming with cramps seizing my belly. Groaning in pain, I wrapped my arms around my stomach, instinctively knowing what was happening. The dampness between my legs was the only verification I needed. Fear ripped through me as I flipped on the light so Melissa could help me.

My heart dropped when I discovered Melissa's bed was empty. Not wanting to attract any attention, I reached for my phone and dialed the number for a cab company rather than call 911. The pain was steady and cramps continued to rip across my stomach as I struggled to gather my belongings. Shrugging into my heavy jacket, I headed out of my room to wait for the cab that would take me to the hospital.

The hours I spent at the hospital passed in a blur. A sympathetic doctor confirmed I had lost the baby. I watched with dry eyes as they gave me a local anesthetic and then performed a D&C to remove any remaining tissue. That was how they referred to it. *Tissue.* As if the thing that had thrown my world completely out of whack had been nothing more than that. My eyes burned from the tears I refused to shed. After the procedure, I was placed in a curtained-off area where I could be observed for the next few hours until they released me.

I received a text around noon from Melissa, asking where I was, while a nurse checked me over one last time. I typed a hasty message telling her I was with the doctor. She fired back immediately asking if I was okay. The nurse was in the process of telling me what to expect over the next few days as my body adjusted to the loss of the baby. My phone chirped again, signaling another message from Melissa.

"Sorry, it's my friend," I said as the nurse paused her instructions. I typed out a quick answer to Melissa, not even paying attention to what I had typed. The nurse waited while I finished and then continued giving me the list of things to watch for.

"You might want to text your friend and tell her you need a ride home," she said kindly as I listened to her instructions in a daze.

"Oh, that's okay. I'll call a cab. My friend doesn't have a car."

"We'd rather you had someone with you for the next twenty-four hours."

"She'll meet me at my dorm," I promised, gathering my belongings.

"Are you sure?" she said skeptically.

"Promise," I said, ready to leave. The knot in my throat from holding back my tears was to the point of becoming painful. An orderly wheeled me outside and helped me into the waiting cab. I needed to make it home and then I could cry. I was scared that if I started now, I wouldn't be able to stop as I thought about how empty my body suddenly felt.

29.

Present Day

4:30 PM

"Okay, so I was a chump," Justin admitted. "It doesn't mean I didn't deserve to know you were pregnant. I should have had a say in some of the decisions. I know it's your body, and in the end you get the final say, but it was my baby too. I should have known about it before you got an abortion."

I felt his pain. I'd lived with it for two years. I should have forced him to listen when I had the chance, but I let pride dictate my actions. I walked away, allowing Justin to believe the worst about me. Maybe I felt it was justice for me to bear the brunt of his accusations since I had contemplated abortion in the first place. It was only after I lost the baby that I realized I could never have gone through with it. I lost something I never realized I wanted until it was gone. Melissa had been heartbroken from the role she had played in the mix-up. She begged me to let her tell him the truth, but I swore her to secrecy. I told her if she cared for me, she would let it go.

Over the tough weeks following the miscarriage, Melissa continued to badger me to tell him the truth, but in the end, I tucked my tail between my legs and ran. Not only from my own pain, but from the destruction I had caused others.

30.

March 2011

Melissa was waiting outside when the cab dropped me off at my dorm. Clouds had moved in while I spent the morning at the hospital and a steady drizzle of moisture was falling from the sky. It seemed fitting that the sky appeared to be weeping.

"I would have gone with you," Melissa greeted me as she helped me into our room, dripping wet.

"Huh?" I asked through chattering teeth as I worked to pull my wet clothes off so I could replace them with something dry.

"I said I would have gone with you," she repeated, sounding hurt.

"That's okay. You weren't here," I pointed out, climbing under my blankets.

"You could have waited for me," she accused, sounding a little miffed.

"Um, no, I really couldn't."

"You mean to tell me you couldn't have scheduled it for a time when I could go with you?" she said in a thick voice.

"Schedule what?" I began to understand. "Melissa, I didn't get an abortion. Didn't you read my messages?" I said, pulling out my phone to show her the text messages I sent.

"Yes, I did. You said you were with the doctor in the first text, and in the second you said you weren't pregnant anymore."

"So you just assumed I . . ." I cut myself off as I looked at my phone and saw she was right. Tears filled my eyes. "When I typed the last message the nurse had been in the process of telling me what to expect after the miscarriage. You get that? *My miscarriage.* I was still kind of in a daze at the time. I wasn't really paying attention to what I was typing," I said.

"What? How?" Melissa asked in a rush as she began to cry.

My tears made it difficult to answer.

"I was knocked down the stairs at Jacob's party. I thought it was just my knees that got hurt," I told her, lifting the blanket to show her my legs, which the hospital had bandaged for me.

"Oh my God. Who the hell knocked you down a flight of stairs?" she asked enraged.

"Some asshat I don't even know," I answered. Melissa never left my side as I let my grief pour out. "I just want to put it all behind me now," I sniffled. "I'm glad no one else knows. I'm not sure I can handle being the subject of gossip and sympathy."

Melissa looked uncomfortable at my words.

"You told Rob," I said, knowing her well.

"I'm so sorry, Brittni. I was upset when I thought you went to get an abortion on your own. I thought you didn't need me," she said as she began to cry again.

"Of course I need you. I was scared to death when I woke up and knew I was losing the baby and you weren't here."

She wailed harder at my words. "I'm so sorry I betrayed your secret. I'm the worst friend ever."

"Wait a second. Melissa, you're not saying what I think you are, right? Please tell me you didn't tell Rob I got an abortion."

She rushed to my side and grabbed my hand. "I was upset. I called him without thinking."

"You were upset? What about me? Oh my God, Melissa. Did he tell Justin?" I asked, jerking my hand away.

"No, no," she replied. "He promised me he wouldn't say anything. Just to be sure, I'll call him and tell him I was wrong. I will fix everything, I swear."

"No you won't. Don't call anyone, don't fix anything. This is between me and Justin. When I want him to know, *I* will tell him. No one else," I insisted.

"Okay. Whatever you want. Please just forgive me," she pleaded, reaching for my hand again.

"I do forgive you," I assured her, knowing part of this was

my fault. "Just please don't say anything to anyone, especially Justin. I would hate it if he felt responsible. I want to try to move on."

Melissa linked her fingers with mine, providing much-needed comfort.

"The irony is I pretty much decided last night I was going through with the pregnancy," I said as exhaustion from the last twelve hours caught up with me. I fell asleep with Melissa's head on my shoulder and my hand resting on my now-flat stomach.

I stayed in bed the rest of the weekend, and by Monday I was feeling marginally better. My body seemed to be bouncing back quicker than my state of mind. I was still feeling weak and gimping around with my road-rashed knees, but I knew missing class wasn't an option. Finals were just over a month away and I needed to ace all of them if I wanted to keep my GPA in my comfort zone. Melissa volunteered to walk me to my classes, but I declined her offer. I loved her dearly, but after a day and a half of her hovering over me, I needed a break.

I was on my way to Smith Hall when a familiar voice called my name. I took a deep breath before turning to face Justin. Our eyes met and I was shocked at the hatred reflected in them.

"Is something wrong?" I asked, worried that maybe his father had done something. "Is it your dad?" I asked, reaching out a hand to comfort him without thinking.

"Don't touch me, you lying selfish bitch," he said, shaking with rage. He jerked away like I was poisonous.

TIFFANY KING

"What the hell are you talking about?" I asked. If anyone should be angry at the other person, it should be me.

"Why didn't you tell me?" he shouted, drawing attention from everyone in the vicinity.

"Rob told you about the baby," I said as more of a statement. "Justin, you don't understand. I—"

"Yes, Rob told me," he said, interrupting me. "How could you keep this from me?" he snarled as the onlookers crowded around so they wouldn't miss a single detail.

"Whose fault was that? You were acting like such an asshole, you never gave me the chance," I yelled. "It's not like you were around. You were too busy hooking up with Shelly to care about the mess you left behind."

"I didn't hook up with Shelly. I took her to one party."

"Right, a party where you had your tongue crammed halfway down her throat."

He looked momentarily shocked at my words. "So I kissed another girl. That sure as hell doesn't give you the right to do something like this without telling me first."

"You're kidding, right? Last time I checked, you're not my father, and you have no right to tell me what I can or can't do."

"When it concerns my baby, I deserve the right to know. What kind of selfish person aborts her baby without telling the father? How dare you take that right from me, you fucking bitch."

I recoiled at his words as everyone around us seemed to gasp at once. From the corner of my eye, I could see people snapping pictures with their phones. I'm sure we were quickly

208

reaching the timelines of every Facebook page on campus. My cheeks felt hot as I searched for the words to set him straight, but all I could focus on was the judgment on everyone's faces.

"It's my body and my choice," I lashed out, ignoring the whispers and comments of the students around us.

"You are a heartless bitch," he said, with acid dripping from every word. "If I never lay eyes on you again, it will be too soon."

I acknowledged his words by turning my back on him and heading toward my dorm. It took all the strength I had to keep myself upright, walking past every stare and snicker until I was out of Justin's sight. My actions had caused a sea of hurt and misunderstandings. I could have set him straight and defended myself, but his eyes held me back. When I looked in them, I saw nothing but anger and hate. The kind of hate that is incapable of understanding. His intention today was clear. He was the judge and jury together, and I was already guilty in those eyes.

Melissa was devastated that Rob had spilled my secret to Justin. She begged me to let her set them both straight. I refused her pleas. I used guilt as a weapon, telling her the only way she could make it up to me was if she never mentioned the truth to either of them. I knew by the look on her face it was a low blow, but I stuck to my guns. She tried to wear me down over the next few weeks as my name rapidly circulated around school. Stares and whispers followed me everywhere I went, making it impossible to put the whole thing behind me. As the weeks progressed, my body recovered, but my will was completely broken. I was anxious for spring classes to end so I could leave. Without telling Melissa, I took the appropriate measures to transfer to a college closer to home for my junior and senior years. I wanted to leave everything behind and go where no one knew the half-truth about what happened.

31.

Present Day
4:37 PM

"I never got an abortion," I admitted. It was a relief to finally have the words out there.

"What?" Justin asked, jerking his head up.

"I said, I didn't get an abortion. I lost the baby that night I saw you and Shelly together. Someone pushed me down the stairs at Jacob's apartment complex and I lost the baby," I said, willing my voice not to break. I had already cried so many times over the past two years that it seemed impossible that mentioning the baby would tear me up again.

He looked like he could vomit. "Why didn't you tell me?" he pleaded.

"In the beginning I was going to tell you about the baby, and then everything seemed to fall apart. I was so scared, and I thought you had moved on. I figured it would muck things up even further if I told you before I made up my mind," I answered, standing up so I wouldn't feel so vulnerable.

"Why did you let me publicly shame you like that? Were you trying to be some kind of martyr?" He stood also, sounding angrier than before.

"God, do you ever think before you speak?" I snapped. "Since you're so into the inquisition here, let me fire a few questions your way. Do you think it's possible that I was completely freaked out over the entire situation? Because you know, pregnancy can do that to a girl. What do you think my frame of mind was when I walked into a crowded room to find you with another woman? Then you shot me that fucking shit-ass grin when you saw me, and don't try to deny it. We both know what the hell you were doing. As for the public shaming, I had just gotten over a miscarriage, so I'm sorry if I wasn't prepared to do battle with you in a public forum. I didn't say anything because you fucking screamed like a lunatic, announcing to everyone that I had aborted our baby. You think at that point I wanted to give you the satisfaction of knowing the truth when you had ripped my heart out and stomped on it in front of everyone? I lost our baby in a painful miscarriage, but even if I had done the awful thing you accused me of, yelling it across campus would still have been wrong. You should have come to me," I said, exhaling the last bit of breath from my tirade.

Justin stood in silence, recovering from the bomb I had dropped on him.

"I was mad," he said quietly as his shoulders drooped.

"Yeah, well, I was hurt," I countered. "Not only that, I had to leave to get away from what you did. You turned me into the martyr, not me."

"I should have handled it better," he admitted.

"You're just saying that because you now know all the facts."

"No, I mean it. I've known for years what I did was wrong. Hell, I knew while I was doing it, but I was like a rogue wave out of control."

I nodded. I could understand that part.

"Why didn't you tell me later? Why did you allow me to continue to think the worst of you?"

I sighed, thinking about the question before I answered it. "I guess at the time I felt like I deserved it. Abortion was one of the options I considered. When you were yelling at me, it almost made everything a little bit better. I was so sad after the miscarriage. You yelling at me shifted the pain away from the loss of the baby to something different."

"You were sad?" he asked, joining me on my side of the elevator.

"It broke my heart when I lost our baby," I said thickly. "I didn't realize how badly I wanted it until I lost it," I answered as one lone tear trickled down my cheek.

Justin reached out tentatively and captured the tear with his thumb. "You wanted our baby?"

I nodded, transfixed on his hand, which slowly moved away from my face.

"You can't touch me," I whispered. I wasn't ready for physical contact after everything we had exposed.

He nodded and dropped his hand but remained standing in front of me. I could see the questions on his face, and I mentally prepared myself for them. Stepping away from him, I sank back down to the floor as the rest of the adrenaline left me. Instead of heading back to the opposite side of the elevator, Justin slid down the wall so he was sitting right beside me.

"Please tell me everything," he said after we had sat in silence for several minutes.

His words opened a floodgate in me and for the next forty-five minutes I confessed everything. Some of it brought back raw emotions and I had to knuckle away a steady stream of tears. Halfway through, he reached over to hold my hand, ignoring my request that he couldn't touch me. I described how awful the miscarriage was, not sugarcoating anything. At times, his grip on my hand tightened to where it was almost painful, and yet through it all he never released it.

"Why did you wait so long to tell me?"

"I figured it wouldn't make a difference."

"Make a difference? Brittni, do you know how hard it was for me to hate you?"

"You made it look pretty easy," I answered dryly as he let out a low chuckle.

"Hating you made the fact that you didn't trust me less painful."

"I did trust you at first, but then I was scared after you broke up with me. Everything was so confusing and you weren't making it any easier. You were being such an a—"

"Asshole," he interrupted. "I was being an asshole," he sighed, rubbing his hand across his head. "I let my insecurities get the best of me and I threw our relationship away. Why did I have to be such a jackass?"

"You were confused. I was acting like a complete zombie." I found myself comforting him.

"So what? You had every reason to be a zombie. I confirmed all your fears by dropping you the second things changed. No wonder you hate me so much."

"I don't hate you. You were the love of my life, the father of my unborn child. I couldn't have hated you if I tried. Believe me, I did try. My friend Tressa had to step up and hate you enough for both of us," I joked through a watery smile.

"One day I'll have to thank her for that."

"For hating you?" I asked, confused.

"For being there for you when I wasn't. For being your friend."

"Yeah, she's pretty fantastic in that category. I've been lucky that way. Melissa and Rob are pretty fantastic too."

"Do they know all the bonehead things I've done?" Justin grimaced.

"Melissa does. She was never supposed to tell Rob, but I suspect he knows, considering he tried to get us together today," I answered.

"I'm surprised he didn't knock some sense into me," Justin

said as the floor beneath us shuddered slightly before starting to move. "Hot damn, we're moving," he said, surging to his feet and pulling me in for an excited hug.

Though my excitement matched his, I couldn't help stiffening in his arms, unsure of how to react. A lot of shit had gone down between us in the nearly six hours we'd been stuck together. Just because we'd cleared the air didn't mean we didn't have a whole lot of baggage and past hurt bogging us down.

Whether he felt my resistance or sensed the doors getting ready to open, Justin abruptly dropped his arms as the doors parted to reveal a crowd of people, including Melissa and Rob.

Melissa rushed forward and gave me a tight hug. "Do you want to kill Rob? I could hold him down so you can at least get a good sock in," she whispered in my ear.

"At the moment, I just have to use the bathroom really bad," I said, dragging her along with me.

"In Rob's defense, he didn't know you two would somehow end up on the same elevator, let alone an elevator that would break down," Melissa chattered away as I hurried to one of the stalls. "Was it awful? I'm so sorry," Melissa continued.

Knowing Melissa as well as I did, I knew no comment was necessary at the moment. I stayed in my stall longer than needed so I could gather my mixed emotions. Having spent the last six hours with Justin with no more secrets between us made me feel jittery like I'd consumed heavy doses of caffeine in a short amount of time.

"Brittni, are you okay?" Melissa asked, standing right outside my stall door.

"Yeah," I muttered, opening the door. "So, how did you find out I was here anyway?"

"Rob fessed up when the building operator called and told him his two visitors were stuck in the elevator. After the first hour, he called me, figuring I'd need to protect him from you once the elevator started moving again."

"Why'd he do it, Mel? Did he think forcing Justin and me to have lunch together would suddenly right everything between us?" I asked, washing my hands.

"Well, he's been pretty upset since I told him what really happened."

"Speaking of which, you swore you'd never tell," I chastised her, placing my hands on my hips.

"Au contraire, my dear. I swore I'd keep your secret as long as he was my boyfriend. As soon as Rob proposed, he no longer fit in that category."

"Really? You're going with the technicality clause?" I asked.

"Look, I was never comfortable keeping it a secret," she said, placing her own hands on her shapely hips. "I did it at the time because I felt so damn bad about my part in everything that went down. It was a bad situation. But just so you know, I never agreed with the idea of you bearing the brunt of it. What Justin did to you in the courtyard was a shitty thing and wouldn't have happened without my big mouth. I needed Rob to know the truth," she added defensively.

"I understand," I said, smiling at her astonished look.

"Really? I thought you would be ready to kill Rob and me by the time you made it off the elevator. I remember you hated elevators and was sick that you were cooped up in one for hours, with your ex no less."

"I'm not going to lie, it got hairy there for a while, but I worked it out."

"And Justin? Did he give you the silent treatment the whole time?"

"Not exactly," I admitted. "We kinda worked some things out."

"You did?" Melissa squealed, making me cringe as a couple of women looked our way.

"Shhh," I said as the bathroom door opened. "We did, but let's not make a big deal about it. I'm not even sure where we go from here. Maybe we'll be friends, maybe not, but at least we don't hate each other."

"Oh my God. I'm so excited," she said, bouncing up and down.

"Mel, chill," I ordered as we headed out of the bathroom together.

We found the guys waiting for us in the lobby. "So, we kinda thought we'd skip visiting my office and maybe grab some grub," Rob said, eyeing me sheepishly.

"You think?" Melissa teased, wrapping an arm around Rob, who was still eyeing me.

"That's fine with me," I answered, throwing Rob a bone. I'm sure the hours he spent wondering what the inside of that elevator would look like when it opened was punishment enough.

"I was dying," Rob said, holding his hand on his chest. "Let's head out.

"You let him off easy," Justin whispered out of the side of his mouth as he walked beside me.

"I distinctly remember hearing someone threaten to kick his ass as soon as we were free from our steel cage. I guess my eyes are playing tricks on me because he looks pretty unscathed at the moment."

"I'm biding my time," Justin replied, flashing me his trademark grin.

"I'm parked over here, guys," Rob called, standing beside a silver SUV that screamed *adult*.

"I figured you'd want to sit up front," he told Justin, slapping him on the back.

"Sure, that's fine," Justin said, shooting me a look before climbing into the front seat of the vehicle.

The ride to the restaurant was loud as Rob and Melissa peppered us with questions about our confined time together on the elevator. Strangely, Justin stayed as closemouthed about what had transpired as I did. After a few minutes of trying, they both graciously surrendered as Melissa launched into a detailed description of the engagement party the next night.

"We wanted to keep it fun, so we decided to do a themed karaoke party," Melissa gushed, ignoring the look Justin and I exchanged as I tried not to snicker.

"Um, karaoke?" I asked, wondering if Melissa had missed the memo where karaoke was no longer cool.

"Yes, Ms. Doubting Thomas, karaoke. I know it's not the

fad anymore, which is why I want to do it. I'm going to help it make a comeback. The kicker is that everyone has to pick a song that best describes Rob and me. Right, babe?" she said, looking at Rob for approval.

"You got it," he said, shooting her the same indulgent smile over his shoulder that I remembered from two years ago. I didn't know whether to laugh or applaud the fact that Melissa still had him hooked so completely.

"Karaoke," I repeated, trying to wrap my brain around the idea as Rob pulled into a crowded parking lot.

"Don't worry, I called ahead," Rob reassured us as we piled out of the car.

"Good man," Justin said, falling in step with me as we headed into the restaurant together.

I tried to sort through how I felt about Justin no longer looking at or talking to me with animosity. For a brief moment, I could almost make myself believe we were all together back at school on a double date. In reality, though, nothing was the same, and I was setting myself up by trying to remember the old days. As we made our way to our table, I maneuvered myself so Melissa and Rob were on either side of me, hoping the buffer would help clear the rest of my mind. What I hadn't counted on was that Justin would be sitting directly across from me. Throughout the meal, I couldn't keep my eyes from finding his time and time again. Each time I looked, he was watching me with the same hooded expression that was hard for me to decipher.

Being thrown off by what his looks meant put me in constant

catch-up mode on the conversation. After having to ask Melissa to repeat herself three times, I finally lied and said that the trauma of being trapped all day had obviously frazzled my brain. I would rather bite out my tongue than confess what the real issue was, especially when I didn't know myself. I was having a hard time figuring out if Justin was being cordial because Rob and Melissa were there or because he'd finally forgiven me and was ready to be friends. If it was the latter, I was unsure how that made me feel. Did I want his friendship? That was the question. That and whether I had forgiven him for the part he'd played.

Regardless, I was able to get through the meal without mishap. Dinner stretched into drinks that helped mellow my frazzled nerves. By the time Rob drove back to his office so Melissa and Justin could pick up their cars, I felt much more in control. I was able to relax as I climbed into the car with Melissa after giving Rob a hug and shooting Justin a smile.

32.

Present Day

I woke the next morning in my hotel room, feeling better than I had in two years. Lying in bed, I allowed myself the luxury of enjoying the moment. Maybe now, once and for all, I could finally put the past behind me. I knew I'd never forget about the baby, but maybe I could let go of some of the grief.

My phone chimed, letting me know I had a text message. I smiled when I saw it was from Tressa, yelling at me for not returning all her texts from the previous day. Instead of trying to text all the drama from the day before, I dialed her number. It took more than an hour to fill her in on everything that had transpired. She huffed and cursed her way through how Rob had tricked me but laughed hysterically when she heard about the elevator getting stuck. She grew quiet as I explained everything that had gone down with Justin.

"How do you feel now?" she asked when I finally ran out of steam.

"Relieved, but I still feel like a Mack truck ran over my chest. You know how I hate to talk about everything that happened."

"He's still a total asshole for what he did to you. He's lucky I never flew there. Otherwise, he'd be dickless now."

"He's different now. Harder, I guess. I think the whole situation changed him."

"Yeah, well, you're different too. He made you go through a tough-ass situation all alone," Tressa snipped, not ready to give up her grudge against him.

"I know. Believe me, I let that be known. Now, tell me what's going on there. How did Ashton's first date go with Panty Dropper?"

Tressa laughed at my question. "Just put it this way, luck has not been on their side. The first night they went out, Mr. Hot Voice ended up in the hospital."

"What?" I laughed as Tressa filled me in on all the details surrounding our friend Ashton's disastrous attempts at a one-night stand. Tears of mirth rolled down my face when she told me about Ashton taking a nosedive on her bedroom floor right before her date. Then he walked in on her with her panty-covered butt in the air.

"Poor Ashton," I said, wiping the tears from my cheeks from laughing so hard. "I wish I were there."

"Whatever. You're too busy shacking up with your ex to miss us."

"I'm not shacking up with him," I denied.

"It's only a matter of time. The hard edge you used to have when you talked about him is missing from your voice. Just don't let the asshole hurt you again, or I'll overcome my fear of flying and drown him in the Pungent Sound."

"Puget Sound," I corrected.

"Whatever. You knew what I meant, and you catch my drift."

"I understand, but you have nothing to worry about. The only thing that happened yesterday is that Justin and I finally have no secrets and now we can move on. Who knows, maybe we can even be friends."

"Translation of 'friends' for you: He's so dreamy. Translation of 'friends' for him: I can't wait to stick it in her."

"Don't be crude, and you're so wrong," I denied.

"Just be careful."

"I will. Trust me, nothing is going to happen.

Tressa mumbled something I couldn't quite catch but loosely sounded like I needed a hard smack to the side of the head.

I ignored her mumblings and told her to text me updates on Ashton and Panty Dropper before hanging up. Checking the time on my phone, I cringed when I realized I had less than half an hour until Melissa would be arriving to pick me up. I hastily plugged my cell into the charger, since talking to Tressa had drained the battery. I was applying my makeup ten minutes later when a knock at my door told me Melissa was early. "Shit," I said, wrapping one of the minuscule towels from the bathroom around my torso before heading to the door.

"You're a little early," I griped as I pulled open the door. It wasn't Melissa. Justin's broad frame was standing in front of me. Yelping with dismay, I clutched what little towel there was before glancing down to make sure it was covering all the appropriate areas. "What are you doing here?" I stuttered out.

"Melissa got called in to work for some paperwork fiasco, so I volunteered to pick you up so we can meet her and Rob for lunch," he answered, entering my room without waiting for an invitation. "Is that okay?" he asked, sitting on the edge of my bed.

"Uh, sure," I answered, trying not to sound flustered, even though he was sitting on my bed. For some reason, it felt oddly intimate. Old memories, I'm sure. "I just have to get dressed," I answered, pawing through my suitcase in a mad attempt to find something that would cover me better than my towel.

"I figured. Towels are so out in the fashion industry," he teased.

I didn't know how to respond. Sure, during dinner last night I'd seen him open up more, showing me that some of the guy I once knew was still there, but I chalked it up to the fact that Rob and Melissa had been there as a buffer. He wasn't flirty like the old Justin, but he was at least friendly.

"I'll be right back," I said, clutching my clothes in front of me and backing up to the bathroom.

"No hurry. We still have a while until we have to meet Melissa and Rob," he answered.

I sagged against the door once it was closed. Having Justin in my room was enough to send my blood pressure through the roof.

I pulled on my panties and jeans with jittery fingers, telling myself it was fine that he was here. Once my pants were in place, I felt a little more comfortable now that I wasn't completely naked. That is, until I reached for my bra, only to realize I'd left it in my suitcase. Biting back a groan of frustration, I weighed my alternatives. I could walk out there in my jeans with the towel wrapped around my chest or I could put on my shirt and walk out to get my bra. Neither option seemed ideal. Knowing Justin as well as I used to, he would definitely think this was a "check me out" ploy. I was screwed either way.

After a full two minutes of weighing the pros and cons, I decided to go with option B. Of course, it was only after I was pulling on my shirt that I realized I had grabbed a fitted T-shirt that hugged my curves. Sighing at the look I was sporting, I left the bathroom with my arms crossed over my chest as I tried to keep the front of my body angled away from Justin.

"Sorry, I'm just about ready," I said, not wanting to make a further spectacle of myself by sprinting the last few feet to my open suitcase, where my bra was dangling halfway out. I maneuvered my body so the suitcase was no longer in Justin's line of vision. Reaching a hand out, I snatched the offending undergarment into my hand, which turned out to be a bad idea since it was snagged on something in my suitcase. My hard tug made it come free with a loud snapping sound as it whacked me in the face.

I silently mumbled a string of curses, trying to control my watering eyes.

"You okay there?" Justin asked, sounding like he was trying to suppress laughter. It was at that moment I looked up from my suitcase and met Justin's reflective stare in the mirror. His eyes were filled with merriment as I clutched the bra in my closed fist.

"I'm fine," I answered, ignoring the fact that I was now sporting a welt on my forehead. I tried to remain aloof as I kept my chin up and stalked to the bathroom with my lips twitching. Closing the door behind me, I could hear Justin's chuckles and I couldn't help laughing at myself. I finished getting ready and before I knew it, we were leaving the room together. My heart skipped when he led me past the elevators toward the flight of stairs. Usually, I requested a ground-floor room, but the hotel had been almost completely booked at the time I checked in. Last night I had gladly hoofed it up the four floors to my room. Seeing Justin bypass the elevators played with my emotions.

We took our time walking down the stairs, exchanging the typical pleasantries. It felt awkward considering our history, but it was better than fighting. We exhausted the topic of weather after the first flight of stairs and Rob and Melissa's engagement party the rest of the way down.

Everything stood still for me as Justin stopped in front of an achingly familiar vehicle.

"Your jeep," my voice cracked.

"I figured since there was a break in the rain, I'd celebrate by taking off the roof and doors. I hope you don't mind?" he asked. Based on the small smile on his face, he knew I would approve.

"Sure," I said, climbing into the vehicle. I kept my face neutral, although emotionally I was soaring.

Justin cranked the jeep, and it was as loud as I remembered. Within minutes, we were able to leave the city behind. The wind whipped around, stinging my face with familiarity. I was enjoying the ride so much it took ten minutes before I thought to question our destination.

"I figured we'd take the scenic route," Justin yelled over the wind.

It felt like taking a trip to the past. My mind became flooded with memories and images of the good times we had shared. We were half an hour out of the city when Justin pulled onto an embankment and whipped a U-turn. The tires spun out on the gravel before gripping the road, taking us back in the direction we'd just come from. I didn't comment, figuring he was a bit turned around. Thirty minutes later, he pulled into the parking lot of a restaurant less than a block from my hotel.

"Scenic route, huh?" I smiled.

"Well, it was scenic for me," he answered softly.

Pulling down the visor, I inspected my reflection, startled by how happy I looked. It had been a long time. Two years, to be exact. I remembered my conversation with Tressa and wondered if I was setting myself up for heartache.

"You're late." Melissa greeted us outside the restaurant.

"We took the long way," I said, nodding toward Justin.

Melissa returned a questioning look before speaking up. "Oh, well, come on. Rob's already inside."

We found Rob sitting at a booth and before I could react, Melissa slid in next to him. I stood for a moment, eyeing the empty side of the booth across from them.

"You want me to slide in first?" Justin asked.

"Huh, oh yeah," I giggled, trying to play off the awkwardness as a joke. I could handle this. We had just ridden next to each other in his jeep. Of course, we had bucket seats with a gearstick separating us, but technically it was the same thing, right? I could almost picture Tressa snorting at my reasoning.

"Is everything ready for tonight?" Justin asked, draping his arm along the back of our booth. I shifted in my seat, rubbing the goose bumps that had popped up along my arms.

"I think so. Brittni and I have an appointment set at the salon while you guys do all the heavy setup," Melissa bragged.

"Oh, so let me get this straight, we get the grunt work while you two get pampered?" Rob mocked.

"Damn straight, but you'll reap the benefits when my nails and hair are all pretty," she said, running her fingers seductively over his bicep.

"Works for me," Rob answered, dipping a tortilla chip into the salsa the waitress had set down.

"Oh brother," I muttered, rolling my eyes dramatically.

Justin laughed outright.

"What?" Melissa asked confused.

"You getting out of work by insinuating your nails will somehow benefit Rob," I answered.

"Are you saying you'd rather lug around tables and chairs all afternoon?" she asked.

"Hell no, but I'm not too shy to tell the guys flat-out they're doing the grunt work." I smirked, dipping my own chip.

Justin and Rob both laughed, while Melissa looked insulted.

"You're supposed to be on my side here. Not three against one."

"I am, Mels," I answered, patting her hand.

After the waitress took our orders, the conversation floated from one topic to the next. We discussed our jobs, or job-in-waiting in my case. Melissa had lucked out and found a job as an assistant to an assistant.

"What if you don't get a permanent spot at your school in Woodfalls?" Rob asked me.

"I guess I'll have to commute to whatever school I can find a position at, or just move there. Hopefully it's a moot point since one of the older teachers is supposed to be retiring soon and her position is basically mine."

"Is it the grade you want?" Melissa asked, digging into her enchilada.

"No," I sighed. "But I'll take what I can get initially."

"Bummer. Maybe you should move back here. I know Melissa would love to have her best friend closer," Rob commented.

Without looking at Justin, I was well aware that the statement had stopped him in midbite. Melissa looked at Rob with a mixture of horror and exasperation as her eyes darted between Justin and me.

"Hon, stop kicking me. It's not like I'm suggesting something ridiculous. Justin and Brittni are no longer enemies, so why shouldn't she move back to Seattle?" he asked, seeing nothing wrong with his logic.

"Because I have a life back home, Rob. I can't just up and leave."

"So you're telling me you have the job you want and a home you like to go to every night?" he quizzed.

"Well, not yet, but there are other things in Woodfalls," I said, very much aware that Justin and Melissa had given up all pretenses of eating while Rob drilled me.

"Like what?" Rob asked, unconcerned, as he took a big bite of his taco.

"My mom and friends, for one."

"So you and your mom are close now?" His ploy for nonchalance was broken when Melissa kicked him hard enough for all of us to hear.

"Look, I'm not dumb, so you can stop kicking him, Melissa, before you do permanent damage," I said dryly. "It's not feasible for me to pack up and move across the country right now just because Justin no longer thinks I'm Satan's mistress," I added. It sounded harsher than I intended, but Rob had forced me into a defensive posture. Justin's only response was to start eating again.

Melissa looked like she wanted to comment but said nothing. An awkward silence settled over our table that lasted through the rest of the meal. I felt bad that I had ruined the mood, but Rob had backed me into a corner. Relieved when the check came, I was the first to slide out of the booth after we paid.

Once we were outside, I waited by Melissa's car while she kissed Rob good-bye. I had the distinct feeling she was still ribbing him for drilling me by the way they both glanced my way. I acted ignorant while I checked my phone for missed messages. I had several texts from Tressa with more Ashton updates. I was smiling as I read them when Melissa joined me.

"What's so funny?" she asked as we climbed in her car.

"My friend Ashton is having a string of bad luck with this guy she's dating," I answered, filling her in on poor Ashton's mishaps.

"I'm sorry about Rob back there," she finally said after I finished.

"It's fine. I know my life isn't going the way I thought it would be at this point, but I don't want it rubbed in my face."

"Oh honey, he wasn't rubbing your face in it. We all just want you back for selfish reasons. I know you have a new life back home, but I've really missed you. Rob is just trying to make me happy."

"I know. Things aren't as easy as they were when we were in college. We have to weigh every decision we make now."

"Very true," Melissa said, pulling into the parking lot of a very posh-looking day spa.

"Wow, extravagant much?" I teased.

"Hey, you only get to celebrate your engagement once," she pointed out as we walked up the discreet path that was hidden from the road with high hedges. "Now, no more blah talk. It's time for some of the finest pampering you'll ever get."

Two hours later, I had to agree with her. I was waxed, buffed, and polished, and practically glowed by the time we were done. Melissa drove me back to my hotel and promised to be back in an hour to pick me up for the party. I opened my garment bag in my room and extracted the black cocktail dress I had bought specifically for the engagement party. Tressa had helped pick it out. At the time, we both had one goal: Get a dress that would make Justin regret ever walking away. Of course, things were different after being stuck in the elevator together, and I couldn't help wondering now if the dress was too much. It wasn't too short since it fell at my knees, but it definitely hugged and accentuated my body in the most flattering way possible. Pulling the dress on, I wished the open back weren't quite so revealing, but I had no other options. Especially since in our juvenile thinking, Tressa and I had also shunned the idea of adding a shawl, feeling it would take away from the dress. After touching up my makeup and redoing my hair in a twist, I slipped on my black two-inch heels and was ready to go. I grabbed my small handbag and left the safety of my room behind before I could change my mind.

I waited in the lobby, deflecting the attention of two businessmen who looked old enough to be my father when Melissa pulled up. Saying my good-byes to the two creepers, I hastily left before either of them could hit on me again.

"Making plans for later?" Melissa teased as I climbed into the car. "You look amazing," she added.

"So do you," I said, taking in her pale pink dress that complemented her blond hair and blue eyes. "Can you believe that? One of them even had on a wedding ring. Seriously? Men can be pigs."

"Truth," Melissa said, pulling away from the curb.

"So, where's your party being held?" I asked, feeling like a complete ass that I just now thought to ask.

"It's in an old warehouse that they refaced last year. It's now the happening place to have parties. Rob does business for the owner, so we were able to get it for a steal."

"That's awesome," I said, watching the sights out the window as we drove. It was hard not to think about how much I loved and missed this city. Even though I had thrown a wrench in Rob's questioning earlier, I had been unable to shake his words. Two years ago, I let something drive me away from the one place that had totally resonated with me.

"What do you think?" Melissa asked, pulling into a dirt lot behind a large industrial warehouse.

"Well, it looks like a warehouse," I said, climbing from the vehicle.

"Don't be a baby. The transformation is on the inside."

"I know," I laughed. "I'm just kidding. It looks great."

Melissa nodded, leading me to the oversized door that was standing wide open. We entered the dim space together and I was instantly taken. The interior was rugged and chic at the same time. There was a stage set back in the far corner of the building. A large glazed concrete dance floor sat directly in front of it, bordered with high tables and plush bar stools. The floor surrounding the dance area was a rich dark wood that had been polished to a high shine. The opposite side of the building held low couches grouped together to form intimate seating areas away from the music. The overall feel of the space screamed *classy*. What drew me in the most were the interior walls. I marveled at the intricate artwork painted across the entire room.

"He's phenomenal, huh?" Melissa asked, following my gaze along the painted wall. Her question left no doubt that Justin was the artist behind the masterpiece I was viewing.

"He always has been," I answered, turning as the guys entered through a set of swinging doors that were hidden on the far side of the room.

Rob let out a low whistle when he saw Melissa. "Babe, you look great," he said, taking her hand and pulling her in for a long kiss.

"So, the grunt labor was worth it while I got beautified?" I heard her murmur as he sealed his lips to hers again.

"You look beautiful," Justin said to me.

"Thank you," I answered, feeling my face blush. It had been so long since he looked at me this way, and yet it felt like not a single day had passed. "You don't look half bad yourself," I answered, taking in the well-cut suit he was wearing.

"This old thing?" he joked, leading me to the bar, where several cocktail waitresses were making last-minute preparations.

I snorted. "Old, my foot," I said, looking up at him with a smile that faltered when I saw the pained expression on his face. I immediately regretted dropping my guard. We were forging a tentative friendship, but it seemed we had a long road ahead.

I turned away to gather myself while I asked the bartender for my favorite cocktail, hoping to settle my nerves.

I could hear Justin clearing his throat like he had a tickle before he broke the silence. "Is that dress backless?" he choked out.

Accepting my drink from the bartender, I raised it to my lips, which were curved in a satisfied smile. Any doubts I might have had about the dress were put to rest. "Is that wrong?" I replied, taking another sip of my drink.

"Depends how many guys you're trying to send to the hospital for heart failure tonight," he said, ordering a scotch neat.

"It's really pretty modest," I pointed out, turning to look at him.

"If that's what you call modest, I'd love to see your version of pretentious," he stated, taking a long drink.

"Are you hitting on me?" I asked as the alcohol loosened my tongue. We were both playing with fire, but I didn't care. The truce we had established the day before seemed to give us the permission to pick up where we left off two years ago, before our relationship had gone to hell.

"Would that be a problem?" he asked, taking my elbow and guiding me toward one of the intimate seating sections.

"I'm not sure," I answered honestly, lowering myself to one of the sofas. "People will probably think we're crazy, and my friend Tressa would most likely have serious issues with it."

"Do you care what they think?" he asked quietly, taking another drink of his scotch.

"They're just looking out for me. Especially Tressa. She knows how rough these last two years have been."

He nodded, contemplating my words. I couldn't help wondering if my candidness would scare him off. For a brief moment, I panicked and wished I could retract what I had said, but rightfully, secrets and misunderstandings had torn us apart before. It was time to put those days behind us and start with honesty.

He raised his drink to his lips, downing the rest of the contents while never taking his eyes off mine. In that moment, he made it clear he wouldn't be scared off. A shiver of anticipation raced through me.

33.

Present Day

Thirty minutes later, I was standing with Rob and Melissa as their guests began to arrive. More than a few of them I recognized from UW. Thankfully, even though they looked surprised to see me, they focused their attention on the engaged couple. I was amazed at how quickly the room filled with people.

Taking to the role of proper hosts, Melissa and Rob circulated the building, making sure they mingled with everyone. I had lost Justin in the crowd shortly after everyone started to show up and told myself it was probably for the best. We were playing a risky game, and taking time to figure things out was the smart thing to do. With that in mind, I forced myself to mingle with a few people I had been friendly with at UW. I was in the process of catching up with a few girls from school when a set of skinny arms crushed me into a hug.

"Brittni," the hugger squealed with adolescent glee.

"Hollie, you're all grown up," I said, taking in the preteen in front of me, who was at least a head taller. "You look beautiful," I added.

"Thank you," she answered, twirling around so I could admire the full skirt. "I'm so excited you're here. Come see Mom and Trav," she said, pulling me away.

I threw an apologetic look at my old friends as Hollie dragged me across the room. "I didn't know you were going to be here," I told her, happily sliding an arm around her shoulders.

"Rob had to invite us. Mom's been like a second parent to him almost his whole life. She wouldn't have tolerated a non-invite," she pointed out.

I grinned at her logic. That sounded like the Trish I remembered. My grin spread to a full-fledged smile when Travis spotted me and squealed much like Hollie had. His hug was every bit as exuberant, and I found myself returning it fondly. It dawned on me at that moment that except for the drunken hug my friend Ashton had given me a few days prior to my Seattle trip, it had been two years since anyone had really hugged me. I forgot how much I had grown to like the hugs from this particular family.

"Travis, you look absolutely dashing. How does it feel to be a college man?"

"It's cool," he said, smiling broadly.

"Brittni, it's so good to see you," Trish said as Travis finally released me.

"You too, Trish," I said, stepping in to give her a tentative hug. She surprised me by pulling me in tightly. "I'm so sorry," she whispered in my ear before releasing me. Tears shone brightly in her eyes and I knew Justin had told her about the baby.

"He told you?" I asked as Hollie and Travis rushed over to talk to someone else they knew.

"He came over last night to talk. I always wondered what drove you two apart. I never realized," she trailed off. "Had I known, I would have helped."

"I didn't know he never told you. I assumed all of you would hate me like he had."

"Oh, honey, I would have never judged you," she said sympathetically. "I'm sorry my son let his pride get the better of him. I could skin him for outing you in front of everyone."

"He told you about that too?" I asked, shocked that he had been so honest.

"He's not proud of his actions, but believe me when I tell you, he's suffered also. The whole situation changed him from the young man he used to be. I know that's little consolation for the pain you went through, but I wanted you to know he suffered too."

"I know he did," I said, fighting the wave of sadness that engulfed me.

"He's learned from his mistakes, and I think he's a better man for it," she said as the subject of our conversation approached.

"Hey, Mom." Justin greeted her with a hug. "Paul's over by the bar and wants to know if you want a fruity drink or a glass of wine."

"Oh, decisions, decisions," she laughed, shooting me a warm smile. "I hope to see you again before you have to head back home."

"I'd like that."

"You two look like you were having a heart-to-heart," he said, handing me another drink.

"You didn't have to tell her. I would have kept my mouth shut," I told him, sipping my drink as we settled at one of the high tables.

He chuckled darkly. "I know, but it was long past time she knew the truth."

"My mom still doesn't know," I fessed up.

"What? The Queen of Knowing Everything never found out?"

I smiled at his description. "She obviously knows something happened, but I let her believe it was just a bad breakup. I know I'm her daughter, but I couldn't trust her enough not to tell everyone. I didn't want Woodfalls to be a repeat of what happened here."

He looked pensive as he digested my words. Instead of commenting, he changed the subject. The conversation flowed easily between us as we caught up on the last two years. We steered clear of any more baby talk, focusing instead on Justin's rapidly growing clientele and my desire to secure a full-time position. After a while, Travis and Hollie joined us with Paul's two kids, Brady and Andrea. Brady was as talkative as Hollie and Travis.

They all rambled on about everything from meeting me the first time to how Trish had met Paul. Eventually everyone left our table when Travis saw someone he knew from school and Brady got sick of our "boring conversation," as he put it.

Justin was called onstage to make a speech about the engagement of Rob and Melissa. He charmed the guests with his humorous insights on marriage and where he saw Rob and Melissa in twenty years. His portrayal of them forty years older was sidesplitting and had everyone in tears from laughing. He then cued the DJ and everyone roared with laughter as he started an awful off-key rendition of Katy Perry's song "Firework." The crowd cheered and groaned with approval as Rob made a production of having Justin removed from the stage by the two bouncers.

Another friend took Justin's spot, singing some old boy band song. The crowd cheered him along, making up their own words as they went. Next, a girl we knew from college took a turn, singing a love song that actually sounded halfway decent. I had to give her credit.

"Looks like your karaoke is a big hit," I told Melissa as she joined our table.

"Told you," she said, smiling at the line of people waiting for a turn on the microphone. "It was cool that Justin kicked it off for us."

"Yeah, that was pretty hysterical. His speech was hilarious too."

"Well, I think he nailed Rob dead-on, but there's no way I'll be that peppy at sixty."

"Oh please. You'll be the spryest chick in the retirement home."

"You know it," she laughed. "You'll be right there with me."

"Yeah, but I'll practically be a youngster."

"Hey, you're only a few weeks younger than me. Don't think I've forgotten your birthday is next week. I plan on taking you out before you leave."

"Don't be silly. It's not like I took you out for yours."

"Only because you were halfway across the country. Now if you move back, I'll force you to take me out."

"You're moving back?" Hollie interrupted. I didn't realize she was standing behind me.

"No, sweetie," I answered, glaring at Melissa, who mouthed, *Sorry.* I had my suspicions that she'd done it on purpose, but she left to talk at another table before I could grill her for it.

"Aw, why? We've all missed you. Especially Justin. He's been a total downer since you left," Hollie piped in as Justin rejoined us.

"Giving away all my secrets, squirt?" he asked, reaching out to muss her hair, which made her shriek with panic. She backed away from the table with Andrea in tow.

"Great speech," I told him as he climbed onto the stool next to mine. I pretended I didn't notice his leg resting intimately against mine.

"It was fun," he chuckled, signaling the waitress for another round of drinks. "What about my song?"

"Well, that was . . ."

"Amazing, inspiring . . ."

"Awful," I laughed. "Don't quit your day job."

"That bad?" he asked, chuckling loudly.

"Just a bit," I said, holding up two fingers to emphasize my point.

He put a hand over his heart dramatically. "I'm wounded."

"I'm sure," I said, taking a sip from the drink the waitress placed in front of me. I could feel the effects of the alcohol as we sat together talking. I wasn't drunk, but I had a definite buzz. Between the liquor and the fact that Justin's leg was still pressed against mine, my senses were on hyperdrive. The music was loud, so we were forced to lean in close as we talked. Everyone else faded into the background as we sat in our own private world.

Eventually, our bubble of privacy was breached when Trish and Paul brought the kids over to say their good-byes. "I can't believe how big Hollie and Travis have gotten," I observed as we watched them head out the door.

"I know what you mean. Every time I see them, they both look an inch taller," he agreed, resting his hand on top of mine. A moment of intensity crackled between us. Looking up from our hands, we gazed into each other's eyes and the past no longer mattered. I no longer cared who had hurt whom, or who had been wronged. All I cared about was the warm familiarity of his touch. My fingers curled around his hand, holding on tightly.

"Is this okay?" he asked, using the pad of his thumb to stroke the outside of my hand.

My only answer was a nod as I watched his thumb with

fascination. Everything inside me hummed to life. Slowly, he seduced my hand with his touch, running his thumb over each curve. Desire coursed through my veins and my breathing became labored. Finally, unable to handle watching his thumb any longer, I looked up to see that his intensity matched my own.

"Do you want to get out of here?" he asked.

I contemplated his words for the briefest of moments. I knew what he was asking. If I said yes, there would be no going back. This tentative friendship thing, which really was a joke, would be revealed for what it truly was. Justin and I could never just be friends. If I slept with him, we would be lovers with baggage. Even though I knew it might be a mistake, I nodded, unable to deny my body what it craved.

We said our good-byes to Melissa and Rob, who saw right through the excuse that I was tired and he was just giving me a ride to my hotel. I gave Melissa a quick hug and promised to call in the morning. I pretended not to notice her happy grin and whispers of excitement to Rob as we left.

Justin placed his hand on my naked back, guiding me toward the parking lot. Any doubts I might have had were laid to rest. An ache spread through me from his touch. I wanted him. No, I needed him.

During the drive back to my hotel, the only time his hand wasn't on me was when he was shifting gears. By the time he pulled into the parking lot, I was completely coiled up with suppressed arousal that was ready to explode. He walked around to my side of the jeep, opening the door to help me climb down. We stared at each other for a moment before he dropped his lips to mine. I pulled him close, wanting him more than I had ever wanted anything.

"Not yet," he murmured, pulling away.

I sighed with impatience, which made him chuckle.

"Come on," he reassured me, leading me through the lobby of the hotel. We reached the dreaded elevators with some of my passion muted as I contemplated telling him I would take the stairs.

Sensing my unease, he tightened his hold on me. "Trust me," he said, dropping a kiss on my head as the doors slid open.

Indecision crowded my senses as I eyed the steel box. I had already spent enough time in an elevator to last a lifetime as far as I was concerned. Pushing past my resistance, Justin guided me through the sliding doors, pushing the button for my floor with his free hand. The doors began to slide closed and before I could panic, he turned my body to face him. He dropped a kiss on me, shifting all my focus from the dreaded elevator ride to a passion-filled thirty seconds of pleasure. He lifted me up so I could wrap my legs around his waist. The sensation of being held in his arms left me shuddering with need. I wanted him now. I didn't care that we were in an elevator and that someone could be waiting on our floor to get on when the doors opened.

"See, that ride wasn't bad, was it?" he asked, lowering me as the elevator doors opened.

"Not bad at all," I answered. It was definitely one way to make me forget my fear. "Of course, I hope you don't mind me dragging you on every elevator ride I take."

"It would definitely make life more interesting," he said, sliding my key card into the slot on the door. The bed jumped right into view as we walked into the room. Were we really going to do this? Could anything good come from it, with the obvious exception of hot sex?

"Are you sure you want to do this?" he asked. I guess my face couldn't hide my hesitance.

"I'm scared of how much I want this," I admitted.

His troubled look disappeared as he swept me up in his arms and closed the door behind us with his foot. His lips devoured mine and I feverishly returned his kisses, wanting it all. He stood me up at the foot of the bed with my back to him, placing his hands on my hips. I could feel him pressed against my bottom, hard and ready as his mouth trailed over every inch of my back. After a moment, I was unable to stand the torture any longer. I twisted around, taking matters into my own hands. He moaned with pleasure as I deeply kissed his neck just inside his unbuttoned collar. His hands moved up my arms, hooking the straps of my dress before gently guiding it down my body to pool at my feet. Justin's clothing quickly followed and he laid me down on the bed. The intensity became almost too much to bear. By the time Justin rolled on a condom, an entire day of anticipation had reached a boiling point. My body vibrated with pleasure as he settled between my legs before entering me with one powerful plunge. The familiarity of the moment made me want to weep as my body adjusted to his. He dropped his lips to my neck, holding still as he slowly rediscovered my body. I moved restlessly beneath him, feeling my release approaching. As I moaned against his mouth, he matched my pace with his movements, reaching a climax seconds after mine.

He collapsed on top of me as we both tried to catch our breath. Exhausted, I closed my eyes, enjoying the feel of him still buried in me. After a few moments, he lifted himself off me and covered me with the blanket before heading to the bathroom to clean up. I wondered what his intentions were now. Would he leave and act like none of this had happened? Would he even say anything? My worst expectations appeared to be true when he returned from the bathroom and picked up his clothes.

I shifted my expression to appear nonchalant. I would not show my hurt. Technically, I had no reason to be hurt. No promises were offered and no illusions were given.

I was searching my brain for something to say when he surprised me by draping his clothes over the back of the chair and adding my dress to the pile. A moment later, he rejoined me in bed.

"You're staying?" I asked, unable to help myself as he flipped off the bedroom light.

"Is that okay?" he asked, climbing under the blanket with me.

"Yes," I whispered. His arm reached around, dragging me flush against his body.

"Good, because I don't think I could leave if you asked me to," he murmured in my ear.

34.

Present Day

Early the next morning, Justin tenderly made love to me as the sun was slowly coming up over the horizon. It was breathtakingly beautiful and I had to bite my lip to keep from crying. Whereas last night had been all about unbridled heat, this morning was about what our bodies remembered about each other. It took every ounce of self-control in me to not declare my love for him.

Afterward, when we were lying in each other's arms, Justin broke the silence. "When do you leave?"

"On Monday," I answered, running my fingers across his palm. "I'm here for a week so Melissa and I can catch up."

"Can I see you again?" he asked, lacing his fingers with mine.

I smiled. "I'd like that. When do you have in mind?"

"How about now?"

I laughed at his words. "Don't you have to work?"

"I'm currently between jobs. I just finished the warehouse venue from last night and have a private job starting next Wednesday. Which means, I'm pretty much free as a bird for the next few days."

"Is it wise for us to do this?" I asked, trying to be the voice of reason.

"We're consenting adults with no relationship attachments dictating what we can and can't do."

"I mean, should we be doing this with our history? Shouldn't this be wrong?"

"Does it feel wrong?"

"No-o-o, but I know it should," I answered honestly.

"Can I ask you a question?" he asked, tightening his arms around me.

I nodded, though I was afraid of what his question might be.

"Have you thought of me at all in the last two years?"

"Of course," I answered, unsure where he was going with this.

"And was it all bad, or did you think about the good stuff too?"

"Both. What about you? Wait, never mind." We both knew what his answer would be. It was no secret how much he had hated me just two days ago.

"That's the kicker. I wanted to hate you, and at times I did, but there was always something inside me fighting for you. I don't know if that makes any sense. You know how I said I ended a relationship recently?"

I nodded.

"Well, I lied when I said it was commitment issues. The more accurate description would be she wasn't you. Despite loathing you at times, I couldn't help comparing every damn woman I've dated the last two years to you. Now that I have you in my arms, I'm positive that's where you're supposed to be."

I digested his words before accepting them. I was no different. Yes, we had ripped each other's hearts out, but I could never get past the good times we'd shared. "How can this even work, though?" I asked. "I leave in four days. I have a life back home that I can't just walk away from," I stated, even though a persistent little voice in the back of my head told me I could if I wanted to.

"We'll cross that bridge when we get to it. I'm not going to ask you to give everything up for me again," he replied, kissing the back of my neck.

The morning melted away as we remained in bed, wrapped together. We eventually fell back asleep for a while in the afternoon before waking and making love again. It was as if our bodies knew we were on borrowed time and they were trying to get their fill. By evening we were both hungry enough to venture out for real food. We hit one of my favorite cafés from college life before strolling along Puget Sound, talking the entire time. It was amazing how quickly we fell back to our old patterns. Two years of maturity had us talking about different issues than what was relevant back then. Adulthood and responsibilities had a way of making a person look at certain issues differently. Suddenly jobs with insurance and how much we would have to pay in taxes made us wish we could run back home. I was thrilled to learn that Justin had proven his father wrong and not only was making a living off his art, but found it profitable.

"I bet that irks the shit out of him," I commented as we headed back to my hotel.

He shrugged. "He's pretty much MIA now. Ever since Mom got remarried we don't see a whole lot of him."

Justin tried to hide it, but I could tell it bothered him. His father might be a prick, but he was still his dad. "Maybe one of these days he'll come around," I said.

"I won't be holding my breath. Besides, it's not like I hold the market on bad fathers."

"True. He could be a complete absentee like mine. It's been years since Mom and I have heard from him."

"His loss," Justin reassured me, patting my hand.

Like him, I shrugged with indifference. I'd given up on having a father figure in my life years ago when the letters I had sent begging him to come to my eighth birthday party went unanswered. After that, I pretty much crossed him off my list. I hardly remembered him enough to miss him anyway.

I changed the subject as we were pulling into the parking lot of my hotel. Justin followed me up to my room. That became our routine during the next few days. We'd go to bed together each night and spend the days rediscovering the city.

As my time in Seattle ticked by, I began preparing myself for the inevitable heartache of leaving. We spent Friday with Melissa and Rob on a boat the guys had rented for the day. Saturday we hung with Justin's family, and by Sunday, I was sick at the idea that I'd be leaving the next morning. I made a spur-of-the-moment decision when Justin was in the shower to surprise him and change my flight to Wednesday morning. I figured I could leave before he had to start his new job.

Justin was thrilled that we had two bonus days together and we decided to keep it secret so the two days could be all ours. Feeling like we had been given a gift, we celebrated by staying in bed all day Sunday. We felt as if we'd been given a stay of execution.

Justin was still sleeping when I woke before dawn on Monday morning. I studied his features in the dim light. He looked younger and more relaxed, like the boy he was two years ago. The love I felt for that boy had been buried so deeply below the hurt that I thought it was gone. In two days, I would be leaving him again and I was scared of the pain that would come along with it. I knew there was a way to avoid it, I just didn't know if I was brave enough to make that decision.

Deciding to let him sleep, I climbed quietly from the bed and snuck into the bathroom to shower. Steam was just beginning to fill the small room when I heard the door open. Seconds later, Justin joined me, and neither of us spoke as he pulled me into his arms, covering my mouth with his. We made love under the hot water cascading down our bodies. It felt bittersweet—like a good-bye. I knew Justin wanted me to stay, but he would not pressure me, not the way things ended before. He would let me go if that was the decision I made.

Over the next two days, neither of us brought up the subject of me staying. Instead, Justin made it his goal to take me to all of our old favorite haunts in Seattle. I chuckled as we sipped coffee at the café on campus where we had first met and he reminded me of how snotty I had been.

"That's because you thought you were God's gift to women," I said, defending myself between giggles.

"What do you mean, thought?" he teased, winking at me. My stomach fluttered. Even after two years, he couldn't help being a flirt.

"Ha, we better slide over a second table so your ego has a place to sit."

"Admit it. You wanted me. Even at that moment," he said, pulling me in close for a kiss.

"More than I was willing to admit," I finally confessed.

"I knew it," he crowed, pumping his fist in the air.

"Oh lord. Don't make me regret telling you that."

"I'll tell you a secret," he said, slinging his arm across my shoulders as we strolled away from the café. He leaned in and placed his lips close to my ear. "I thought you were the most beautiful woman I had ever seen when you gave me a piece of your mind that day. I fell for you hook, line, and sinker. I had to force myself not to follow you like a lovesick puppy when you stomped away." His words made my heart clench.

"That's just because you wanted to get in my pants," I said, keeping the conversation playful. I couldn't afford to let myself dwell on our impending separation.

"Well, that too," he laughed, placing a soft kiss on my temple.

I tried laughing with him, but it was a forced effort.

We kept things light as we soaked up the last of our remaining time together. I could tell it was difficult for us both when Wednesday showed up like an unwanted bill that was due immediately.

Justin drove me to the airport that morning. We could try to act differently, but the mood was somber. I stared blindly out the window, not paying attention to the passing landscape.

My heart felt like a brick with each mile. I had no idea how I could walk away from him again. We were both silent as he pulled his jeep into the parking garage and unloaded my bags. I gripped his free hand as we walked inside, not ready to let go.

Eventually, we hit the security checkpoint and he could no longer accompany me.

"I'll call you tonight," he said, cupping my face.

I nodded as my eyes began to well up. I felt like I needed to say something more

"I'm here—whatever you decide," he said reassuringly, pulling me into his arms. It was as if he could read my thoughts.

"I'll never regret this week," I murmured, burying my head in his chest.

"Neither will I," he answered, stroking my back.

Unable to stand the pain any longer, I tipped my head back

and captured his lips before turning and walking away. I told myself I wouldn't look back. That it would only make it hurt more, but I couldn't help myself. He was standing off to the side, watching me. It threatened to bring me to my knees, but I blew him a kiss. With each step after that, I had to fight the urge to turn and run back to him. This was the second time I'd walked away from him and the finality of it was crushing.

35.

Present Day

Woodfalls was covered in an unseasonably early blanket of snow when I drove my car down Main Street past my apartment. I was mentally and physically exhausted from my trip and would have liked nothing more than to curl up in a ball on my bed, but I knew Tressa would kill me if I didn't come by to see her first.

I pulled into her driveway and couldn't help smiling at the small obscene snowman on the front lawn. The carrot nose had been moved down below his belly, obviously the handiwork of Tressa's thirteen-year-old brother, Chris, and most likely his partner in crime, John. Putting my car in park, I climbed from my car, smiling again when I noticed the backside of the snowman resembled a nude person.

Without bothering to ring the doorbell, I opened the front door to Tressa's house.

"Brittni, you're back," Stephenie, Tressa's mom, greeted me, looking up from the blanket she was crocheting.

"I just got in. Is Tressa in her room?"

"Yeah. She missed you while you were gone," she answered.

I nodded but didn't answer as I took the stairs two at a time up to Tressa's room. Without knocking, I pushed open the door.

"Black, I like," I said, taking in her recently dyed hair.

"I felt like shaking things up. You know, get some tongues wagging here in Deadfalls," she said in her typical sarcastic tone. "I thought you were coming home Sunday," she added, opening the bottle of black nail polish that was lying next to her knee.

"I missed you too, sugar lips," I answered, picking up a bottle of purple polish.

"Aww, shucks, are we dating?" she asked, batting her thick eyelashes at me. "I'm not sure how I feel about eating peaches."

"Ew, don't be crude," I said, smiling halfheartedly.

"You look like shit. Did Mr. Ass Face show his true colors again?"

"No," I snipped.

"Holy shit," she said, knowingly. "I told you he'd win you back. Don't tell me you're in love with him again."

"I'm not in love with him."

"Right, and I'm Mother Theresa," Tressa said dismissively.

"Look, I don't know what I am. I'm still trying to figure things out."

"Figure out what? Either you're into him or you're not."

I shrugged without saying another word, wishing it was that simple.

We spent the next half hour catching up. She told me about the nightmare date she'd gone on over the weekend. I loved Tressa to death, but her taste in guys was atrocious. Somehow, she was a magnet for assholes. Behind the tough exterior she liked to portray, she had crazy insecurities where guys were concerned. I personally blamed her ex-boyfriend, Jackson. He'd basically stripped away her confidence during the several years they had dated. I was convinced it was his own insecurities that made him feel the need to belittle Tressa. The guy was a total momma's boy. He made Tressa second-guess her appeal.

Once we had exhausted Tressa's disastrous date, she tried to bring up Justin again. I brushed off her questions, claiming to be tired as I rose from her bed. Truthfully, it was a subject I had to work out on my own. I knew what the look on her face meant when her eyebrows came together, but she dropped the issue. I threw her a quick kiss good-bye before fleeing from the room.

Five minutes later, I pulled behind Mr. James's hardware store, where I rented the small apartment above. Hauling my suitcases from the trunk of my car, I trekked through the snow to the wooden staircase. By the time I made it to my one-room flat, I was both physically and mentally exhausted.

I dropped onto my pull-out couch that also served as my bed. I couldn't help thinking how bleak it suddenly seemed. Just a week ago, I was satisfied with my life. I was ready to finish the last of my intern hours so I could officially become a teacher. Now, what I was missing was glaringly obvious.

I decided I'd better call my mom. If word spread—and it would—that I was home and I hadn't called her, shit would hit the fan.

"Hey, Mom. I just wanted you to know I made it back okay."

"Oh, Brittni. You should have stopped by."

"I know, Mom. I'm sorry, but I was too tired."

"Well, come on over and rest here. You can tell me about your trip, and I'll make you something to eat."

"No thanks, Mom. I really am too tired to leave."

My phone buzzed, indicating I had another call. As I looked at the Caller ID, my first genuine smile of the day spread across my face.

"Hey, Mom, I have to go, okay? I'll call you tomorrow."

"Okay, honey. Make sure you call me. Bye."

I tapped the screen to take the incoming call. "Hi," I answered.

"Hey, you made it back?" Justin asked.

"Yeah, a little while ago. I miss you." The words slipped out before I could retract them.

"I miss you too, sweet stuff. More than should be humanly possible."

"What are we going to do?" I asked despairingly.

"We're going to take it one day at a time. We'll talk on the phone every day, and in three weeks, when I finish this job, I'll come see you."

"You will?" I asked.

"Well, yeah. I mean, I already bought my ticket, if that's okay?" he admitted hesitantly. "Brittni? Is that cool?" he asked again, breaking the silence when I didn't respond.

"Heck yeah," I finally replied, letting him off the hook. "Were you worried there?"

"Yes. Don't screw with me like that."

"Sorry. I was just teasing," I said. For the next hour, we continued chatting about nothing in particular. It was a double-edged sword. I loved hearing his voice, but it made the distance between us even more obvious. He promised to call the next evening before hanging up.

The next day turned out to be a huge bore, since I no longer had classes and wasn't needed at the school. I drove the few short blocks to Mom's house for dinner. I was thankful to have something to occupy my time.

"You look rough," she greeted me as I walked into the kitchen, where she was finishing a pot of chili.

"Gee, thanks, Mom," I said dryly, grabbing a handful of crackers from the package on the counter.

"Just making an observation. I guess your 'conference' was pretty tedious," she stated, letting me know she had seen through my excuse.

I sighed. I was no longer sure why I had felt the need to keep her in the dark on every aspect of my life. "I went to Seattle for a friend's engagement," I said, throwing it out there.

"And to see the boy who broke your heart two years ago," she said, stirring the pot.

"Yes," I answered.

"And did you two fix what was broken?"

"How did you know it was something broken and not just a typical breakup?" I asked.

"How did I know? Honey, I don't get my nosey nicknames by sitting back and cooling my heels. I knew the moment you came home all broken inside that some boy had done that to you. Only love can break a gal's spirit like that. I waited for you to come to me and tell me. I figured you'd get around to it when you were ready," she said, pulling two bowls from the cabinet.

"You never said anything."

"That's because I know how much you value your privacy. I know my runaway tongue embarrasses you, but it's who I am. I figured I owed it to you not to pry this time."

I felt so ashamed. For years I'd kept her in the dark, punishing her for who she is. I gave her an awkward hug. "I'm sorry, Mom. I never meant to make you feel bad."

"It's okay, honey. I know we're different, but I want you to know that doesn't mean I don't love you."

"I love you too," I said, sinking down at the bar with my bowl of chili in hand.

"Tell me about your trip and why it made you unhappy."

I decided to go back to the very beginning. I filled her in on everything from meeting Justin at the café to spending Thanksgiving with him that year to the first time he told me he loved me. Our untouched chili cooled as I told her about the pregnancy and then the miscarriage. I was surprised when tears rolled down her cheeks and she reached out to grasp my hand. I even told her how Justin had outed me for an abortion I never had. Finally I moved to my recent visit to Seattle. Through my whole confession, my normally talkative mom remained silent. She gave me a hug that didn't feel nearly as awkward as the first one before reheating our chili.

"I'm so sorry, honey, but I'm confident you and your young man will figure it out."

"You are?" I asked surprised.

"Honey, you may be my flesh and blood, but you and I are as different as night and day. You see something you want and you go after it, no matter how scary it may seem."

I mulled over her words as we both ate our chili in silence. In retrospect, I knew she was right. I was never one to not rise to a challenge. Only once had I ever let a situation beat me down. Feeling lighthearted, I headed home so I could be there when Justin called. I had no sooner sat down on my couch when my cell phone rang. I greeted him much the same way I had the night before, by declaring how much I missed him. Thankfully he seemed equally miserable, so I didn't feel nearly as codependent as I thought. We talked for several hours, neither of us wanting to hang up. The rest of my week pretty much followed the same pattern with the exception of subbing a couple of days at the elementary school and the high school. The highlights of my days were the text messages Justin would send me and our nightly calls.

Two weeks after returning home, I finally got a call from

Ms. Miller, officially offering me Mrs. Duncan's full-time position when she retired at Christmas break. The feeling of excitement that I was so sure would come when I finally secured a full-time position never manifested. I was appreciative but hated that there was yet another thing to tie me to Woodfalls. That night when I talked to Justin, I could tell by the lack of enthusiasm in his voice that he felt the same. He then delivered the blow that his trip would have to be delayed since his client had commissioned him for another job. I tried to interject cheer into my voice as I congratulated him, but my heart wasn't in it. This was why long-distance relationships were impossible.

The next morning I felt marginally better when I woke to a text from Justin. I sent a return message and a few seconds later my phone rang.

"Morning," I greeted him. "Sorry about last night. I just miss you so damn much."

"I miss you too. I'm sorry about my trip being delayed," he sighed. I knew without even seeing him that he was rubbing a hand over his head.

"That's okay. Maybe I can come for Christmas," I said, not sure if I was being too forward.

"Really?" he asked, sounding more excited than I'd heard him in the last few days.

"Sure," I said as the idea took hold. "I don't start until after Christmas break, so I'll have those two weeks off."

"That would be amazing," he said.

"I think so too," I said happily, not dwelling on the fact

that Christmas was still months away. We talked for a few more minutes before he had to return to work.

"I'll call you later tonight," he promised.

"You better," I threatened. "Bye."

"Bye, I love you," he shocked me by saying just before he hung up the phone. Glancing at the phone in my hand, I wondered if I'd heard him right. We had both avoided saying the words. It got to the point where I wondered if we would ever be able to say them again. Sitting there with his words still swirling around my head, I knew without a shadow of a doubt that I loved him too. I always had and always would. I belonged with him. He was the love of my life.

Looking around my empty apartment, I realized that all the things I thought were tying me to Woodfalls merely needed to be untied. Grabbing my keys, I tore out of my apartment. Five minutes later, I was running up the stairs to Tressa's room, glad she had no classes.

She was in the middle of typing something on her computer when I burst through her bedroom door. "Well, it's about damn time," she greeted me.

"What?" I asked, momentarily confused.

"You're leaving, right?" she asked, setting her computer to the side.

"What? How? Did you tap my phone?" I asked.

"No, you turd. I can tell by your face. You've been a Debbie Downer for the last two weeks, and suddenly you burst into my room like you just won the lottery. It took you long enough to decide," she added, glaring at me.

"You knew. How did you know when I didn't even know?"

"Oh please. You talk about Seattle like it's your mother ship, and Justin like he's your alien lover or something. I can't believe you waited this long."

"Waited this long?" I asked. "I thought you would think I was a total ass for moving across the country for some guy who broke my heart. Not to mention, I have no idea how I'm going to tell my mom or Ms. Miller, who finally offered me the job yesterday. I'll be leaving a lot behind," I added defensively.

"Your mom will recover, and Ms. Miller will have to hire someone else."

"Yeah, but what about you?"

"Brittni, seriously? I've known you'd be leaving since you got home. I've had two weeks to adjust to the idea. I'll miss you like a pussycat misses her tomcat, but I get it. Dicks before chicks," she smirked, tossing a pillow at me.

"Gah, you're so crude," I stated, returning her smile. "Are you sure you'll be okay? Maybe you should move to Seattle with me."

She snorted loudly. "I could never leave Deadfalls. It's in my blood. I know I make fun of it, but I love this old town. I'm going to miss your twat-face though, and you better not forget about me," she said. She stood and gave me a ferocious hug.

"I love you," I said, squeezing her tight.

"I love you too."

I left my best friend behind a few minutes later after she

promised to box up my belongings for me. My next stop was the school, where I turned down the job offer. With a few hours to kill, I went home and packed everything I could into my car, knowing Tressa would send me the rest. I contacted my landlord, Mr. James, and thanked him for renting me his loft. By four o'clock, I was ready to go with only one other person left to tell. I was just pulling into the driveway of the house I'd spent the first eighteen years of my life in when my mom pulled into the driveway next to me.

"You'd think I wouldn't be the last to know," she said, looking at my carload of belongings.

"I'm sorry, Mom. I wanted to wait until you got off work to break the news to you," I said, following her into the house with a lump in my throat.

"He knows I'll hunt him down if he breaks your heart again, right?"

"Yes, ma'am," I answered.

"And I won't tolerate sporadic visits like when you were in college, you hear me?"

"Yes, Mom," I said, grinning with relief that she was willing to let me go. I had been so sure it would be a battle, but I was right, the strings just needed to be untied.

"And I wish you would wait until morning to go, but I can tell by the determined look on your face there's no talking you out of this."

"No, ma'am," I confirmed, giving her a hard hug that she returned wholeheartedly. "I love you, Mom."

"I love you too," she said, walking me to my car. "You better call as soon as you stop for the night, and no driving past eleven, since that's when the drunks hit the road."

"Promise," I agreed, giving her a quick kiss on the cheek before climbing into my car.

Maybe it was the finality of leaving, but backing out of the driveway, I suddenly felt more love for my mom than I ever had. Not because she was letting me go, but because she had always accepted me for who I was. Finally, I realized I owed her that in return. The GPS indicated my destination was thousands of miles away, but I didn't care because I knew I was going home. The sign telling me to visit Woodfalls again soon came into sight, and I laughed openly when I drove past it.

36.

Present Day

I was a hundred miles into my trip when Justin called. Wanting to keep my news secret, I lied and told him I was on my way to the city to see a movie with Tressa. It killed me not to tell him the truth, but I bit my tongue. Heeding my mom's warning, I pulled into the parking lot of a hotel at around eleven o'clock. I made sure to call to let her know I was off the road. I was so amped I could hardly sleep, and by six the next morning, I was back on the road. My car ate up each mile as if it sensed my hurry. The only time I stopped was to fill up on gas, make quick bathroom breaks, and to hit a drive-through. The day passed quickly and by eleven that night, after twenty-four hours of driving time, I was more than halfway there. I was giddy with excitement, knowing that soon I would be back in Justin's arms.

I looked at my phone after I checked into my hotel room, feeling guilty that I had let his nightly call go to voice mail. I was afraid I couldn't trust myself not to blurt out the truth. Listening to the voice mail made me feel even worse. He sounded lonely, but the result would be worth it. I sent him a text message saying I was sorry I missed his call and that I would talk to him tomorrow. Sleep came easier than it had the night before. As excited as I was, I guess all the driving had me exhausted. Even the buzz I maintained all day from sucking down one Red Bull after another was long gone. I lay down on the bed, intending to rest my eyes for a minute before showering. Before I knew it, I was awakened by the jingle of my cell phone sitting on the bed next to me. Luckily I had remembered to set the alarm before I crashed. I still had on the same clothes from the day before, but I felt surprisingly refreshed. After a quick shower, I hit the road before the sun came up.

By the time I made it to my next hotel stop that evening at eleven, I was less than five hundred miles away from Seattle. I couldn't believe how many miles I had covered in the past three days. The god of road trips must also be on my side because I had managed to avoid highway patrols and state troopers the entire way, which was good considering I hadn't exactly been paying attention to the posted speed limits. I spent a few minutes talking to Justin on the phone before giving him the excuse that I was feeling a little under the weather to get off the phone. I felt like a kid in a toy store, eager to get what I wanted. Tomorrow I would claim my prize.

The next day I was less than fifty miles away when Justin called, and I couldn't decide if I should answer. Choosing to wait one more hour for the big surprise, I let it go to voice mail again. I was pulling into the parking lot of his building when he called again. Gleefully, I answered the phone this time.

"Hello," I said, climbing from my car.

"There you are. You've been hard to reach," he said, sounding stressed.

"Sorry, it's been a crazy couple of days," I answered, climbing the steps to his condo.

"Anything I can help with?" he asked as I located his door.

"I think so," I said, raising my fist to knock on his door. "I'm wondering about what you said to me the other night," I added, knocking.

"I've been worried about that. Just a sec, someone's at the door," he said.

"I was wondering if you were serious about the love part?" I asked into the receiver, grinning broadly at him. He looked like he might pass out before gathering himself.

"Hell yes," he answered, dragging me into his arms.

"That's good, because I love you too," I said, seconds before our lips came together.

Epilogue

"You ready, babe?" I called, closing my suitcase.

"Just about," Justin said, looking up from the painting he was working on.

"Um, hon, you know we have to leave for the airport in twenty minutes?"

"I know. I just wanted to finish this," he said, turning the painting so I could see. "What do you think?"

"It's beautiful," I whispered, taking in the painting of the land we had purchased that week. It would be several years before we could afford to build the house of our dreams on it, but for now at least, the land was ours.

"You can see yourself growing old here?" Justin asked, sliding his arms around me.

"Only if you promise to mow all that grass," I teased, looking down at the ring sparkling on my finger.

Justin had proposed on a cliché date, despite his vows not to. I had to admit though, it made for a memorable New Year's Eve. At least he bucked the traditional route of a romantic dinner with onlookers. Instead, he popped the question just as the clock struck midnight beneath the stars while we sat in his jeep. Even though it was the middle of winter, he had removed the roof and doors for me and filled the jeep with heavy blankets. Wine and fine cuisine was traded for steaming cups of coffee and pizza from our favorite place. In the parking lot of Olympic Sculpture Park, with the stars shining down, I had just declared it the perfect way to spend New Year's when Justin handed me a cup of coffee with something taped to the side. I had laughed with glee when I saw it was a ring.

Now, admiring the ring on my finger, I couldn't believe how much my life had changed since leaving Woodfalls. I was engaged. I loved the school I was working at. Things had managed to come together after all.

"Ready?" Justin asked, pulling me back to the present.

"Absolutely. I can't wait to see everyone."

"Do you have your mom's gift?" Justin asked, locking the door behind us.

"Yep, it's packed in my suitcase," I said, following behind him.

"Do you think she'll like it?" he commented, loading up our bags.

"I told you a hundred times while you were painting it. You are a brilliant artist. Of course she is going to love it."

"Well, *brilliant* might be a strong word. *Masterful* works though," he replied.

"There's the ego I know and love."

The five-hour plane ride passed quicker than I expected, and before I knew it, we were driving past the Welcome to Woodfalls sign. I guided Justin down Main Street to Mom's house. She had insisted we stay with her while we were in town. I conceded graciously, since our relationship had changed so much these past six months. It was ironic that I had fought the trip to Seattle for Melissa and Rob's engagement party, and in the end it had changed so many aspects of my life.

Mom was outside doing some gardening when we pulled into the driveway. I climbed from the vehicle and gave her a big hug, surprised at how happy I was to see her. Justin stepped in to give her a hearty hug when I was done. They had met at Christmas when she decided to fly to Seattle to see us. For weeks before her visit, I had stressed over spending the holidays with her and Justin's family together, but all my fears were silly. She took to his family as quickly as I had, and they all loved her. Observing her outside Woodfalls, I realized I had always viewed her too harshly. She was just overly friendly with everyone. She liked to know what was going on. That was my mom.

"Brittni, honey, you look lovely," she said warmly. "I'm glad to see your young man has shaped up," she added, looking sternly at Justin.

"Yes, ma'am," he answered, winking at her. His wink had the same effect on her as it did every other woman. I couldn't help smiling as she giggled.

"How is everyone?" I asked, knowing I'd get a full report. Justin smiled at me as she launched into a detailed description of everything I had missed. For once, I didn't mind it at all. It felt like home, and before I knew it, it was time to change and leave for the Annual Woodfalls Spring Fling. Every spring, the residents of Woodfalls would gather for a nighttime dance under the stars to celebrate the end of winter. Sometimes Mother Nature would throw a monkey wrench in the festivities by dumping a late-season snowfall, but this year she had graced us with a mild evening. I was stepping into my dress when Justin joined me. I couldn't help admiring him as he stood before me dressed in slacks and a short-sleeve button-up shirt. His tattoos were visible down his arms. For just a moment, I forgot about our plans and considered spending the evening wrapped in those arms.

"Would you like me to zip you up?" he asked, turning me so my back was facing him. I sighed with pleasure as his lips trailed across my neck before zipping me.

"You look delectable," he said wickedly, placing another kiss on my neck.

"Hmmm, so do you," I answered, tilting my head back so he could have my lips.

He obliged without hesitation. I pressed closer, feeling intoxicated from his touch.

"We'd better go," he said, grinning.

"You're such a tease," I complained.

"You'd be mad if you missed this," he pointed out.

Mom rode with us to the dance. We chatted the entire time, pausing only to give Justin directions to Jessup Park where the Spring Fling was being held. As he pulled into the gravel parking lot, I gasped in delight at the fairy-tale sight before our eyes. Many of the trees along the lake had been wrapped with thousands of twinkling lights, while white Japanese lanterns hung from the branches of other trees, swaying gently in the breeze. A large dance floor had been placed near the lake with dozens of tables and chairs scattered about. The residents of Woodfalls had gone all out.

"Brittni," a loud voice boomed. I turned to greet my best friend.

"Tressa," I mimicked her, throwing my arms around her. "Tressa, this is my fiancé, Justin. Justin, this is my best friend, Tressa."

"I still owe you a knee in the nuts," Tressa greeted him.

"Tressa," I chastised, chuckling, despite myself.

"Would a punch to the arm work?" Justin asked, turning so his arm was close to her.

"Works for me," she said, hauling off and punching with all her might.

I had to hand it to Justin, he barely grunted. I knew from past experience that Tressa's sucker punches hurt.

"Now it's nice to meet you," she said, smiling at him. "You ever hurt my girl like that again and it'll be a knee to the crotch, okay?"

"Sounds fair," Justin said, draping an around my shoulders. "But I wouldn't hold your breath. I don't make the same mistake twice."

"That's what I like to hear." She glared at him in her typical way to let him know she was serious before turning to me. "You won't believe this, but the city council finally decided to spring for a DJ this year."

"Shut up," I replied. Woodfalls was steeped in tradition, which meant we were usually stuck with the musical stylings of the Johnson siblings each year. It wouldn't have been so bad if they actually knew any songs from our generation.

"I know, right? I almost shit myself when I heard." She was interrupted by her mom calling her to help carry a cake to the buffet table. "Oh, hell. I'll be back when I'm done being Cinderella," she complained before heading off.

"So, yeah, that's Tressa," I said, smiling wryly.

"I like her," he said as another car pulled in.

"Hey, that's Trent James," I said, watching him climb out of the car. He looked like something right out of a computer lab. "What's up, Trent?" I greeted him.

"Oh, hi, Brittni," Trent answered, pushing his glasses up the bridge of his nose. "Is Tressa here?" he asked, glancing around nervously.

"Yeah, she's over by the gazebo," I said, smirking as he looked flustered. "Do you want me to call her over here?"

"No, that's okay. I'll talk to her later," he said, scurrying off.

"What's all that about?" Justin said, taking in my smirk.

"Oh, nothing. Trent's had a crush on Tressa forever, but she claims he's too nerdy for her."

"Should we join your friends?" he asked, linking his fingers through mine.

"You looking for more punishment?" I teased. "Woodfalls residents are an acquired taste."

"I think I can handle it."

Two hours later, I was pretty sure he wanted to eat his words. He'd been patted on the back, lectured, smothered in hugs and kisses, and even threatened again by Tressa, just for good measure.

"Told you," I giggled as we slowly circled the dance floor.

"As long as you're by my side, I'm good," he said, dipping his head down to place a warm kiss on my neck.

"I'm never leaving again," I said, admiring the diamond ring that sparkled on my hand.

Why Lightweights Shouldn't Drink

ASHTON

"Come on, go," my friend Tressa said, trying to push me out of my chair. "What good is a bucket list if you're too chicken to do any of it?"

"Zip it," I said out of the corner of my mouth as I apprehensively eyed the situation in front of me. It seemed like a good idea on paper, but actually committing to it suddenly made me nauseated. I took a long pull from my beer, hoping that would help calm my nerves. "God, that's disgusting." I grimaced as the foul liquid poured down my throat. "I don't know how people drink this crap," I complained, slamming the bottle back down on the table a little harder than I should have.

"You're stalling, Ash. Besides, this was your idea. Pick up a random stranger and bang his socks off," Tressa quipped. "You need to seize the opportunity before someone else does, otherwise you'll be SOL, and your only choice will be Old Man Jones over there," she added, making our friend Brittni snort loudly.

"Shush," I said, elbowing her in the gut. Tressa had one volume level—loud. Her words traveled from our table to the many other patrons throughout the only bar in this sleepy little town. Joe's was the hotspot here in Woodfalls, and Friday was your only good chance to meet someone if you were single and on the prowl because Saturday was family karaoke night.

"Ow, bitch," Tressa said, rubbing her stomach. "It's not like the grumpy old fart can hear us anyway," she said loudly in his direction.

"Gahhhh, shush, Tressa. He's going to hear you," I said, sliding back down in my seat.

"Chillax, drama queen. He doesn't even have his hearing aid in. Watch," she said, shooting me a mischievous grin. "Hey, Mr. Jones, I really want to blow you," she said loudly.

She managed to get the attention of about a dozen guys with that one, including Mr. Jones, who whirled around, studying us with his beady black eyes. His gray, bushy eyebrows came together in a unibrow that looked like a giant caterpillar on his forehead.

Brittni snorted again as she shook with laughter. I squirmed uncomfortably on the hard wooden bench, fighting the urge to point at Tressa like we were in kindergarten and had gotten busted for throwing spitballs or something.

Tressa returned his stare head-on, smiling sardonically until he turned back around.

"Sheesh, girl, you're lucky he didn't take you up your offer," I said, stifling my own laughter.

"Hey, you never know what he's sportin' in those dusty old overalls." Tressa winked.

"Gross," I shrieked.

Tressa just shrugged, unconcerned. I couldn't help admiring her self-assuredness. She didn't care what people thought about her. She was loud and seriously inappropriate, but hilarious as hell, despite the tight leash her boyfriend tried to keep her on. We'd only been friends for four months, but I had grown quite fond of her in the short period of time. Both she and Brittni had welcomed me into their friendship circle without a second thought. They acted like I belonged. Not because they felt sorry for me or pitied me like everyone else had done for so many years, but because they genuinely seemed to like me. Brittni wasn't as flamboyant or inappropriate as Tressa, but she had a wickedly dry sense of humor that kept people on their toes. And then there was me. I wasn't completely sure what I brought to the group, but that's why I was here. Somewhere over the last five years, I'd forgotten who I really was.

"All right, time to stop stalling. Get off your ass and pick up that tall, dark, he-can-have-my-panties-any-day seximist," Tressa said pointedly, looking at the stranger we'd been eyeing for the last fifteen minutes.

"Maybe I should do something else on my list," I said, pulling a rumpled slip of paper out of my bag while desperately trying to ignore the butterflies that had suddenly decided to hang out in my stomach. I gently smoothed out the creases as I contemplated the items scrawled on the paper.

"You're kidding, right? This town has a population of like negative ten, and he's the hottest thing to walk in here in forever. When are you going to have the opportunity to have one night of hot wild sex with a stranger like that again?"

"That's my point. Don't you find it a little weird that we don't know this guy? This town is pretty much off the beaten path. He could be some mass murderer. How do you know he wouldn't put my head in his freezer or something?"

"Sweetheart, after a night with him, you'll want a freezer to cool you off," Tressa said, eyeing him with open admiration. "Besides, if you don't make your move, I'm totally claiming him," she added, adjusting her shirt so the tops of her ample breasts peeked out from the thin camisole she was wearing under her button-up see-through shirt.

"So, you wouldn't mind that you don't know him and that he could very well chop up your body into a million pieces? Not to mention what Jackson would say if he found out," I said, reminding her of her boyfriend.

"Wow, seriously, chill, Ash. She's just trying to give you a spark. Besides, you were a stranger here once too, and you didn't show your true crazy for a couple days," Brittni teased. "Now get up there and sex that possible serial killer up."

"You two are a riot," I said, choking down the last of my beer, which tasted like elephant piss, or at least what I would assume elephant pee would taste like. "All right, wish me luck," I added, finally sliding out of the booth. "If he chops me up into little pieces, neither of you gets those boots of mine you want so bad," I threatened. I made my way up to the counter where the object of our interest was perched. Considering my shaky legs, I wasn't exactly as subtle as a prowling jungle cat. Tressa was right. Finding a perfect candidate for a one-night stand was slim to none in a town the size of Woodfalls. Strangers were far and few between. Couple that with the fact that he was drop-dead gorgeous and his sudden appearance was like a gift from God. Not that good-looking was a prerequisite. The only requirement I had set was that he know nothing about me or my past. I wanted one night where someone wanted me for me, not because they felt sorry for me.

"Hey, Joe, can I get a shot?" I asked, sliding onto the bar stool next to the tall-dark-panty-dropping-worthy hunk.

"Sure thing, Ashton. How'd you like your beer?" Joe asked, drying a small shot glass with a cotton towel he had tucked into his apron.

"It tasted like pee," I confessed.

Joe threw his head back as a loud roar of laughter erupted out of him. "Drink a lot of pee, do you?" he asked.

I opened my mouth to answer him sarcastically when the object of my fascination let out a low rumble of laughter. Seizing my opportunity, I gulped down the bourbon Joe had placed in front of me and swiveled around to face the stranger next to me. The liquor burned its way down my throat, leaving a fiery trail all the way to my belly, but it was eclipsed by the liquid fire that burned through me when my eyes finally met his.

"Can I get you another?" he asked softly in a radio-DJ-like

voice that you would hear on a lonely Saturday night, encouraging listeners to call in with their favorite weepy love songs.

"Sure." I eyed my empty glass as my body responded to his sexier-than-sin voice. I was a sucker for a deep voice—or an accent, especially British or Australian accents. Neither, though, could compare to his rich deep voice that seemed to vibrate through me. I realized in that instant I had left a crucial item off my bucket list. Having an intimate conversation with someone with a voice like his should have topped my list.

"You all right?" he asked, looking bemused as Joe placed another shot in front of me. I started to answer his question and mentally kicked myself when I realized I'd been staring at him like he was a tall glass of water on a hot summer day. Matter of fact, I was about ninety-nine point nine percent sure I may have licked my lips in anticipation.

"Absolutely. How 'bout you?" I asked, trying for a seductive throaty voice that just went wrong. "Thanks for the drink," I added, sucking down the liquid confidence in an attempt to calm my frazzled nerves.

His bemused expression turned to outright amusement as he took in my watery eyes, which had resulted from my quick gulping of the whiskey shot. "Another?" he asked with raised eyebrows.

"Why not," I answered, though the room was already tilting slightly. I could count on one hand the number of times I'd actually had a drink growing up. They all centered on the time my life had slipped drastically off course. I'd gone hog wild for a couple of weeks until I realized drowning my sorrows in alcohol only made me sick and didn't solve anything anyway. After that it wasn't a viable option. Needless to say, my time in high school and college had been pretty lackluster.

Tall, Dark, and Dreamy chuckled softly beside me as he flagged down Joe for another round. Holding up his own shot glass, he waited until I raised mine to meet his and then winked at me as we clinked glasses. "Damn." My breath hitched. I was a sucker for winking too. Something about it made my stomach tighten up in anticipation and my breath quicken. Not to mention, having Mr. Seximist behind the wink made other areas tighten up too, while a certain other area began to throb. It took me a moment to distinguish the throbbing as desire. My one and only sexual encounter had been four years ago, after prom, and it didn't last long enough to ever cross over into the desire category. It was the means to an end. I had wanted to feel normal just for one night, and by the end of the dance, I finally coaxed Shawn Johnson into ending my virgin status once and for all. He'd resisted the idea at first, but my constant touches and whispered comments finally muddled his brain enough that he caved. The actual act lasted less than two minutes and hurt like a bitch, but in the end, I was glad I'd gone through with it.

It was ironic that one wink by Mr. Voice had me crossing my legs in an attempt to distill the ache that was slowly beginning to radiate between my legs. He'd managed to excite me more in three minutes of flirting than Shawn had done in an entire evening of slow dancing, grinding, and sloppy kisses.

I was pulled away from my thoughts by a low chuckle. *Son*

of a bitch, not again, I thought, blanching inwardly. He'd busted me gawking at him like a lovesick teenager again. *Okay, pull it together*, I reminded myself. *Focus on why you're here.* I welcomed the warm buzz from yet another shot of bourbon and the uncharacteristic confidence that came with it. Licking the last drop of amber liquid off my bottom lip, I watched with satisfaction as his eyes settled on my lips. I could do this.

"You know, you keep winking at girls like that and one of them is bound to take it as an invitation," I said.

"Sweetheart, I only wink at the girls I'm interested in," he answered smoothly, tipping his own glass to his lips.

The desire I had been trying in vain to control unfurled inside me, making my nipples harden beneath the black lace bra I'd had the uncanny foresight to don that evening. The dull ache between my legs morphed into a steady throbbing that even my crossed legs could not ease.

"Is that so?" I asked, arching my eyebrow in what I hoped was a seductive manor.

"It's a fact, sweetheart," he whispered close to my ear.

I clamped my lips together so I wouldn't embarrass myself by moaning out loud as his warm breath rustled the hair at the nape of my neck. I resisted the urge to sweep my long dark hair out of the way to give him more access.

"You're pretty cocky," I said as he signaled Joe for another round. My head was already spinning, but I figured another one couldn't hurt.

"Not cocky, sweetheart, confident," he answered huskily,

reaching for our drinks with one hand when Joe brought them over.

I reached over to relieve him of my glass, but before I could retract my hand with my drink in it, he snagged my pinkie with his. Looking at our now-linked hands, I watched as he slowly raised my hand to his mouth. I gripped the glass tightly as he brushed his lips across my knuckles before releasing my hand.

Suddenly, the drink felt ten times heavier with the sudden absence of his hand. I worked to keep the glass upright in my shaky hand as I raised it to my lips. Gulping the contents, I set the glass down and took in his slightly blurred features.

"You okay?" he asked as I swayed slightly on my bar stool.

"Absolutely. I do this all the time," I lied.

"I'm sure," he mocked, softly signaling Joe for another round.

"You can bank—" My retort was cut short when my cell phone chirped in my purse.

"I need to use the ladies' room," I breathed, rising unsteadily to my feet as the floor tilted slightly beneath me. "I'll be right back."

"Do you need some help?" he asked, cocking his eyebrow at me.

"Um, I'm pretty sure I know how to pee on my own," I answered, feeling flustered.

He chuckled. "I meant getting to the bathroom. You looked like you were a bit unsteady there."

"I'm good," I clarified before strutting away. It took all my willpower to keep my gait steady as I made my way across the scuffed wooden floors to the bathroom. Tressa and Brittni were leaning against the bathroom counter waiting for me when I entered. It was all part of the plan we had set up. They were here for the status update.

"So, is he a serial killer?" Brittni asked as I headed for one of the stalls.

"Hold on, I really do have to pee."

"He looks like he's into you," she added, switching on the faucet so I could pee in peace.

"Of course he's into her. She's smoking hot," Tressa interrupted. "I bet he's already suffering from a case of blue balls," she added, laughing as I heard the smacking of flesh.

"Do you always have to be so crude?" Brittni asked, disgusted, as I flushed the toilet and opened the stall door.

"He's not the only one," I muttered, filling the palms of my hands with soap before sticking them under the faucet, which was still running.

"Ooh, things a little damp downstairs?"

"Oh my God, Tressa, seriously?" Brittni said, taking another swipe at her.

"That's one way to say it. Put it this way, he'd slide in pretty damn easy right now, if you know what I mean," I giggled, bracing my hands on the counter as the floor beneath me continued to sway.

"You okay, slick?" Brittni asked, really looking at me for the first time since I'd entered the bathroom.

"Fine," I answered, moving my eyes from the slow-rolling floor.

"She's buzzing," Tressa crowed, taking in my glassy eyes and flushed cheeks.

"I sure am." I cracked up, not entirely sure why I found it so funny.

"Are you sure you're up for this, you lightweight?" Brittni asked, placing her hands on my shoulders so she could study me critically.

"I'm fine, Mom," I teased. "I just decided to take the liquid courage route."

"So, you're going through with it?" she asked, looking worried.

"Duh, that was the plan," Tressa chastised.

"I know, but I thought she'd chicken out," Brittni retorted like I wasn't even there.

"Hey, standing right in front of you," I said, waving my hands exuberantly in front of them like I was trying to land a plane or something to that effect. "Besides, I have to do it, it's on my list," I pointed out.

"Right, it's on your list. I still think it's ridiculous for someone our age to have a bucket list."

"I told you a million times. It's for a study I'm doing for the master's program I'm hoping to get into," I lied, smiling brightly at her. "It's a study on living life to its fullest in a limited time frame."

"So you've said a hundred times. I just think a study on males that have the best pecs or dreamiest eyes would have been more productive."

"That's so cliché and overdone. Having a nice six-pack

usually translates to 'conceited asshole,'" I answered, sweeping the lip gloss Tressa handed me across my lips. "Thanks," I told her, handing the wand back. I tried not to focus on the irony of my new friends having no qualms about sharing their makeup with me. Back home, most people refused to touch anything I had touched. They were all assholes. What I had wasn't contagious.

"You better get back out there before Mr. Blue Balls thinks you ditched him," Tressa interrupted, giving my back a light shove toward the bathroom door. "Text us if he turns out to be an asshole."

"And make sure he bags his junk," Brittni piped in.

Giggling at their advice, I twisted around before exiting the bathroom and threw my arms impulsively around both their necks. "I love you guys," I said, knocking their heads together from my exuberance.

"Okay, we love you too," Brittni complained, trying to extract my arms.

"Yep, she's toasted," Tressa commented, rubbing her head where it had knocked against Brittni's.

"Maybe we should hang around to make sure she doesn't embarrass herself," Brittni mused.

"No way, you guys promised," I reminded them. "If I'm doing this, I'm going in without a safety net."

"Fine, but your scrawny ass better text us first thing tomorrow morning, or we're sending out the armed forces to take down Mr. Seximist," Brittni warned, giving me a quick hard hug.

"Don't worry, Brit, he looks harmless enough. Besides, I've

taken at least twenty pictures on my phone. We'll nail that bastard's ass to the wall if he hurts her," Tressa said from behind me as I pushed open the bathroom door.

"Don't worry, my head will make a beautiful mantelpiece," I threw over my shoulder as I sashayed across the room toward the bar.

"Hey, stranger," I said, boldly sliding onto my bar stool.

"Whoa there," Mr. Hotness said as my ass misjudged the middle of the seat and teetered on the edge, making the legs of the stool wobble. Hotness reached over and grasped my arm to steady me.

"You're hot."

"Why thank you," he said chuckling.

"I mean, your hands are hot . . . no, I mean, your touch is hot . . . shit. Never mind," I mumbled as he chuckled next to me.

"It's not the first time I've been called hot, sweetheart."

"Vanity isn't a virtue," I pointed out, picking up the shot glass that had magically filled itself in my absence. "So, what do you do, Mr. I Know I'm Hot?" I asked, realizing that in all our flirting we'd neglected to exchange names.

"Nathan," he answered, holding out his hand for me to shake.

"Ashton," I parroted as his hand engulfed mine. His touch was sure and sensual at the same time, making my poor hand feel bereft once he let go.

"I'm a freelance journalist."

"Freelance journalist? What does that entail?" I asked, intrigued.

"Lots of traveling and a knack for being able to dig out the truth. I've been fortunate enough to be able to pick my assignments," he answered, turning on his bar stool to face me. His knees knocked against mine, which my body was keenly aware of as our legs settled, intimately touching each other. "I'm actually on my way to my next assignment. What about you?"

"Right now, I'm working at Smith's General Store over on the corner of Main and Stetson," I answered defensively, waiting for his judgments. I didn't bother to mention the barely dried ink on my BA in human psychology, or the fact that up until four months ago, I had been planning my internship at the local hospital back home. Those were need-to-know facts that he didn't need to know.

"I think I met the owner when I arrived today. Fran, right? She's quite an old card," he replied warmly, surprising me.

"Yeah, she is. Don't let her age fool you. She's sharper than people a quarter of her age. That store has been in her family for more than a hundred years. Each generation it's passed down to the next. Fran should have passed it down like fifteen years ago, but she claims hell will freeze over before she allows her 'sniveling, no-good, lazy nephew to run it into the ground.' She says she reckons she'll stay until she breathes her last breath or her nephew finally decides to man up. She says she won't be holding her breath on the latter . . ." I rambled on. Obviously, the multiple shots had turned my tongue into a nonstop chattering mess.

"That sounds like the person I met," he said, chuckling

softly. "So, have you lived here all your life?" he asked as Joe set another round in front of us.

Running my finger around the small base of the shot glass, I weighed his question, contemplating how I wanted to answer. "No. I moved here four months ago after my dad died," I lied, giving him the standard answer I'd given everyone else when I moved to town.

"Really?" he asked, studying me critically.

I was slightly taken aback by his response. I'd been greeted with nothing but sympathy when I'd let the lie slip on previous occasions. I always felt a twinge of guilt over it, but knew in the end it was necessary. "It was quite sudden," I answered defensively.

"I'm sorry for your loss," he replied, finally offering up the words that I had grown accustomed to hearing.

"Thanks," I said, not sure if his sympathy was genuine. Maybe he really was some psycho who traveled through small towns collecting heads and storing them in his trunk. I sucked down the contents of my glass once again. My brain was teetering on the edge of remaining focused on the noticeably rock-hard pecs beneath his shirt and becoming drowned by the liquor party that was flowing through my bloodstream. My tongue became numb while the buzzing in my head intensified, making me wish I could rest it on the bar. I contemplated climbing up on the bar so I could lie down, but even that seemed like way too much work. Instead, I tried to focus on my last coherent thought, knowing it had something to do with my head.

"Are you going to put your trunk in my head?" I asked, finally able to make my tongue work.

"Excuse me?" he asked, amused.

"Wait. I mean, are you going to put your trunk in me?" I asked, though the question still seemed slightly off.

"Is that what the kids are calling it now?" he asked with open amusement.

"Wait. What did I say?" I asked, shaking my head in a feeble attempt to clear it.

"Well, darling, you asked if I was going to stick my trunk in you. Is that an invitation?"

"Well, shit. I meant, are you going to put my head in your trunk?" I asked slowly, making sure the word placement was correct.

"Just your head?"

"Unless you keep the whole body, but won't your trunk get full if you keep the whole body?" I reasoned, pleased that I was able to form a coherent question even if it was related to my decapitation.

"I'm more a breast kind of guy," he said, smirking.

Laughter bubbled up out of me. "So, your trunk is full of boobies?" I asked, giggling uncontrollably.

"Boobies?" he snorted. "I haven't heard that word in like twenty years."

"Twenty years? How old are you?" I asked, giggling again at the idea that my one-night stand would be with an old man.

"Twenty-nine. What about you?"

"Twenty-nine? That's not old."

"Who said I was old?"

"Didn't you?" I asked, confused over why I had thought he was old.

"I only said I haven't heard them called 'boobies' in twenty years. It's actually closer to sixteen years, to be precise."

"So, 'boobies' is a thirteen-year-old-boy word?" I snickered again, not surprised at all. I'd been known to crack up over word choices for years. It was official. I had the mind of a thirteen-year-old boy.

After that, the conversation took on a hazy quality as Nathan ordered more drinks. I lost track of what my thirteen-year-old mind said, but I was pretty sure I asked Nathan to put his trunk in me again, which was what I was going for before the booze messed it up.